Late of
this Parish

by the same author

MORE DEATHS THAN ONE
REQUIEM FOR A DOVE
DEATH OF A GOOD WOMAN

MARJORIE ECCLES

Late of
this Parish

St. Martin's Press
New York

Library of Congress Cataloging-in-Publication Data

Eccles, Marjorie.
Late of this parish / Marjorie Eccles.
p.   cm.
"A Thomas Dunne book."
ISBN 0-312-11019-7
1. Mayo, Gill (Fictitious character)—Fiction.   2. Police—England—
Fiction.   I. Title.
PR6055.C33L3   1994
823'.914—dc20   94-420   CIP

First published in Great Britain by HarperCollins Publishers.

10 9 8 7 6 5 4 3 2

Late of
this Parish

CHAPTER 1

It had been a day of cheerful sunshine and blue skies interspersed with dark rainclouds and showers. Easter, with its hope of rebirth. Good Friday, and reminders of death.

The Town Hall was that evening crammed to capacity, the audience listening with varying degrees of enjoyment and attention to the massed choirs of Lavenstock's three churches singing the *St Matthew Passion*. The women members of the choirs wore black for this occasion, the female principals purple. The mothers of the choirboys had washed and starched their surplices and ruffs to a dazzling white and their faces looked as angelic as choirboys' faces were supposed to look. They were surpassing themselves with their singing.

Mayo stirred, trying to bring back his wandering attention, easing his long legs into the too-narrow leg-room. He was finding it difficult to keep his mind on the music, and that was a major irritation because music was one of his chief pleasures and not only had he paid good money for a ticket to this charity performance, he'd moved mountains to make sure he got here. And now murder, however much he tried not to think of it, would keep jumping to the forefront of his mind. As a Detective Chief Inspector, it was a familiar enough subject to him in all conscience but one he could have done without that evening. Maddeningly, morbidly, thoughts of violent death would keep intruding as a sinister and distracting counterpoint to Bach's benign harmonies. But he was a policeman first and foremost and there was a rapist on the loose, and at the back of his mind the ever-present thought that there might soon be another victim— one who wouldn't be so lucky as the previous five.

There were other things bothering him, too.

Briefly, rain drummed on the roof, almost drowning the

music. The next moment the lozenges of stained glass in the windows were lit by shafts of evening sunshine and he caught a glimpse of his daughter's shining fair-gold hair from his eye corner. Julie, whom he had thought he knew through and through—until last night, when she'd come home from college and delivered her bombshell. As a police officer of long experience, Mayo had come to consider himself shock-proof—only to find he wasn't. Not when he was personally involved.

He sighed and closed his eyes. All right, don't fight it, he told himself. Go along with it, think about it if you must. And naturally, as soon as he'd given up the attempt to concentrate on the music, his whole attention was grabbed by it, caught by the melodious power of the voices of the Christus and the Evangelist, and the majestic, sonorous chorales invoking the scene of the Crucifixion. As the first part came to its sombre conclusion he opened his eyes, his glance refocused and came to rest on a woman sitting two rows in front, slightly to his left.

She was seated in a corner, half obscured by a pillar, and presumably thought herself unobserved. He could see a regular profile, a round curve of cheek, a fan of thick eyelashes, heavy dark brown hair waving almost to her shoulders. Not young, still a good-looking woman—but it wasn't that which held his attention. Quite clearly he could see a rain of tears pouring silently down her cheeks.

The flow was splendidly unchecked, without any furtive dabbing at her eyes. At first he thought it was emotion engendered by the ineffable music, but then he thought no, it's more than that, there's personal sadness there as well. Music did that to you. Capable as nothing else was of giving profound pleasure and solace, he knew only too well how it could also touch unbearable chords of memory and pain.

He saw her again as they emerged into a Town Hall Square garden full of the mingled smells of rain-washed earth and traffic fumes. Darkness had fallen and the street lamps shone on wet pavements, light spilled from illuminated shop windows, passing traffic sent hisses of water from under their wheels. She stood on the steps, assessing the necessity or otherwise of opening her umbrella. Deciding against it, turning up the collar of her mac, she began to walk quickly down the street towards the municipal car park. She was above middle height, generously proportioned and carried herself well. There were no traces of tears now. Her chin was lifted, her mouth had an upward curve, she looked warm and vibrant. He thought: There is the face of one who has come to a decision.

Later, in the restaurant, he couldn't help being aware of heads being turned towards their table. He'd always had a natural prejudice towards believing his daughter beautiful. Now, bursting with pride, trying to look at her objectively, he knew that his opinion was not entirely coloured by love. She seemed to have grown, in a way utterly amazing to him, straight from pony-tailed schoolgirl into a self-possessed young woman, without any of the attendant horrors he'd dreaded. Tall and rangy, she wore casual clothes and no make-up. Her eyes were slate-grey like his own, under decidedly-marked brows, the barley-blonde hair was exactly the colour Lynne's had been. Apart from that, she was unlike either Mayo or his dead wife, uniquely herself. She was barely eighteen and he was beginning to wonder if he hadn't made the mistake of congratulating himself too soon on how she'd turned out. He felt he didn't know her any more, that now there were whole sections of her life which were suddenly foreign to him.

He picked up the menu and scanned it to hide any traces of dismay he felt at this. It was in French and though he could find his way around it as well as the next man, he said, 'You'd better decide what we're to have. You're the expert.'

'Not any more.'

'Julie—'

'Let's eat first.' She smiled, wide, entrancing. 'Promise I'll try and explain properly then.'

He thought he'd better have a bottle of wine to make it easier on himself, or at least half. Julie didn't drink and would be driving home.

'Don't go on at me, Dad,' she began when they'd reached the coffee, looking suddenly young and vulnerable, all her assumed sophistication gone. 'I've made my mind up—I really do know what I'm doing.'

'Oh aye.'

'And *please* don't go all Yorkshire on me! It's not that I don't still enjoy cooking but I can't make a career of it, I can't imagine why I ever thought I could. The thought of spending my whole life thinking of nothing but food revolts me. Especially all that meat—it's really gross! Look at them,' she said, with an exaggerated shudder, averting her eyes from the sight of a man cutting up a bloody steak so rare as to be almost alive, 'devouring their fellow creatures. It's cannibalism! Well, it *is*, isn't it?'

Mayo was glad that he had, as a special deference to her new-found idealism, ordered the same vegetarian dish as she had. It hadn't been as bad as he'd feared. But he wished she'd been less graphic. At this rate he was never going to be able to look a lamb chop in the face again.

'I wasn't intending going on at you,' he answered mildly, swallowing the urge to shout his frustration and ram down his fist and generally come the heavy father. What about her course at the catering college? What about the cherished plans for her own restaurant? What about the rest of her life? Not to mention the secondary consideration of his own disappointment. 'Have you thought what you're going to do instead?'

'For the moment, I'm going to stay with Gran. I've rung her and she says I can.'

At once, Mayo felt better. It wasn't that he wanted to shift responsibility, but his mother, an active and sensible woman in her mid-sixties, a former teacher, wouldn't let

Julie do anything irrevocable just yet, giving him time to get to grips with a situation he had never envisaged but one for which he felt he was perhaps partly responsible. Julie had begun to take over the cooking when her mother had died. He had praised her, perhaps over-extravagantly, amazed at her capability, and plugged it as a career when, left to herself, she might never have thought of it.

That night, the rapist's wife returned from an extended visit to her lover and threatened her husband with what she'd tell the police if he didn't agree immediately to what she wanted. She meant divorce on her own outrageous terms. Two hours later he tried unsuccessfully to shoot himself. When he came round in hospital to find a policeman at his bedside he knew he could have saved himself the agony. His wife had told them what she knew, anyway.

Another case wound up. Nearly time to close the files and catch up on some lost sheep. To put thoughts of violence in their place, where they belonged.

But by morning, murder had occurred again, though not on Mayo's patch.

This time it was in Hurstfield, twenty miles away. A bomb had been planted at the Fricker Institute, the research department of Fricker International, manufacturers of pharmaceuticals. It was sheer good luck that the only casualty was a security guard, blown sky-high. Bad luck that he had been a married man with three children.

CHAPTER 2

Castle Wyvering stood on a high eminence where aeons ago unyielding rock had forced the River Stockwell to change its direct course down the broad valley and make a sweeping curve around it. The valley road bypass had given the village a degree of isolation, since the road into Castle

Wyvering was exceedingly steep, narrow and winding and led nowhere else except down the hill on the other side to rejoin the bypass. In any case there was little enough to encourage people to stop for at the top, nothing but the tumbledown old Saxon castle at the farthest end, the venerable church of St Kenelm at the other, with a straggling main street between the two. The street sported a few shops, a Mobil garage, the Drum and Monkey and some small cottages. Behind these was a short terrace of good-sized houses with plunging gardens and a magnificent view overlooking the valley. Outside the church was an attractive green known as Parson's Place, surrounded by the rectory and a dozen or so houses of varying antiquity, whose inhabitants lived in more or less harmonious propinquity. Uplands House School, a boys' boarding and day school of minor repute, was situated half way up the hill, the village school at the top of it. A tiny market was held every Friday. There was no industry as yet. And that was about it, the last outpost in the Lavenstock Division of the county constabulary, a parish of some three thousand souls.

Not much, put like that, but few who lived in Wyvering had any wish to leave. The desire was all on the other side. Plenty of potential newcomers were anxious to invest in a piece of pleasant, peaceful, timeless England but so far the inhabitants had successfully resisted all attempts at such invasion. Except, that is, for the building of a group of small houses on the duller side of the hill. Originally meant as low-cost housing for young local people, who were unable to afford their escalated prices when they were finished, most of them had eventually been bought as retirement homes by elderly city people who formed a small, clubby enclave within the larger whole.

The sun came out brilliantly as Laura Willard was tidying her office at the boys' school before leaving. Instantly the dark secretary's room next door to the headmaster's study sprang to life, its gloom dispelled by the gleam of the sun on the old dark panelling, bringing out the still-rich reds and blues in the worn square of Turkey carpet. She allowed herself a moment to breathe in the freshened air before closing the window, although she was much later leaving for home than usual. It was guilt that had kept her: she wouldn't be here for the open day tomorrow, and so she'd done as much as she could today. However, as a consequence she'd missed the last downpour and with luck might reach home before the next. She'd cycled to and fro in the rain all week and she was sick of it but she disliked driving and used her father's sedate old Vauxhall only when necessary to get into Lavenstock or further afield for necessary shopping.

The Head's study and her own room were situated in the arm of the reversed L-shape of the school. The main wing stretched to her right, the rain-soaked stones glowing with a deep intensity as the rays of the late afternoon sun touched them. Even the scaffolding on the west tower didn't mar the prospect and she felt suddenly pierced to the heart with pure joy: with the beauty and grace of her surroundings, the lovely grouping of buildings, the smooth stretch of the playing fields beyond, the line of huge old chestnuts down the drive, all seen with a new clarity through the lens of her own present happiness. Don't, a cautionary voice warned, don't be too sure, and she shivered as if someone had walked over her grave. She wasn't used to rewards for anything she hadn't worked for and couldn't yet quite accept the idea that here it was: love, the blessed condition that other people seemed to take for granted.

She snapped the window-latch down, made sure her desk was cleared and that she'd switched off her word-processor, an infernal machine which she still regarded warily, like a wild caged animal that might at any moment take a retaliatory bite. A few minutes later she was trundling her bike from the shed to ride down the drive under the still dripping trees.

At that moment an untidy mob of the younger boys

surged out from behind the main building. Kitted out for sports practice, scuffling amiably, elbowing and tripping each other up as they made for the playing fields, their unbroken voices shrilled across the front lawn. Bringing up the rear was Jonathan Reece, the geography master who occasionally took them for games, looking tough and muscular in his blue tracksuit, his fair hair haloed by the sun.

'Shut up, you lot, quieten down and get a move on or it'll be raining again before we get there.'

The voice of authority brought the boys into slightly better order. One hung back to speak to him—Bedingfield, naturally, a budding Mafioso if ever there was one, despite his cherubic appearance. Jon slowed down to listen, smiling down at him and throwing a careless arm across the boy's shoulder as he did so, then shooed him on with the rest. Tossing his hair back, a typical gesture, he was following the boys at a jog when he saw Laura and stopped to wait for her.

'Hi, Laura. Did you leave those pamphlets out for the parents tomorrow?'

'They're on your desk . . . I'm sorry I shan't be here to help, Jon.'

'Consider yourself lucky. You realize I'm missing my weekend in London because of all this fandango?'

'It's good of you,' she answered, thinking privately that might be no bad thing, considering the recklessly aggressive way he drove his car. 'I know your weekends off are important.'

'Sure. Recharge the old batteries, become human again. But some of us must rally round Richard. Sorry, didn't mean you, you've worked like stink to get everything ready.' He smiled brilliantly, his charm-the-birds-off-a-tree smile, which still didn't take the edge off his resentment. It had been another dig at David, who was registered for a weekend conference near Brighton and wouldn't be at tomorrow's open day, either.

He looked on David Illingworth, the senior science

master, as a blinkered intellectual, not a fair assessment. Whereas David looked upon him as all beef and brawn, which wasn't fair either; there was more to Jon than that. He might not possess a brilliant degree like David, but he was what was known as a good all-rounder, a reader, a music-lover, confident and sure of himself, thought by some, including himself, to be the obvious candidate to step into the Headmaster's shoes when Richard Holden retired at the end of the school year.

'Don't look so worried,' he said, 'it won't last.'

This time he meant 'when I'm Head'. She'd known him for some time and knew how to interpret what he said, though she still wondered occasionally what went on behind that square-cut, fresh-complexioned and apparently guileless face.

Voices clamoured across the lawn and Jon said, 'Must go. Little perishers are getting restless. Ciao, then, Laura.' He was off at a sprint and in a minute she heard his whistle blowing, saw him charging down the field, throwing himself into it with his amazing energy as he did into everything.

She was sorry in a way that he was in for a disappointment about the Headship. He was naïve enough to believe he couldn't fail, which had possibly been true before David had arrived on the scene, a force to be reckoned with. One who could very easily overtopple Jon's ambitions, although Jon was still a front runner with many of the school governors, including her own father, who had hoped—very nearly decreed—that she should marry Jon. She was horrified sometimes when she thought how narrowly she'd escaped.

It might so easily have happened. I might well have given in, she thought, done what my father and Jon both want, though it was only when Richard had announced his retirement after his heart attack that it had apparently occurred to Jon that a wife was an asset to an aspiring headmaster. Despite being aware of this humbling fact, three months ago she'd been on the brink of stifling her doubts and agreeing when he'd asked her to marry him.

Time's running out, Laura, began the litany whenever she looked in the glass. No grey in the thick dark hair yet, still all your own teeth, lines only of laughter—but it won't be long. Thirty-six next birthday, too old soon for children. And there was the real pain: never to feel a small warm body in her arms, or walk with a child's hand held in hers. The only child she had was her father. Tied to him and no way out, except by marrying Jon Reece.

It had been a shock to Jon's self-esteem when she had refused him, but one from which he'd quickly recovered. He might even have been relieved. All his life, things had fallen into his lap. Perhaps that was partly why she'd refused him, to show him that she at least was immune to his charm. She liked him, but no more. And even at the ripe old age of thirty-five, the blood leaps, the heart dictates more than the head . . .

She'd been right to hesitate. Because now here was David and there was no hesitation at all, nothing but the certainty that nothing must spoil it this time. She would do anything, anything at all, to prevent that. But her father was implacably opposed to him, with the result that for months she'd felt torn in two, vacillating between being convinced that she had a right to a life of her own and knowing that she could never face the consequences of direct opposition to him.

Heavy drops fell on to her head from the wet branches above as she reached the top of the hill, mounted and rode along the main street until Dobbs Lane and the turning for the houses on St Kenelm's Walk.

From where he sat, in the comfortably cushioned window-seat of the second house in Parson's Place, the Reverend Lionel Oliver just caught a glimpse of Laura, hair and skirts blowing, as she cycled up Dobbs Lane and turned into St Kenelm's Walk. She was one of his favourite parishioners, willing, able—and nice to look at, too. A sweet young woman and a good child to her father to boot, not like some offspring. He sighed, turned his handsome profile to his hostess, sipped the last of his sherry and suggestively tipped up his glass to catch the very last drops. The sherry was excellent, as always, fine and dry, an eminently civilized sort of drink. Much to be preferred to the very dry martinis his hostess, Miriam Thorne, was in the habit of drinking. Several of them by now. Miriam was never half-hearted about anything.

Large, bossy, vigorous, generous and with a wild bush of untidy carroty hair, she drained the latest martini and looked meaningfully at the clock. After having been married to Denzil Thorne for nearly twenty-five years the Rector's pre-supper visits and mildly flirtatious attentions were not unwelcome, but she was a busy woman, organizing herself and others to the last degree. As well as teaching modern languages at Uplands House, she was a tireless worker for the church and most of the other local good causes. No one ever came to Miriam for advice and went away without it.

'Another sherry, Lionel? Though I'm going to have to turf you out shortly. Denzil will be home pretty soon and I've got work to do—and it must be nearly dinner-time at the Rectory. Wouldn't do to let the shepherd's pie get cold.'

This last was said not with any intended malice; Miriam was not a malicious woman, although the cooking at the Rectory was a subject better not mentioned and her careless laugh intimated that such mundane dishes and regular mealtimes were an unnecessary bore. Her own cooking was slapdash, but often successful.

'Oh,' he answered indifferently, 'Catherine won't be expecting me yet. She'll still be busy in the summerhouse with her little drawings, I dare say.'

Miriam raised an eyebrow as she reached for the sherry, but said no more and the Rector, reminded of something he would rather ignore, resolutely turned his back on the offending prospect of his own garden next door, or rather that part which could be seen from Miriam's back window. Unfortunately this did not happen to be the section kept tidy by his jobbing gardener. Not the well-tended lawn and neat flowerbeds immediately outside the french windows, alas, but the semi-wild, overgrown, ever-encroaching acre, now lush with the burgeoning foliage of a wet May, which ran steeply down to the river. The part which Catherine, with surprising obduracy, insisted on leaving as it was. Ah well.

Watching the quick frown of displeasure gradually clear from the Rector's face, Miriam guessed he had again put aside the problem of Catherine and old Willard and decided that she herself would certainly have to do something about it, if only for Catherine's sake. For a man of the cloth Lionel Oliver could at times be peculiarly insensitive.

He was an attractive man of considerable charm, extremely good-looking, perhaps more so now than in his youth. Now that his thick smooth hair had acquired that distinguished silver patina like the very best old Sheffield plate, and especially when wearing his long black cassock, a garment that seemed specifically designed to accentuate his height and the leanness of his still youthfully trim figure. He was generally regarded as well-intentioned and urbane, pompous it must be admitted, but good-humoured if not pressed too much.

He had married circumspectly, the daughter of his bishop, and although preferment had not come as swiftly as he had hoped (and believed he deserved) there were compensations. While the Rectory was by no means to be compared to the Bishop's Palace, and Bishop Lionel admittedly had an enviable ring to it, life in Parson's Place was agreeable and undoubtedly created less demands on him than a bishopric would have done. As a rural dean he presided over several parishes, which made him busy but not overworked. Here he could serve God with the ritual and ceremonial he regarded as paramount, conduct his elaborate services and his daily recital of Evensong without interference. He would dearly love to be known as 'Father' but few in Wyvering would go so High.

And he could always, for instance, find time for a cup of tea or a glass of something with Miriam in this pleasant little house. It was a harmless custom which offended no one, least of all Catherine, who if she was even aware of it gave no indication, merely smiled vaguely whenever Miriam's name was mentioned.

'Well, all I can say is that old Willard is a spiteful old man and Denzil a fool for getting involved,' Miriam declared energetically, refilling his glass and dismissing the subject they had been discussing, though not from her mind. How facile that sort of judgement really was, she thought, putting the sherry decanter firmly back on the sideboard. For no one was in a better position to know that Dr Denzil Thorne was not a fool than she, his wife—but, though he might be the Director of the Fricker Institute, Miriam sometimes thought he possessed no common sense whatsoever. So willing, so eager, so much more obviously good than either of the two neighbouring clergymen. So like a lovable but not very well trained puppy dog, leaping up with great licks of unwanted affection. Poor Denzil. Tiresome Denzil, putting his foot in it with Catherine—but not to be underrated. He could still on occasions surprise her with his insights and this kept her irritation at bay. She was really rather fond of him.

As for old Willard . . . one still tended to believe that a dog-collar automatically conferred goodness and simplicity on the wearer. Nothing could be further from the truth where that selfish old tyrant was concerned. Laura deserved better after dancing attendance on him all these years and now that she had the chance to get away Miriam hoped she'd have the sense to take it this time, and to blazes with her father. There were times recently when Miriam had noticed an expression on her face that could only be described as quietly desperate.

The Rector said, turning to a topic that mention of Denzil

had brought to mind, 'So the police are no further forward with their inquiries about the bomb at the Institute?'

'The police?' Miriam rolled her eyes to heaven to show what she thought of them. 'Fat lot of good they're being! Nearly a month and they still haven't a clue who planted it.'

'Some misguided animal rights activists, of course,' he replied with conviction. 'Protesting against experiments. One must admit to a certain sympathy with their point of view but it's difficult to support the logic of their thinking.'

'I'd give them animal rights!' Miriam returned, raking back her hair with her fingers. 'What about people rights? What about the babies with leukæmia, mothers with cancer? Do they have any thoughts for the rights of the man who was killed, his wife and children? He was only the security guard, only doing his duty.'

The Rector blinked, slightly taken aback, though he should have been used to her vehemence by now. Miriam was always so forthright, so sure she was right!

The clock on the mantelpiece chimed a silvery six, and as it did so a car was heard to draw up outside with an unnecessarily noisy application of brakes. The wide uneven floorboards protested at Miriam's not inconsiderable weight as she went to the small front window, peered out and gave a little shriek. 'Good heavens, it's Philly! And the naughty girl never told me she was coming home!'

It was a very small room, with windows back and front. Lionel craned his neck and was rewarded by the sight of young Phyllida Thorne, in a tight black sweater, an extraordinary hairstyle and a skirt of inflammatory length. Slamming the door of her little black MG and with a great display of shapely legs and a clinking of attendant chains and bracelets, she walked round to unlock the boot.

'Gracious!' he said, echoing Miriam's exclamation a little faintly as at the same moment the passenger door opened and a young man of immense elegance slid out, 'she's brought Sebastian!'

Miriam was halfway to the front door and didn't hear him. The Rector finished his sherry in one unwise swallow and felt the familiar disagreeable sensation in the pit of his stomach as he watched his only child walk round to join Philly and extract an ominously large holdall from the car boot.

When Laura walked into the sitting-room, her father was seated in his wheelchair in front of the french windows, facing the garden that plunged to the valley, the inevitable book on his knee. He didn't turn round as she came in, always a bad sign, and her heart sank. She forced a smile to her lips, cheerfulness she didn't feel into her voice. 'Well, I see he came. Did you have a good old natter?'

The Reverend Cecil Everard Dalby Willard, sometime headmaster of Uplands House School, spun slowly round, looking pained. 'Bernard Quentin and I had an interesting conversation, yes, if that's what you mean.'

'And a good tea, too, by the look of what's left,' she answered, refusing to be needled by the veiled sarcasm in his clipped, dry voice.

She had come home at lunch-time and left everything ready. Homemade buttered scones and jam, a date and walnut loaf, Bath Olivers and gentleman's relish, a Dundee cake. The small table laid with her mother's best lace cloth and silver tea service, the electric kettle already filled. Her father could manage, he always made tea for himself and any visitors he had, but if not, surely even a bachelor don from Cambridge was capable of plugging in the kettle? No matter, she'd no intention of staying at home as her father clearly thought she should, as if her job at the school was a hobby she could pick up or discard as and when she felt so disposed, like knitting.

As she feared, he stayed wrapped in his black mood all evening. As a rule, Laura welcomed visits from his old friend Bernard Quentin for their therapeutic value. Her father's body might be weakened but his intellect remained unimpaired, as sharp and abrasive as ever, and the stimulus of conversation and argument with Quentin did him more good than a whole bottleful of his tablets, enlivening him and making him more like the man he used to be, less of the enfeebled and disagreeable old man his stroke had made of him.

Tonight, however, Quentin's visit seemed to have had quite the opposite effect. Her father was at his worst, querulous and demanding. He needed his pills immediately, he wanted to know why she was spending so long in the kitchen. He threw down unfinished *The Times* crossword, which he always saved to do during the half-hour before supper. Clearly, something had put him out. She thought at first it must be the saga of those wretched badgers again, and cursed Denzil Thorne and wished Mrs Oliver could bring herself to be a little more detached on the subject. Or that he might be going to bring up that business of Danny Lampeter again.

At supper, she learned that it wasn't either the badgers or Danny, this time.

'Quentin is publishing his book on the Middle Eastern question', her father said. 'At last.' Pushing aside his lasagne, he added petulantly, 'I really cannot see why you insist on making this stuff, you know it's too rich for me. I can't eat any more.'

She was on the verge of apologizing (not for the lasagne, it was one of his favourite dishes) but stopped herself in time. She knew him better than that. Whatever disappointment he felt about his own unpublished work he would not want anyone, even her, to show they were aware of his disappointment. He had never at the best of times had the humility to take the slightest sympathy.

After she'd cleared the dishes and washed up, Laura sat drinking her coffee in front of the sitting-room window. She never tired of the view from here, the perspective it put on feeling and emotion. The feeling of littleness against the immensity of the landscape, surrounded by sky, was always overwhelming. Tonight, the sky was spectacular with a theatrical, Turneresque beauty. Purple thunderheads piled up in the west, shot with unearthly rays of silver light from behind. A band of clouds lay below, wine-dark streaked with gold. The river was a still ribbon of pewter far beneath her and tiny Dinky cars crawled imperceptibly on the curving road. And all of it in tune with her own excited apprehension, the tremulous fear that filled her whenever she thought of what she was about to do.

'More coffee, Father?'

He was asleep, his mouth slightly open, and she sat watching him, filled with pity. She knew how deeply he felt about his failure to finish the book he'd been working on, a complicated study of the comparative religions of pre-Reformation Europe. The fact that it would have been completed now had it not been for his stroke must be profoundly galling to him. Intellectual faculties intact, he simply no longer possessed the considerable physical stamina necessary to sustain such a Herculean labour. He had seemingly accepted this, acknowledging that although contemplated for many years, the work had been begun too late in life, after his retirement and shortly before this illness overtook him. Whereas Bernard Quentin was twenty years younger and worked in the fullness of his health and strength. All the same, it was perhaps understandable that his friend's achievement should have upset her father. But why had it upset him so much?

The clock in the hall hissed the usual warning before booming out its nine deep strokes. Her father woke, reached out his good arm for his cup of weak, decaffeinated coffee and finished it. She took a deep breath and turned her back on the view, facing the room furnished with things familiar to her for most of her life: a long, low room, dominated by the number of books in it. The shabbiness of the furnishings had acquired a certain distinction through long association —the comfortable sagging armchairs, the worn old rugs, the faded brown velvet curtains, the set of black and white cathedral etchings and sepia photos of people long gone, known only to her father. There was nothing of her own personality stamped on the room, nothing to her own taste.

She decided to speak. Although aware that it might not be the best time to reapproach the subject that was uppermost in her mind, something in her naturally impulsive nature impelled her to do so. She had to give it one last try, to hope that he might make the effort to understand her. She said abruptly, 'I do wish you'd meet David and talk with him.'

Her father didn't answer immediately. His eyes, watching her, were hooded, like an old turtle's. His withered neck, rising from the clerical collar he still insisted on wearing, reinforced the impression. 'Illingworth and I have already met several times,' he said at last.

'I mean to talk. To discuss our marriage.'

'I fail to see any point in doing so, since as far as I'm concerned there can be no prospect of a marriage. You know my beliefs, and after a lifetime of seeing them work in practice I am glad to say they are still quite unshakable. A Christian marriage, once made, is for ever.'

'Even when it's become a travesty? When it's tearing two people apart, when there's nothing left to salvage?'

'There is always something left.'

'Not always. Sometimes, divorce is the only way out. Father, I know how strongly you feel about this and I respect your views, but surely we can come to some sort of compromise? We wouldn't expect you to actually marry us, even though I've always hoped you would when the time came.'

'I think,' he answered, reducing her to the level of one of his errant ex-pupils with a smile colder than was perhaps intended, 'that isn't a proposition even you could have considered very seriously.'

She said nothing because in her heart she'd known not to expect miracles. He wouldn't change, perhaps he couldn't. The idea that his daughter might go against him and marry a divorced man despite his wishes seemed never to have entered his head. To him it was unthinkable. And perhaps it was, she thought drearily. She could never match him in argument and the habit of believing he was always right was hard to break.

'Nor, I might add, will I support his claim to the Headship, on that and other grounds. I am still on the board of governors, don't forget—and there will be others who think as I do.' He paused as if about to add something else, but merely said abruptly, with one of his sudden swings of mood, 'I'm sorry if you're feeling hurt over this, Laura. One cannot avoid that when faced with making moral choices, none of us can. But, my dear, are you sure you're not being led into something you would certainly regret because you are—how shall I put it?—of an age to think that life is passing you by?'

Her nails bit into her palms in an effort to stop herself answering. She would have liked to think he didn't realize how witheringly unkind his comments could be—but how could he *not* know? And what moral choices could he be faced with, sitting here all day? she thought, her resentment mounting. And what could he know of love? She was ignorant of the state of her parents' marriage. Her father had been middle-aged when she was born, she remembered her mother only as a pale, gentle ghost. But although she forbore to speak, what she was thinking must have registered on her face.

'Oh yes, there are moral decisions that even I am faced with,' he said, looking at her with a kind of pitying understanding. 'For instance, what should one do if one comes into possession of some potentially damaging information —which could destroy a person—but if not revealed could be equally damaging to others? Where does one's duty lie then?'

He knows, she thought, motionless with shock. Somehow he's found out. No, not found out. Specifically learned from

Bernard Quentin who was a Fellow of the same Cambridge college David had recently belonged to.

It would be better for everyone, himself included, said a voice in her head, if he were to die now. The thought came unbidden into her mind, clear and fully formed. Appalled, it took her a moment or two to admit that in its unrealized state it had been there before, not once, but many times.

CHAPTER 3

Wyvering was asleep, its lights extinguished. Below, dark as silk under the moon, the river flowed silently in the broad valley. Down in the beech hollow further along its course six badgers—a boar and a sow and four cubs—came out of their sett one by one and began to make for the clearing where the garden ended just above the river.

Still and patient through long practice, Catherine Oliver leaned her elbows against the sill of the summerhouse, watched and waited. Disregarding the stiffness in her joints, wrapped in many layers of clothing, a Thermos of hot soup to hand, she had spent many similar nights watching the badgers and other night creatures, just looking, committing to her unfailing memory the lines of their bodies and their movements so that she could later draw them.

The moon rose higher and an owl swooped silently to the ground. A small animal screamed in death. A few moments later the badgers arrived, lumbering like so many amiable old drunks, grunting and snuffling over the bread and milk, dried fruits and nuts she'd left out for them, a regular source of food they'd come to expect. But tonight the exquisite pleasure of watching them was marred by the thought of the badgers found dead last week. Shot, the RSPCA had said. It was an offence against man's laws and against nature. She suspected that old Willard was at the bottom of it, that the deed had been done at his instigation, but how could that ever be proved? Inoffensive creatures, the badgers were not rooting up his lawn for spite, only for food, for the leatherjackets and worms under the turf. How could he hate them so? But he did, and he had a gun; he shot grey squirrels from his wheelchair.

Another thing—how could Denzil Thorne have been such a crass fool as to tell Willard she fed them? Knowing as he must that it was calculated to enrage him?

Catherine Oliver was generally regarded as an unassuming and forgettable woman (when she was thought of at all as a separate entity from her husband), careful about voicing her opinions, as befitted a clergy wife. There was a gleam in her eye and a twist of irony to her unpainted lips that might have warned her detractors if they had but taken the trouble to look so far. At the moment her mouth was set in a hard, uncompromising line as she watched the badgers. Normally peaceable and tolerant, there were some things about which she was inflexible.

A sound fell on the night air. Only a soft footfall, but the badgers froze, and then they were gone. A figure in dark rollneck sweater, jeans and tennis shoes appeared in the clearing.

'It's only me, Ma.'

'Seb! Oh, Seb, you've frightened the badgers away.'

'Wouldn't you rather see me than the badgers?'

'Not at this particular moment. You're supposed to be asleep in bed.'

He laughed softly as the old childhood remonstrance came from her, as though he were still twelve years old. He stood for a moment silhouetted in the moonlight before coming into the summerhouse, a handsome, slimly-built figure just under middle height, the smile on his curly mouth showing very white teeth, his eyebrows winged above his slanting eyes. 'Thought I'd like to talk to you on your own, that's all.'

'Well, that's nice,' Catherine said, but she sighed as he entered. 'Would you like some soup? It's homemade.'

He said very kindly, 'No, thank you, I'm not hungry,' and forbore to shudder as she poured viscous unnameable brown liquid from the flask for herself. Leaning back against the doorframe with his hands in his pockets, he watched her as she sipped. 'Well, what's all this about this book, Ma?'

She stayed with her hands clasped round the plastic mug for a long time before raising her eyes and speaking. 'Philly, I suppose. It was Philly who told you.' Philly also worked in London, for a publisher of children's books, wore very tight, very short skirts and was reported on occasions to use language that would have made a sailor blush. 'I haven't told you because I didn't want it generally known, not just yet, not until nearer the publication date.'

'You don't want *God* to know is what you mean, isn't it, Ma?'

This was an inadmissible joke, not for any irreverence to the Deity but because Lionel Oliver's second name was Godfrey. But Seb was unrepentant, his black eyes dancing, full of wickedness. In the moonlight, with his dark sculpted curls and his faun's ears, he looked pagan, lacking only the cloven hoof, reed pipes and pair of little horns to complete the picture.

Where had he come from, this clever, charming, unknowable child of hers? Catherine had asked herself time and again. Which errant genes of hers and Lionel's had shaped him? They were questions to which there was never an answer. From babyhood, when he'd arched his back and screamed and spat out food he disliked and then turned on his mother a toothless smile of heart-melting sweetness, there had been no coping with him. It was no better as he grew older, during several years at the expensive school where he was predictably popular but never did more than the minimum required work, disappointing his father unbearably. From which school he had been expelled for allegedly failing to respond to authority. In what way this had occurred remained shrouded in mystery; the headmaster had been evasive and Seb uncommunicative and apparently uncaring, and even Lionel had been unable to get to the bottom of it. A faint suspicion had crossed his mother's mind that Seb had engineered the whole thing for reasons of his own but she dismissed this as unworthy.

Nevertheless, he had left school without regrets and then, amazingly, proceeded to land himself a job in the City which paid him an enormously inflated salary. He now had an expensive flat in the Barbican, wore beautiful suits and shirts and, being Seb, owned a motorcycle—not much ridden—instead of the mandatory Porsche. Catherine was vague about what he actually did, except that it was to do with money. She loved him to the depths of her being, tried to understand him, and despaired of him. His father also loved him but had given up trying to understand him years ago.

'Why don't you want him to know?' Seb pressed now. 'No, don't answer that, I think I can guess. He'd be jealous, wouldn't he?'

'Sebastian, you are not to say things like that!'

'But it's true, isn't it? Admit! He's the only one allowed to be the big wheel around here.'

'I am not,' she answered, trying to be severe, 'ever likely to become a big wheel, or even a small one. I've written a little book and illustrated it with some of my drawings, that's all. That's hardly going to make much of a stir.'

'Don't be too sure of that, Ma. It's been very well received, according to Philly.'

'Has it really?' She was transformed.

And a little afraid. Because it was going to take Lionel —and everyone else, of course, she qualified—a little time to adjust to the idea that she'd been even moderately successful at something that was uniquely hers. That she wasn't just the Rector's wife, the unobtrusive woman who wore neat shirtwaisters and her brown hair cut in a short, easy style that she could manage herself.

'You're going to be rich and famous, me old darlin'!' He

threw a careless arm around her shoulders and kissed her.

Delighted as she herself was, both by the news he'd given her and his unwonted display of affection, she smiled. 'I shall be neither, silly boy. Certainly not rich,' she added ironically, and told him why.

Seconds passed. Sober now, he let his hands rest on her shoulders. 'You're a dark horse and no mistake,' he said at last. 'I only hope you know what you're doing.'

'Oh I do, I do.'

'Well then, that's it,' he answered awkwardly, dropping his arms and changing the subject. 'It's terrific news, really, Ma. I'm over the moon for you. Promise I can have the first signed copy?'

'Darling, of course you can. But there's months yet before publication.'

Several months' breathing space which in fact she'd been counting on. But if Phyllida Thorne knew already, everyone else soon would. Now she'd have to tell Lionel. Well, after the weekend. She began to pack up her things, ready to return to the house. The night was ruined anyway.

Sebastian began to help in a desultory way. 'You know, he couldn't have been responsible for having those badgers shot. Old Willard, I mean,' he said suddenly, looking up from fiddling with the cap of the Thermos, returning voluntarily to the topic he'd found himself up to the ears in as soon as he came home. 'He's not like that.'

'Isn't he? He shoots squirrels.'

'Grey squirrels. Tree rats. That's different. They were brought into this country and now they're doing tremendous damage to the environment. Not to mention spreading diseases.'

She eyed him for rather a long time before answering. 'Is that what he wanted to see you about this afternoon? To indoctrinate you further?'

'No. I was the one who wanted to see him.'

'Is anything wrong, Seb?'

'No,' he said again, his tone noticeably cooler. 'Should there be?'

'I've had the feeling, since you came home . . .'

'Of course there's nothing wrong. You're just being Mumsy.'

'I expect so.' She sighed. 'Anyway, it's very good of you, darling, to take the trouble to visit an old man like that.'

'I just happen to like the old boy. He's never wishy-washy in his opinions, he sees things so directly, without sentimentality.'

'Without feeling, you mean. Even for his daughter.'

'Has it ever occurred to you that Laura might rather enjoy playing the martyr?' he asked, with unexpected perception. 'After all, nobody can make her stay with him. She could make provision for him if she wanted.'

Catherine, however, was a woman who saw things in black and white. She couldn't understand how Willard, a clergyman whose life was presumably dedicated to truth and integrity, should find it possible to be so devoid of charity, and not only on the subject of Laura's freedom. 'That's hardly fair to her,' she said.

'Isn't it?' He picked up a bit of dry stick and began breaking pieces off, tossing them into the clearing, then walked ahead of her up the steep path with his springy, athletic stride, her satchel of belongings over one shoulder, the flask under his arm. This part of the garden, which she had created and looked after herself, was a small area of peaceful seclusion, uniquely beautiful to everyone except Lionel, who deplored its untidiness. Skillfully combining nature with art, it had a romantic wildness which pleased the eye and made it a habitat suitably natural for the wild creatures she encouraged—if sometimes impractical from the human point of view. When he came to an awkward bend in the path where an artistically-placed cotoneaster posed a threat to life and limb he stopped and turned, offering her a hand to negotiate the steep step up. 'Sorry about all that, Ma,' he said when she stood beside him. 'I know you've got in for the old boy, which isn't like you, but you're wrong about him, you know, dead wrong.'

She shook her head, smiling, to put an end to the argument and being occupied with her own thoughts said nothing more as they toiled on. It wasn't until they reached the top and were walking across the moonlit lawn to the house that she spoke again. 'You've become very friendly with Philly lately, haven't you?'

He laughed. 'If you mean are my intentions serious, the answer's no. Nor are Philly's. She's got other fish to fry. She wouldn't consider a decadent like me. She thinks I'm a broken reed, that my life's devoted to money and pleasure. Though I've never pretended to be intense about everything, like her.'

Catherine was deeply indignant that anyone should think her son a broken reed, while reluctantly admitting there might be a grain of truth in Phyllida's assessment. She often wished he had it in him to be intense about anything. But who was Phyllida to accuse Sebastian? Catherine couldn't see what he had meant about her—if anyone was more frivolous than Sebastian, it was surely Phyllida Thorne.

The following morning, Saturday, Philly was having breakfast alone in the kitchen, her mother having attached herself to the hall telephone where she was likely to remain for some time, when her father threw open the door and burst in with Taff, a bright-eyed and chunky Welsh corgi, at his heels. In an instant there was pandemonium. As the dog bounded noisily into the kitchen the cat, spitting, leaped like a performing flea on to Philly's knee. She was a very old but by no means moribund black Persian called Florence whom Philly had had since she was thirteen, and who hated Taff with a loathing which was fully reciprocated in every way. They could never be left alone in case either one of them killed the other.

Taff was commanded to shut up and sit and eventually did so, though with great reluctance. Florence subsided warily under Philly's stroking hands. Order temporarily restored, Denzil proceeded to scoop muesli into a pottery bowl for himself and a similar-looking concoction into a not dissimilar bowl for Taff, only just avoiding taking the wrong one for himself.

'What was the fuzz doing here, earlier on?' Philly asked, as he eventually sorted things out, sat down and began pouring milk.

'The police? Oh, just someone to talk to me about increasing safety precautions at the Institute.'

'Haven't they found who put that bomb there yet?'

Her father, his mouth full, shook his head.

'They must have some sort of lead, surely? Well, no, even if they had, I don't suppose you'd know.'

Denzil hoped he had imagined the stress on the 'you'. He sometimes felt his status here in this house was about on a par with that of Florence and Taff, only just above that of the inanimate furnishings, and about as much use. He'd have been the first to admit that he was hopelessly inefficient about the small details of everyday living but the fact was that neither his wife nor his daughter had any idea what went on in his mind. This didn't much trouble him. It suited his purposes, in fact. As his alter ego at the Institute he cut an altogether different figure. There, he was well-liked and though easy-going and friendly, was respected for his abilities and had authority. Philly was correct, however, in assuming he didn't know much about the police inquiries or how far they'd progressed. Even if he had known, he would never have dreamed of passing on what he knew to anyone else.

'Bloody fuzz, you'd think they'd have come up with something by now,' Philly said scornfully and seemed about to add a few more choice adjectives but changed her mind. It was no fun when he remained unshockable. The last time she'd displayed the extent of her vocabulary it was his turn to shock her rigid when he'd responded in like manner, using words that even she'd hesitated over. She'd been more circumspect since then.

'They're doing their best. Not much to go on,' Denzil said pacifically.

She turned impatiently but then said seriously, 'The trouble with you, Pop, is that you're so bloody long-suffering. Hasn't it even occurred to you that you might have been killed?'

Her voice had taken on a rough edge and he reflected with surprise that Miriam could have been right after all in being ready to believe that the reason Philly had come home so unexpectedly was because of a belated need to reassure herself that he was all right after his near miss with the bomb. Belated indeed—the bomb outrage had occurred almost a month ago—but he pushed aside a more unbearable thought as to why she might be here. All that had happened long ago, it was all over. If Miriam was right in her supposition, it pleased and touched him out of all proportion to the act. Philly was clever and had her mother's energy and, like her, her life seemed to be organized to a T and full to overflowing with things unimaginable to him. At any rate, there was normally no room in it for spontaneous, unplanned gestures of affection.

'Killed? What gave you that idea?' His bright-eyed smile lit up a face as ingenuous as a baby's. His hair was wispy. He was going bald. His figure was sagging into a paunch and he never ceased to be surprised that he could have produced so spectacular a daughter. He never ceased to worry about the life she lived in London, either—perhaps because neither he nor her mother had been privileged to be told anything much about it. But she was secretive by nature and always had been and was unlikely to change, so there was little to do but accept the situation. 'I was nowhere near the place,' he said.

'Only by good luck. Mum says you were there only about ten minutes before. Why were you? So early on Saturday morning? Easter?'

'My dear child, like a few more people who had equally lucky escapes, I'd certain things I had to do, work to see to . . . the Institute can never really close completely. But let's not talk about that.'

Their eyes met. He wondered what she was thinking, if she remembered. It suddenly occurred to him that she probably thought it irrelevant whether her parents approved of her lifestyle, since there was so much she didn't approve of in theirs. She held the cat cradled to her, watching him as he spooned in the last of his muesli. She was rather like a bedraggled little kitten herself, one that had been out in the wet, with those startlingly blue-green eyes in her sharp little triangular face, her spiky, gelled dark hair, claws sheathed at the moment but ready he knew to scratch at any time.

'All the same, it was a near miss, wasn't it?' Her gaze on his face was intent, and perhaps he didn't imagine the concern behind it. 'I was in Bognor that weekend with Seb and I didn't hear about it until I got home.'

'*Bognor?* With Seb?'

She correctly interpreted the frown that appeared between his brows. 'Now, Pop, don't be so stuffy!' she said impatiently. 'Seb's OK. He's good fun—and Mr Loadsamoney at the moment—but don't go getting any ideas. I've already told him it's his motorbike I love and not him.'

He wasn't sure he was keen on the idea of her racketing around on the back of a Harley Davidson, either. He pushed aside his empty cereal bowl, and looked at her, careful not to show the dread he felt at the thought of where her fearless and headstrong nature might take her.

But with unexpected gentleness she said, 'You shouldn't worry so much about me, Pop. I'm a big girl, now. I'll be all right.'

He wished he could believe that. But nothing she'd done so far gave him too much cause for hope.

CHAPTER 4

Did other fathers, Mayo asked himself, fatalistically accept that they must in some mysterious way be to blame when their daughters suddenly became as incomprehensible as some creature from another planet? He suspected that most of them did, that it was all part of the contemporary human condition. But that didn't make it any easier to cope with. Julie had come home after three weeks with her grandmother, still of the same mind. And left again after three days.

'All she'll say is she doesn't want to make any major decisions yet—only little things that don't matter, like chucking up a career and leaving college and knocking around the world like some blasted gipsy.' He added tonic to gin for Alex before subsiding into a chair on the opposite side of the hearth with his own whisky. 'Before her teeth fall out and she's married and saddled with six kids and a mortgage, to be precise.'

Alex grinned and sipped her drink. 'Didn't we all. Ancient as I am and feel, I can still remember the urge.'

Well, maybe. He thought of himself at Julie's age, twenty-five years earlier. Recalled a vague restlessness, the feeling that the world was out there and why weren't you out there with it? But had he ever wanted to kick over the traces so completely? He found his memory for things like that was growing dimmer, the older he became. Still not quite yet into the sere and yellow, he sometimes felt that he understood so little of people of Julie's generation he might have been born before the Flood.

'It's endemic in the student population,' Alex said calmingly. 'She'll be all right when she's got it out of her system. Itchy feet, they all get it.'

'Not half way through a college course!' He didn't want

to be smoothed down. He wanted to be allowed to give vent
to what he felt.

'Especially half way through a college course. All right,
they don't all pack it in, but at least she's not doing it
without thought—give her credit for that.' Alex settled back
into the sofa with her high heels kicked off and her feet up
on a small table, anything but the crisp, efficient police
sergeant she'd been an hour before. Their free time coincid-
ing for once, they were in Mayo's flat, he was doing the
honours and had in mind for their strictly non-vegetarian
meal a large mixed grill, including pork chops and kidneys.
Then afterwards, hopefully, she would stay on, though he
couldn't ever be sure of that. Just glad to pick up whatever
crumbs were on offer, you poor old mutt, he told himself,
knowing it wasn't true, because such terms between him
and Alex could never be acceptable to either.

'You'd better believe she's serious about it, Gil. It takes
courage to do what she's done. She must've known what
your reaction would be.'

'Good God, I'm not that frightening! Am I?'

Alex looked amused. 'Well, maybe a bit Victorian papa
—thinking about your daughter not being a sweet, biddable
little girl any more. Sorry, shouldn't have said that. Not
my business.'

'No, what you say makes sense, I suppose—but what
d'you mean, it's not your business? Anything to do with me
is your business, I hope.' He thought about pressing the
point, but he'd no desire to spoil a good evening before it
started. They'd achieved a compromise which for the
moment suited them both. If he were honest, he'd admit it
was a truce rather than a compromise but it was for the
time being working, and he wasn't going to push his luck
by breaking the rules and asking her to marry him yet
again. There'd been a time when he'd thought she wouldn't
marry him because she wasn't yet completely free of Liam,
her Irish ex-lover. Now that he'd apparently gone into
limbo (and bad cess to him, bloody Liam of the Sorrows)

and no longer appeared to occupy her thoughts so much, he had to realize she had ambitions beyond marriage: a career she didn't intend jeopardizing by the demands of a husband and maybe children. She'd seen too much of that happening with her female colleagues, she said. There was some truth in that, but the threat of her promotion hung over him like the sword of Damocles—and perhaps over Alex as well. He sensed a tension in her tonight—but he was always on the edge of apprehension with Alex. Moodily, he swivelled the ice around in his glass and switched problems again. 'What gets me, I suppose, is that I can do damn all about it, though I won't give up without a try.'

'No, Gil, I suspect you won't.'

He acknowledged this with a wry smile. There was silence between them while she slowly felt herself relax. It was very easy to do that up here in this quiet top-floor flat. Carly Simon, in deference to her own tastes, on the turntable. The tick-tack-tocking from the old clocks, knackling away from every corner of the rooms—something she'd once thought might well drive her mad but which she'd grown used to and and would have missed had they gone. The evening shadows growing long in Miss Vickers's garden below and the scent of the wallflowers her brother had massed into the borders wafting in through the wide open windows. The flat had a different look about it. Not noticeably tidier, mind, but warmer, more personal, less of a bachelor pad. Julie had departed northwards again only yesterday but she'd left traces of her presence. Records, magazines . . . there were even some fresh flowers inexpertly stuck into a vase, certainly not Mayo's doing. One bloom is worth a thousand words—a bunch of daffodils to express regret: I'm sorry, Dad, I love you but . . .

Alex knew that all these authoritarian father noises Mayo was making were no guarantee that he wasn't deeply worried about Julie, though she thought there was no need. She herself thought that Julie would probably regret later what she was doing now, but there was a core of good sound common sense in the girl, which he'd admit to when he'd had time to come round. Meanwhile, a daughter apparently hell-bent on wrecking her chances, as he saw it, was something he regarded as unfinished business, which wasn't in his book.

'Half your problem is you're going to miss her dropping in and stocking up your freezer with all that delicious food!' she teased, trying to lift his mood.

'Not if it's nut rissoles, I'm not—and half way to Australia's a bit different from college, two hours up the motorway, you must admit.' He leaned back, rolling the malt round his tongue, savouring it before swallowing. He looked tired as well he might, having been out catching thieves until dawn, but he was used to that and a good night's sleep would make up for it. His big frame sagged in the chair. She must remind him to get his hair cut. It was beginning to curl up at the back in the way he hated. Suddenly he grinned, looking ten years younger. 'Hell, no. To tell you the truth, for the first time ever I'm not sorry to see the back of her for a while. I'm not sure I can take any more at the moment. I've had vegetables and peanut butter and going green rammed down my throat till I'm up to here! What in God's name's got into her? She never used to be like this.'

'Oh come on, if you don't have ideals at eighteen—'

'It's not just ideals. I could understand that—or try to. But she's in a funny mood. Dangerous. Dammit,' he said, sitting up again, 'I won't *let* her go traipsing round the universe!'

'She's not under age, Gil. Nothing you can do, though I suppose you'd feel better if she wasn't going on her own.'

'She's not going on her own, that's the whole point! Didn't I tell you, there's a boy—a man—another student anyway. Some sandalled weirdo who's put all these screwy ideas into her head.'

'Ah.' So that was what had really been bugging him. 'No, you didn't tell me. That does make a difference.' She looked thoughtful but before she could elaborate on what the difference was, the telephone rang.

Mayo swore and let it ring.

'It won't go away.'

Muttering under his breath he got up to answer it. While he listened to what was being said at the other end, Alex heard the clocks begin to chime in unison, one very slightly off-synch with the others. Like their relationship, she thought. Just one degree off being perfect.

'Just a minute.' Mayo held his hand over the instrument until the chimes stopped, using the time to gaze thoughtfully at the wall in front. 'Go on.'

By the time he put the receiver down, Alex knew that this was destined to be yet another evening gone for a burton.

It was a thwarted but resigned Mayo who sat back in the passenger seat while his sergeant, Martin Kite, put his foot down on the stretch of road in front. Tough luck that Castle Wyvering was situated at the furthest point of the division, just inside the boundary—another mile or two and it would have been Hurstfield's pigeon. After a while, he settled down. Having had DC Farrar with him over the last couple of weeks while Kite had been conducting an investigation into a series of break-ins at local supermarkets, he was more than usually appreciative of his cheerfully capable sergeant by his side once more. Farrar was OK by his own lights— bright and alert and plenty of initiative, even if he did know it all and dressed like a male model. In fact nobody—least of all Farrar—could understand why he'd twice failed his promotion boards.

'Manage to get something to eat before we left, did you—?'

Kite only just bit back the 'sir'. He knew Mayo found too many of them boring and unnecessary between them but years of discipline and training made the habit hard to kick. He'd better watch it, though, or there'd be some caustic comment. Very sarky he could be when he wanted, the gaffer. Still, like most of the team once they were used to him, Kite considered himself lucky to be working with Mayo. He was fair, if you were fair with him, not soft but not case-hardened, either. He'd arrived in Lavenstock with a sharp reputation behind him. Wariness had changed to respect, respect to liking—though most of the team would have been hanged, drawn and quartered before they'd admit this.

Another of Mayo's little ways that Kite had grown used to was that he was inclined to forget about food when the job was under way. Not everyone shared this tendency. Especially Kite, whose metabolic processes kept him as thin as a long drink of water but demanded frequent stoking. He had, however, learned to suss out where he stood regarding meals and act accordingly, hence the question.

'An omelette,' Mayo answered, sounding glum. As though it had been hastily gobbled and lay heavily on his stomach. 'Left a mixed grill behind and all.'

'Shame. We had Lancashire hotpot. Sheila's a dab hand —lashings of onions and the potatoes all crisp and brown.'

'I should be so lucky.'

Kite looked smug and thought of Sheila and his two kids, and pitied Mayo. And envied him because he might, or might not have, Alex Jones. Or maybe pitied him for that, too. Sergeant Jones wasn't anybody's soft option.

Mayo asked abruptly, 'What's the form then, Martin?'

Kite relayed what he'd been told: that a parson by the name of Willard had been found dead in his church. That the doctor called in hadn't been the dead man's usual one, but a locum who wasn't satisfied that it was a natural death. That Ison, the police surgeon, had been contacted at a formal dinner party and would arrive as soon as he could. In sum, no more than Mayo already knew. He added, ever optimistically, that it would like as not turn out to be nothing.

'Let's hope you're right, and we can all go home.' Not every suspicious death was murder and not every murder by any means required a prolonged and intensive investigation. More often than not, the murderer would be waiting for them, shocked and speechless at what had happened in a moment of uncontrolled rage, wife, husband or some other relative dead at their feet. 'The Press'll have a field day, if not. Imagine the headlines!'

Kite was more concerned with finding his way. Surely there should've been a signpost before this, he was asking himself when Mayo spoke again, asking to be put in the picture about this benighted spot they were making their way to. 'I suppose you've been here before?'

Kite, locally brought up, was used to briefing his chief, as a comparative newcomer to the district, when it came to the more distant parts of his bailiwick, though by now there weren't many parts he wasn't familiar with, nearer to hand. He thought for a moment. 'Not a lot to it, as I recall, but not a bad place. Remote. High up. Castle ruins. Last time I came here was on a school outing and all I remember is seeing who could roll fastest down the grass on the castle hill . . . Here we are.'

The sign for Castle Wyvering had at last made itself manifest and he executed a smooth right turn, steering the car into a dark narrow road made darker by the trees arching together to form a natural tunnel above it. Winding upwards, it passed on the way a pair of large wrought-iron gates with a gold-lettered notice-board announcing the entrance to Uplands House School. There was no other sign of habitation until, leaving the trees behind at the top of the hill, at a point where the ruins of an ancient castle stood dramatically silhouetted against the rapidly darkening sky, the road levelled out and turned sharply into Wyvering itself.

Most of the houses were in darkness as they drove down Main Street, itself unlit save for the brash fluorescent anachronism of the Mobil garage and a few television screens flickering through uncurtained windows. Smoke curled lazily from chimneys. Two men having a late gossip and a smoke over their garden fences turned to watch the police car as it sped by. More lights, and sounds of muted revelry issuing from the Drum and Monkey. Otherwise, silence.

'Strewth! Bet it all happens here of a Saturday night,' Kite remarked, so disgusted he almost overshot the narrow turning which PC Wainwright, the local policeman, had declared they couldn't miss. Having spotted it just in time, he braked and turned right, slowing to negotiate an exceedingly narrow street of small, very old houses whose upper storeys leaned towards each other.

Dobbs Lane gave no indication of what was waiting at the end, where it opened out into what was in effect a kind of miniature cathedral close. In the middle, in its own churchyard, was St Kenelm's church, a grey sandstone edifice with a strong square tower, gilded by the rays of the setting sun. The churchyard stood on a green sward and surrounding it was a narrow road of houses of vastly disparate styles and sizes, their doors and windows opening directly on to the pavement. Mayo drew in his breath with pleasure. Although erected haphazardly over the centuries, the buildings had grown into a natural sympathy with each other and most of them, he was glad to see, had escaped the tarting-up that always set his teeth on edge. Quiet and harmonious, Parson's Place lay undisturbed by the twentieth century.

Undisturbed except for two cars, one of which was Wainwright's police car, ignoring the No Parking sign outside the church gates. As Kite drew up to join them, a black furry object stirred in the shadow of the lychgate, revealing itself as a huge Persian cat which glared at them and then lifted its tail and stalked off, all offended dignity, on its stocky legs.

Dr Hameed, the locum, with Wainwright in attendance, had apparently been writing up her notes while waiting for them at the back of the church. She was small, slim and brown, her face a perfect oval and her expressive eyes large and dark and not a little disdainful. There was gold in her ears and a faint emanation of chypre issued from her. She was fashionably dressed in western clothes. 'I don't have much time,' she told them crisply, consulting her watch, 'but I'll give you any information you need before I leave. I have been asked to call on Miss Willard. Her father dying like this must have been a great shock to her.'

Her accent was that of the educated Indian, pedantically correct and precisely enunciated, with a borrowed touch of the pukka memsahib and a corresponding put-down effect; it seemed a safe bet from the colour of PC Wainwright's ears, glowing like traffic lights, together with his mortified expression, that he'd recently said something which had put him at the receiving end.

'I understand and you won't be kept longer than necessary, ma'am, though I'd appreciate it if you could wait for our police surgeon,' Mayo replied, putting what was virtually a command in the form of a request out of consideration for the wait she'd already had. 'Meantime, perhaps you could tell me what you found when you arrived that made you suspicious.'

Her eyebrows lifted, rather as if she thought he was questioning her integrity, and she said stiffly, 'I think we should look at the deceased.'

'Shall I tell the Rector you're here, sir?' asked Wainwright, anxious to assert himself.

'Not for the moment. Doctor?'

The young doctor snapped her case shut with thin and delicate hands before leading the way through the elaborately-carved wooden screen separating the tower from the nave. Mayo and Kite followed her in procession down the aisle, their footsteps muffled by the strip of matting down the centre. Her legs, Mayo noticed, were nowhere near equal to the rest of her.

It was dimly-lit and very cold and he was sharply aware of the smell, peculiar to very old churches, an amalgam of stone and ancient dust, a chilly damp that any amount of modern central heating would never entirely dispel, over-laid with the scent of massed spring flowers, beeswax and Brasso. A faint breath of incense and he was back in his pre-agnostic High Church days, a very young thurifer swinging the censer in some festival procession. Death was too recent for it to have made its own olfactory presence felt. But it was also there, an odour in the mind.

At the foot of the chancel steps, facing the altar, stood a wheelchair, and here Dr Hameed paused. The ruby light of a sanctuary lamp glowed richly on flowers, white linen and lace, on an elaborately-painted reredos behind the altar and on the four highly-polished silver candlesticks and the brass lectern. But it was barely sufficient to light the area around the body in the chair and, peering into the dimness, Mayo called for more lights.

His voice, though not unduly raised, sounded shockingly loud in the silence, irritating him by making him feel the weight of some mysterious guilt, as though he'd committed some undisclosed indiscretion or was showing disrespect in a hallowed place. He could almost feel the child's conviction that here in church was where God lived and was sure to find out your sins and punish you if you were not unnatu-rally good as he looked at the prospect of the gloomy body of the church before him, inhospitable and intimidating by contrast with the resplendent altar. And the stained glass windows, which would be rich with colour against the light of day but were now, with the coming night pressing behind them, blank black voids, like dead eyes which had seen and condemned.

More lights suddenly sprang up as Wainwright pressed switches he had found at the back of the church. 'Good man,' Mayo said. Grunting, he turned abruptly away, dis-missive of his fancies, and gave his full attention to the man in the wheelchair.

The body was that of a very old man. There was a rug across his knees and he wore a tweed jacket and a clerical collar. A tweed hat with a narrow brim lay some distance away as if it had rolled there. He had slumped backwards and his head was resting against the back of the chair, revealing a scrawny neck above the dog-collar. His sparse hair was in disarray and his face was blue. His skeletal hands hung loosely. Mayo gently lifted one of them and found it icy cold, but slack.

He stood looking down intently at the dead man. 'Was this exactly as you found him?' he asked Dr Hameed.

'His head had fallen forward. I had to lift it to examine him. I haven't moved him otherwise.'

'When did you get here?'

'Just before seven, about twenty minutes after I got the Rector's call. I believe he was the one who found him.'

'So Mr Willard here wasn't the incumbent?' The doctor frowned and raised her eyebrows and Mayo waved a hand in apology. 'Sorry, my mistake, I assumed he was Rector here. Where is the Rector now?'

'He took Miss Willard away. She insisted on coming here to see her father when they told her. I estimated he had died about half an hour before I got here, possibly just before he was found. He was Dr Dickerman's patient and I was aware from his notes that he'd suffered a stroke some time since. I presumed he'd had another but as I'd never seen him before, I couldn't of course sign the death certificate.'

'Would you like to hazard a guess as to the cause of death?'

'I examined him carefully and I noticed the petechiæ— the minute hæmorrhages in the mucous membrane of the eyes and around the mouth, and I *diagnosed*,' she corrected him coolly, 'that he had been asphyxiated in some way. A pillow or something soft over the face, perhaps . . . It's easy enough, when someone is old and can't struggle.'

By nature Mayo was obsessively observant, and by training had learned to take note of every detail, however apparently insignificant, to be one step ahead of witnesses. After

one glance at the cyanosed face, and noticing the apparent
absence of marks on the neck, and the pinhead spots, he
had anticipated what Dr Hameed might say and his eye
had already searched the immediate vicinty for a possible
means of asphyxiation, finding nothing, however. No squab
cushions on the bench pews, and the kneelers were stiffly
padded needlepoint ones, probably worked by women of
the parish. If the old man's life had been smothered out,
the means had been removed. Yet her words echoed in his
mind as he looked around: 'A *pillow, or something soft* . . .'

'Just a minute, Doctor.'

A step or two took him to the foot of the deep-blue car-
peted chancel steps, beyond which he was careful not to go,
wary of unnecessarily contaminating the scene. Behind the
Communion rail stood the raised altar, its green silk-
damask frontal embroidered in gold. On the right side of
the altar, between the central silver Cross and one of the
tall symmetrically-placed white candles in their silver
candlesticks, sat a small blue velvet cushion, corded and
tasselled at each corner. On it was placed the Altar Service
Book, a dark blue morocco-bound volume tooled in gold.

Not all that soft, the cushion, but probably still a viable
means. And if it had been used to smother out the old
man's life, there would be traces—fibres from the attacker's
clothing, or saliva stains the lab could match up with the
victim's. In order to get hold of the cushion, someone would
have had to walk up the chancel steps and cross the carpet,
remove the missal and pick up the cushion, then reverse
the procedure after using it. He would have left something
of himself behind, something of the traces we all leave of
ourselves as we move through the days: dead hair, dead
skin . . .

'There's your means, Martin,' he said to Kite, who had
followed him to the chancel steps. 'Your probable means,'
he added with due caution, because he might be jumping
to conclusions in a way he was always warning Kite
about, though he didn't think so. Policemen didn't rely on

hunches, they relied on feelings based on what experience of rogues and villains and the means they used had taught them, and his gut feeling this time told him he was right. Sure enough at least to be satisfied in his own mind that there would almost certainly be sufficient grounds to set up further inquiries.

'Make sure the SOCOs give this bit the works,' he said to Kite. 'Particularly the cushion.'

'Will do.'

Dr Hameed was still standing by the wheelchair, mute and now seeming suddenly awkward and ill at ease. Her head was bowed as she looked at the body, and her hair with its black sheen, knotted into a bun at the back, her brown face and undeniably exotic appearance seemed strangely alien in the cold, grey English church. He wondered what she was making of it all. She murmured, as he approached, 'It's the first time I've come across anything like this. Not since medical school. I couldn't be sure . . . I hope . . .'

She raised liquid brown eyes and put a hand on the pew as if to steady herself and he thought for a startled moment he'd overestimated her self-possession, and that she might even be about to pass out on him. He was sorry if he'd been too sharp in his judgement of her. 'Don't worry, the police doctor's on his way.'

'Of course.' Her chin lifted and she immediately became aloof again. 'But I hope he won't be long. I'd like to be on my way. I still have to make another call.'

'On Miss Willard, that's right. You did mention. Where is she? At the Rectory?'

Wainwright coughed. 'Rector was going to take her to his neighbour's, next door. Mrs Thorne's by way of being a friend of Miss Willard's, sir.'

'I hope you don't intend questioning her tonight, she'll be in no state for that.' The doctor's voice was sharp, but Mayo made non-committal noises, knowing that he would, as always, play it by ear.

'She's been out all day and only got back just before the Rector found her father,' Wainwright said.

At that moment the door at the back of the church opened and Mayo saw Doc Ison walking towards him. Wiry and indestructible, the police surgeon walked quickly down the nave, a raincoat over his evening clothes, evidently in a hurry to get things over and back to the function he'd left. But a man to rely on, not one to skimp doing whatever was necessary. A tentative sort of friendship had developed between the detective and the doctor during their time of working together and he greeted Mayo cordially, but without wasting time on preliminaries. Within minutes he had his coat off and the sleeves of his dress shirt rolled up, his notebook out, and was deep in consultation with Dr Hameed.

Mayo left them to it for the moment. Kite went out to the car to prepare for wheels to be set in motion, to have the necessary officers and the Scenes of Crime team alerted, and Mayo sent Wainwright to ask the Rector if he could spare time to speak to him. Left alone, he prowled around with his hands in his pockets, idly read the notices at the back of the church and flicked through the guide while his mind turned over and considered which line his inquiries were going to take. The church had that peculiarly indefinable air of great antiquity, tangible evidence of which was in the dusty hammer-beam roof and pale, barely discernible frescoes on the crumbling plaster of the south wall. The building was otherwise well maintained and kept in a spotless condition, no doubt by a band of those willing helpers who can invariably be found, even in this Godless age, to dust and polish and arrange flowers. The monumental brasses shone and the pews were well beeswaxed.

It had overtones to it, this old man's death, something he couldn't pin down but felt in the pricking of his thumbs. Murder, yes. Which without in any way condoning, he could understand. For human nature being what it was, deaths of this sort did happen from time to time. The old could all too easily become an insupportable burden, particularly on unmarried daughters who were expected to devote their lives to looking after them. Situations specifically designed, it seemed to Mayo, to lead to nothing but trouble, and it continually surprised him that anyone could show amazement when trouble happened, when years of resentment surfaced and the burden was not to be borne any longer: a momentary aberration when everything added up to just too much, a second's temptation, a pillow over the face, all over in a minute. When the victim was alone and in a helpless condition, preferably subdued with sleeping pills, conveniently in bed.

He sat down and thought yes, why here and not at home? Well, why not? A stroke or heart attack, which was presumably what the killer had hoped it would be taken for, could happen anywhere, and the obvious suspicion of a domestic murder would hopefully be averted. Then time and circumstance must have been propitious for the killer.

The clock in the tower was exact to the minute. It had just tolled eight and been checked by Mayo's pedantically-correct wristwatch when the door opened and an elegantly tall, silver-haired man in a long black cassock, came through the screen, genuflected towards the altar and then approached him.

CHAPTER 5

'Lionel Oliver,' the clergyman introduced himself, advancing towards Mayo with a springing step and outstretched hand. 'I am the Rector here.' He announced the fact in a mellow and resonant voice pitched to reach the back of the church and holding more than a hint of a Celtic lilt, as though reading a first verse from *Hymns Ancient and Modern*. Lowering his tone, he added, 'This is a very terrible thing. I shall of course be happy to help in any way I can.'

'Thank you. If you could spare me a moment to tell me what happened when you found Mr Willard, sir.' Mayo indicated a pew and sat down with the Rector beside him.

'Certainly.' Oliver complied and collected his thoughts for a moment. 'He was already here when I arrived to say Evensong at six-twenty. He invariably joined me, when he was up to it.'

'Which door did you use?'

'Which door? Oh, I came in through the vestry, as I always do if I have to robe. I thought at first when I saw him that he was at prayer. His head was bowed but then when I got nearer, I discovered he was dead, poor fellow.'

'How did you know he was dead? Did you touch him?'

'I felt his pulse, certainly, though there was no need. I am not, as you'll appreciate, unfamiliar with death.' Oliver paused. 'It wasn't entirely unexpected, you know, he'd been ill for some time. I never dreamed, however . . . Surely it cannot be true that he didn't die naturally? As I said, he wasn't a well man and there were no signs of violence that I could see.' His glance strayed, with a sort of appalled fascination, to where the two medicos were bending over the wheelchair, their murmuring voices only just audible. He added, 'The doctor didn't say how he'd died.'

One up to Dr Hameed.

'I'd rather not say anything yet either. We shan't know for certain until after the post-mortem, but meantime there would appear to be reasonable grounds for treating it as a suspicious death. So it'll be necessary for the time being to lock up the church, at least until the Scenes of Crime people have finished.' A dismayed look passed momentarily over the Reverend Mr Oliver's face, but was quickly erased. 'After that, we'll let you have it back as soon as possible. Also, as soon as it's practicable, I'd like you to check that there's nothing missing from the church, sir. I see the altar silver's still there. Presumably there's more—communion plate and so on?'

'Yes, and some very valuable old books, but I can tell

you now there's nothing missing. When the doctor told me of her suspicions I immediately checked both the Rector's safe and the churchwardens'. I could think of no other possible reason why the poor old fellow should have been killed, unless he'd interrupted a thief—though like everyone else we have unfortunately to keep the doors locked nowadays. Mr Willard himself had a key. I didn't like the idea of him waiting outside if he happened to arrive before I did, which was normally the case. And if I wasn't able to be here, he could come along and say Evensong himself, without any bother.'

Mayo could have wished that the Rector had been slightly less swift in his reactions. He hoped by what he'd done that he hadn't queered the pitch for the SOCOs. 'Who else besides yourself and Mr Willard had keys to the church?'

'Only the churchwardens, Brigadier Finlay and George Washburn. Anyone else who needs to get in is handed a key by one or other of us. There's a notice by the gate advising anyone who wishes to look round the church where to apply. We do have a few visitors, especially in summer. The brasses, you know, the memorials . . .'

'Do you keep the belfry locked?'

'The belfry?' The Rector looked puzzled. 'Oh yes indeed, always. The stone steps are worn and most dangerous. I have the only key.'

'A good many people would know it was a regular habit of Mr Willard's to come to Evensong?'

'Everyone who knew him.' Appalled, he stopped and stared at Mayo. 'What am I saying? Surely, no one who knew him would even contemplate such a thing!'

'I can assume from that he was popular and got on well with everyone?'

The Rector fell silent, tracing the grain of wood along the pew rest with a long, well-manicured finger. Mayo waited patiently, gazing at the two fourteenth-century marble effigies of a knight and his lady, which the church guide had told him were of Sir William de Wyveringe and Eleanor his wife. Their hands reverently placed together in prayer, his feet resting upon his dog, they lay side by side eternally asleep on raised table tombs, their eleven children depicted along the sides. His crest had been a wyvern—a heraldic winged beast with a serpent's tail and the body and head of a dragon—in punning reference to his name. According to the pamphlet, even to this day the local pronunciation made the village 'Wyvern'.

'To be strictly truthful,' Oliver said at last, choosing his words with some care, 'Cecil Willard was never a man who was universally loved, I think, but good gracious me, which among us can claim that? I must confess I've had one or two small differences with him myself from time to time. He was a little querulous and short-tempered, especially since his stroke, but that doesn't constitute a right for anyone to take his life!'

Mayo didn't doubt the Rector's sincerity, though couldn't help feeling there was something vaguely theatrical about him, as if he were playing a part, just a little too much Welsh grandiloquence about his pronouncements. Mayo suspected that he dearly loved the sound of his own voice, and nothing better than a sermon.

He was also, Mayo felt, hedging his bets, getting his oar in first in case someone else felt inclined to inform the police that he and the old reverend hadn't been the best of friends. Putting the best construction on it by admitting to a little peccadillo in case some greater one might be suspected. A perfectly natural reaction. But the question had rattled him, Mayo was sure, and he wondered why.

'Let's begin by getting a general idea of the set-up here. Was Mr Willard your predecessor?'

'No. He was Headmaster at Uplands House School until his retirement about seven or eight years ago, when he bought one of the houses just around the corner in St Kenelm's Walk for himself and his daughter. A very scholarly man, a historian. Working on a book. He was of course a regular worshipper and communicant here.' He paused. 'I think you should know that my wife saw him coming into the church tonight, at about six. That was the time he almost invariably arrived, in order to spend some time in prayer before the service. I came in myself at six-twenty and found him dead, so I dare say she was the last person to see him alive. Except, of course ... Yes, well ... ' The pause lengthened as he hesitated to say what he was thinking. Or had he just realized that any person who found a murdered body might naturally be the first suspect? Probably not.

'That should make it possible to establish the time of his death fairly precisely, then. I take it she saw no one else?'

'She was in the bedroom at the time, getting ready to go out, and happened to see him through the window—the Rectory is just opposite—but she'd no reason to stand there watching. Mr Willard going into the church was hardly an occasion for surprise. I still feel he must have disturbed or interrupted someone . . .'

'Possibly.' It was something that would be borne in mind, though as a theory it had its drawbacks, the chief being the method used to silence Willard. Far more likely, from the sort of yobs who set out to steal church silver, would have been a hefty bash on the head. 'Is the church ever left unlocked accidentally?'

'Not often. But I have to say that not everyone is as careful as they might be locking up before they leave so it does happen occasionally.'

'Who would've had reason to come in here today?'

'Various people may have been in and out. I've popped in myself several times. And of course, it's Saturday, when fresh flowers are put in the vases. Let me see, who's on the flower rota this week?' The Rector threw a quick glance towards the graceful twin arrangements set on pedestals either side of the altar. Wine-red tulips, white lilac and some frothy greenish flowers Mayo couldn't recognize. He said immediately, 'No need to look, it will be Mrs Holden, the headmaster's wife at the boys' school, she always does them so beautifully. The school's just down the hill, Uplands House.'

'Yes, we passed it on the way here.'

'She would have arranged them this afternoon—but the key was dropped back at the Rectory, so she's unlikely to have left the door unlocked.'

'What about Mr Willard's family? You mentioned a daughter, I think?'

'Laura, yes. There's only Laura. A dear girl, a saint, really.' Mayo felt this could be a comment which perhaps told him more about Willard's character—and maybe Oliver's judgement—than it did about the daughter. 'What I mean is,' Oliver qualified, 'she has devoted these last few years quite unstintingly to looking after her father. She's always put him first. She was his secretary at the school before he left and continued the job under the present head-master. They say she knows the routine inside out, which will be useful for the new, incoming Head when he takes over in September, whoever he may be.' He stared thought-fully in the direction of the altar. 'Unless she gets married.'

'Is she likely to?'

The Rector said vaguely that he'd heard rumours, but couldn't be specific. Mayo closed his notebook and thanked the Rector for his help. 'Perhaps now I could see your wife, Rector.'

But it appeared she wasn't available, having disappeared before the arrival of the police to attend some meeting apparently deemed too important to cancel, even in the circumstances.

Then the saintly Laura Willard had better be the next person he spoke to, Mayo decided, never mind Dr Hameed's warning. She would undoubtedly be distressed, but that couldn't be helped. Regardless of the fact that she might well be responsible for her father's death, despite the Rector's eulogy on her character, she would in any case have questions to answer. He must have information about

Willard's life, his friends and his enemies, anything which might have relevance to the man's death. At the very least she should have some idea who her father had seen that day, who'd visited him and so on. She was the most likely person to be able to give him this information.

The Rector, handing over the church keys and with a final bemused look towards the activity in front of the chancel steps, left, followed shortly afterwards by Dr Hameed. Mayo joined Ison who was packing up his instruments and who proceeded to give him a brief résumé of his findings, which did not differ from those of Dr Hameed. 'Bright young woman, that,' he remarked. 'Have to be a PM, of course. I'll hang around until Timpson-Ludgate arrives— not here, though, I'm off to grab a sandwich at the pub. Your boys caught me before I'd even started my soup and I'm hungry. Coming?'

'Too much to do, Henry, sorry.'

Shutting his case, Ison paused and looked down at the body in the wheelchair. 'Poor devil wasn't long for this world anyway, in the natural course of events, but somebody helped him on his way, take it from me. I hear there's a daughter, poor soul. Ah well,' he finished, buttoning himself into his coat, 'tell them where they can find me when T-L arrives.'

The implication of Ison's remark about the daughter wasn't lost on Mayo. Ison's tone clearly indicated that that clinched it, and maybe it did. It was the obvious solution and the obvious solution fairly often turned out to be the correct one. Maybe this was a run-of-the-mill domestic murder after all.

But if Laura Willard had wanted to get rid of her father, why hadn't she simply dosed his cocoa with a sleeping pill before smothering him when he was asleep in bed? Trying to divert suspicion from herself by doing away with him in the church was surely being unnecessarily devious, not to mention unnecessarily risky.

*   *   *

'Poor Laura! All this hassle and then having to cope with the fuzz on top. Honestly. That's enough to make *anybody* throw up,' declared Phyllida Thorne. 'Is she feeling any better now?'

'I stopped them from questioning her.' Triumphantly her mother began slinging coffee mugs back on to their hooks, with much attendant danger to their handles. 'Told them she'd been sick and that the young Indian doctor had given her something to make her sleep and she was already dozy and would soon be out for the count. The Chief Inspector chap wasn't very pleased but I can't help that. Anyway, she was awake enough to give him permission to go and poke around the house—though I'm not sure she should have, and what he expects to find I don't know. She'll be able to face things better after a good sleep. What she really wants is David—but he isn't due back until tomorrow evening, and she won't let me ring him to let him know what's happened.'

'Good old Mum. I'm glad to see someone around here's capable of standing up to that lot. David—that's David Illingworth, the new man, isn't it? Bet Papa Willard wasn't very happy about that!'

He wouldn't have been if he'd known everything, thought Miriam, deciding she didn't want to discuss Laura's affairs with Philly. She was sharp and might prise out her things that Miriam herself had only guessed at, leading to an argument about Sebastian, which she didn't want. How we all keep our own secrets, thought Miriam: Laura now, normally as open as daylight. Catherine, hiding from Lionel the fact that she'd written that book. Philly, who didn't always tell her parents when she came to visit her friends in Hurstfield. Sebastian, keeping his own counsel about almost everything . . .

'The new man!' she repeated, ignoring the second part of her daughter's remark. 'You talk as if he was the last of a string. He's only the second man Laura's ever shown any interest in, to my knowledge.'

'You know what I mean. What's he like? Not another wimp, I hope. It's time something good happened to Laura, she deserves a break.' Philly swung her legs. She was sitting on the edge of the kitchen table, biting into a crisp apple with her sharp white teeth.

'He's certainly not a wimp, whatever that might imply. No oil-painting, I'll grant you, and frightfully intellectual. Fairly intimidating to talk to, and very abrupt. Anyone else and I'd think he was shy, but it's more likely he's just impatient with lesser mortals.' Aware by Philly's quizzical look that she was damning with faint praise, Miriam stopped. 'If he suits Laura, what does that matter?'

'Not a lot, I agree. But crikey, she does pick 'em, doesn't she?'

If there had previously been a shade of reserve in Miriam's acceptance of David Illingworth, it vanished as she had a momentary vision of Laura's face, seen that morning. She said decidedly, 'He's going to be very good for her, she looks happy for the first time in ages, and she's really coming out of her shell. So smart lately you wouldn't recognize her. You should've seen the outfit she had on today.'

Philly contemplated one slim, bare brown foot. 'Well, whatever, this one has to be an improvement on Jon Reece.'

Miriam's eyebrows rose in astonishment. 'Jon? What's poor Jon done to deserve that? There's nothing wrong with Jon that I can see. Unless,' she said severely, 'being popular with everybody—and amusing and good-looking into the bargain, is wrong. What's more, he may be Headmaster by the end of the year—well, either him or David.'

'Mum, you're priceless!' Philly said, in the way she had of making her mother feel as though their roles were reversed and it was she who was the child, a feat of not inconsiderable skill when dealing with Miriam. Then she added obscurely, 'You don't see what's under your nose, do you?'

CHAPTER 6

'Must be like living in a goldfish bowl, Parson's Place,' Kite remarked. 'Not somewhere to be having it off with the neighbour's wife.'

'I don't know, looks to me as though most of the front windows'll overlook the valley. There's no view from this side. No garages, either, two entries and one way round the square. But somebody may've seen something.'

The house-to-house inquiry would find out if anyone had. As it looked at the moment, whoever had killed Willard must have gone in behind him and left before Oliver went in. Twenty minutes at the outside. Leaving plenty of time for a row to develop and tempers to rise. But imagine, Mayo thought, imagine walking up to the altar to get the cushion and coming back with it, with the old chap watching all the time, knowing what was going to happen and not being able to do a thing about it. No, he'd rather not imagine that, he thought, sickened.

He telephoned Howard Cherry, the Detective-Superintendent, to give him a brief rundown on what was happening. Cherry listened in his usual attentive way and then said, 'I'll let the powers that be know and then I'll be along to have a look around myself as soon as I can, but I have to pick my daughter up from a disco first. I don't imagine you'll be finished just yet awhile.' Not yet—but no later than we can help, Mayo thought, yawning, his lack of sleep beginning to make itself felt, hoping mightily that Cherry would get a move on, tell Cinderella it was an early night for once.

Meanwhile, since Laura Willard was in no condition at present to be questioned, and Mrs Oliver was not at home, Mayo decided to take himself along for a brief look around the house where Willard had lived, taking Wainwright with

him and leaving to Kite the logistics of setting the investigation in motion. Kite made it plain he'd rather have been
with him than coping with all the mundane details, but
hard cheese. All part of the pecking order, mate. It was
Mayo's prerogative to leave him to it, just as it was Cherry's
to keep *him* waiting all bloody night if necessary.

She'd a bit of a nerve, Mrs Oliver, scooting off like that,
knowing she was a key witness to the time Willard had last
been seen, he thought as they walked round the corner.
Probably another bossy, self-possessed woman, much the
same type as Mrs Thorne, to whom he had spoken a few
minutes before.

He was a little intrigued by Mrs Thorne. A large woman
whom he judged to be normally good-tempered and probably loquacious, in this instance she had become suddenly
tight-lipped when questioned, insisting that Laura Willard
should be left alone. She'd reluctantly allowed him a few
minutes with Laura after warning him that she'd been given
sleeping pills and would be drowsy, and had subsequently
sent him packing before there was any chance of being able
to conduct a proper interview, which he felt he couldn't
decently insist upon in view of that young woman's evident
exhaustion. While conceding that Mrs Thorne was showing
concern for her charge, Mayo, who could recognize evasion
at fifty yards, left her alone for the moment. Interviewing
the lady would have to wait until a more convenient time
presented itself.

Two roads led off Parson's Place. One was the narrow,
overhung Dobbs Lane, the other St Kenelm's Walk. Things
had changed since Saint Kenelm had walked there. It now
began with half a dozen Georgian houses on the left-hand
side and led to a path, fenced with iron railings, which
overlooked the broad sweep of the valley and the river
below and came eventually to the castle. On the opposite
side of the road to the houses was a high brick wall which
had at some more affluent and leisurely period been con-

structed to hide the sight of offending washing lines and privies in the backyards of the houses which fronted Main Street.

The Willard house was the third one on the Walk. As the two police officers rounded the corner an ambulance was preparing to draw away from No. 2. 'Hello,' Wainwright said, 'that's old Mrs Crawshaw's.' He quickened his steps and spoke to the uniformed woman driver for a moment as she closed the back doors and then watched her quickly reverse out of the street and drive off. 'Seems she's been taken bad, poor old soul. Lives alone but she managed to get to the telephone. Dr Hameed's had a busy night.'

As the noise of the engine receded it was very quiet. Not a soul was in sight. In a town a crowd would have materialized within seconds at the sight of an ambulance. 'Not very curious round here, are they?' Mayo remarked.

'Oh, I wouldn't bet on that! But the young married couple that live at No. 1 are away on holiday. And Mr and Mrs Vigo at No. 4 wouldn't hear the last trump. Here's the Willards' house. Shall we go in, sir?'

Wainwright was a young family man, painfully slow to Mayo who was used to quicker reactions in his men, but eager to be helpful and endowed with plenty of common sense. He'd been the village plod for some years and was seemingly content to stay in a place where he didn't often have to work unsocial hours, the place was to his liking and he knew everyone, at least by name. The Reverend Willard, he said as they went into the house, had been known to him personally, in a manner of speaking. That is, Wainwright had called to see him officially on the occasions when Mr Willard had had cause to make complaints.

'In the habit of making them then, was he?'

Wainwright scratched the side of his nose. 'Well, he'd been a bit touchy, like. Couldn't abide these motorbikes some of the young lads had and he'd had this thing about garden bonfires and then, last week, there'd been that business of the badgers.'

'Badgers?'

'Come and see, sir. You'll better understand what I mean.' Wainwright extended a thick arm from the sitting-room towards the garden.

Threading his way between old-fashioned leather club-type chairs with sagging seats and velvet cushions, Wain-wright, followed by Mayo, opened the french window and stepped out onto a wooden ramp that gave on to a stone-flagged area. This in turn led to a stretch of garden in which flowering shrubs and spring bulbs, though leached of their colour by the now bright moonlight, were making a lavish display. That part of the garden which lay beyond the lawn and the mixed borders was invisible from the house, evidently having been constructed on the steep slope descending to the valley.

'Wonderful views from this side of Wyvering in the daytime.' Wainwright's eyes brightened with pride, as proprietorial of his patch as though he was personally responsible for its attractiveness. 'And very particular about his garden, Mr Willard was. Had somebody in to do the rough stuff, of course, but he used to potter about in it himself, do what he could. He told me his daughter had bought him a set of those long-handled tools that he could use from his wheelchair. Proper upset he was when he saw what the badgers had done to the lawn, and can you wonder? It used to be like a bowling-green.'

It was a shambles now. If a herd of pigs had been let loose to root they could have done no worse. Holes the size of a pudding basin had been dug by powerful claws, eruptions of torn-up turf marred its flat surface.

'You reckon *badgers* did that?'

'And not for the first time,' Wainwright answered, enjoying Mayo's untutored townie surprise. 'Every time he got it patched up, the dang things'd come and root it up again. Not a lot you can do about it, neither, them being a protected species.' Wainwright admitted to being a keen gardener himself and it was evident where his sympathies lay.

'Upsetting,' Mayo agreed as they re-entered the house. 'But what did he expect you to do about it?'

'Oh well, the thing is, he reckoned there's folks around here who've been encouraging them, like. Putting food out. Disgraceful, he thought that, and he made no secret of it,' Wainwright explained, looking as though he thought it was pretty disgraceful himself. 'Then last week, there was three of the animals found shot and the reverend was accused of shooting 'em.'

'Good Lord. Could he have done?'

'Not directly, because the RSPCA chap reckoned they must've died immediately and they was found a goodish way from here, near what they call their sett, down by the river. But the person that accused him thought he could've put somebody up to it as you might say.'

'Who accused him?'

The question obviously embarrassed Wainwright. His country-fresh face flushed even more deeply and his give-away ears glowed. 'I reckon it was Mrs Oliver, the Rector's wife. That's what she *thought* had happened, at any rate.'

No wonder the Rector had been upset at being asked if Willard had had any enemies when it seemed that his own wife might have fallen into that category. 'What do you think yourself? Is it likely?'

'She's a lovely woman, Mrs Oliver. A real lady, quiet and nice to everybody,' Wainwright answered obliquely, his words cancelling the mental image Mayo had formed of her. 'But she has this thing about animals. Organizes collections for them in the village and writes letters to the papers and all that sort of jazz. Can't abide cruelty to them.' He added, looking at his shoes, 'No more can most decent people, and I'm not meaning to say she'd've gone so far as to kill the old chap for it, neither. That's just daft.'

Mayo stood with his hands in his pockets, his apparently vague gaze wandering. This was the main sitting-room, but evidently the old man had used it as his study. There were all those books, for one thing. You could hardly move for them. Spilling off the shelves on to every surface which might accommodate them, even the floor. A big desk stood in the corner and a good many rather dull pictures and photographs adorned the walls. There was a dim, overall impression of Edwardian brownness and shabby, undemanding comfort.

'Anything else you can tell me about Mr Willard's relationships with other people?' he asked. 'Or anything at all that might throw a bit of light on his death?'

Murder on his patch was unprecedented and had evidently shaken Wainwright, but his daily duties didn't normally call for the exercise of such imaginative insight and he couldn't easily bring it into play now. But at least he knew his fellow-villagers. 'Everybody's pretty law-abiding round here, no trouble much to speak of. There's young Lampeter, of course,' he offered after further cogitation. 'Danny Lampeter. He does the garden here for the Willards two or three times a week, and it was him Mrs Oliver reckoned had actually shot the badgers. But he swore he hadn't and he doesn't have a gun, neither was they shot with the same gun as Mr Willard has. His is only a Webley airgun, capable of doing a bit of damage mind, but not a twelve-bore shotgun, like the one that was used on the badgers.'

When Mayo had sorted out what the constable had said from what he actually meant to say, he asked, 'But if Lampeter shot the badgers at Willard's instigation, presumably he was on Willard's side?'

'That's as maybe,' Wainwright said obscurely. 'There's no accounting for them Lampeters.'

'What d'you mean? Has he been in trouble before?'

'Once or twice before he went in the army. Joyriding and nicking radios from cars, that sort of thing, but nothing since . . . nothing I can lay a finger on, at any rate. Mind you, hard to say what he lives on since he come out the army. He lives with his sister, Ruth. She keeps the post office—and him and all, I shouldn't wonder. Thinks the sun shines out of his backside, but he's a lazy devil. Odd jobs here and there, that's all he seems to do.' He added thoughtfully, 'Never seems short of a bit of the ready, though.'

Having finally ascertained that the badger-shooting had been the most disruptive event to happen in Castle Wyvering for at least a year, and that nothing more sinister which could account for Willard's death had been brought to Wainwright's notice, Mayo let him go.

He wouldn't dismiss this quarrel about the badgers; passions were often aroused by much less. But he had other ideas as well, after seeing Laura Willard.

Pale and distraught as she'd been during those few moments he had been with her, he had recognized her immediately as the woman he'd seen in the Town Hall on Good Friday, over a month ago now, during the *St Matthew Passion*. Although subsequent events had erased the incident from his memory until now, seeing her again, he remembered her tears. And the certainty he'd had that during the performance, she had come to some sort of momentous decision.

When the constable had left, Mayo took a quick look round the house. Two attics, three bedrooms and a bathroom upstairs, one attic bare, the other used for storage. Two of the bedrooms not in use but furnished with heavy, old-fashioned mahogany bedroom suites. The third was evidently Laura Willard's. Totally unlike the rest of the house, it was frilly and feminine, done up in lavender and white with lacy cushions and a flounced spread and thick pale carpet. As disconcerting as a swansdown powder-puff in a nun's cell, he felt it said a good deal about her and what her life with the old man must have been like.

Downstairs again, he saw why the sitting-room had been used as a study. Willard had slept in a small room that had perhaps once been his study and now, because of his disability, had been turned into a bedroom. Like the sitting-room, it was lined with books. Apart from that, there was a single bed with a crucifix over it, an invalid commode, and a small table in the corner spread with a white cloth and on it the needs of a sick man: alcoholic rub, soap and talc, and enough bottles of pills to kill an army, if one had been so disposed. On the night table was a Bible, a stack of books, notebooks and pencils.

There was nothing of interest to him and he went back into the sitting-room and turned his attention to the desk but was brought to a halt before he began, momentarily defeated by the chaos thereon. If an uncluttered desktop was supposed to denote a clear and decisive brain, the owner of this one should have been a moron, but that was contradicted by the numerous books of a scholarly nature, their margins annotated in pencil, the many reference books with markers inserted at frequent intervals between their pages. Willard appeared to have been working on some sort of manuscript, probably the one the Rector had mentioned. Scads of almost illegibly handwritten papers covered what was left of the desktop, piled anyhow on top of one another, almost obscuring the telephone. He glanced at some of them and saw there was much rewriting and crossing out, though a slight film of dust indicated they hadn't been looked at for some time.

In the end he gave the top up as a bad job for the time being and turned to the drawers. Here he found bank statements showing comfortable balances, a large envelope of share certificates in all the recently privatized public utilities, the deeds to the house and insurance papers. One drawer was full of old letters and another held a jumble of defunct ballpoints and paperclips, plus a large stiff-backed foolscap diary, a current three-year affair with a day to each page.

As he flipped through this, it became apparent that Willard, like many another writer before him, had been incapable of seeing an empty space without scribbling on it. Many were the observations tucked in here and there in his small crabbed handwriting, the testing out of a felicitous phrase in the margins or on unfilled days, of which there were plenty, Willard being an invalid with his diary consequently fairly free of appointments. There were a few with his doctor and chiropodist, and it seemed he had been active enough to participate as a member of the parochial church council and to be a governor of Uplands House School. In fact, the approaching Monday held a reminder of a school governors' meeting.

The space for today was blank. But on Friday—yesterday—he'd had an appointment with someone called Quentin at 2.45 and on the same line a time, 6.30, was written. Was that when Quentin had been expected to leave? Possibly it denoted another appointment, for next to it the initials S.O. were scribbled. Beneath that was written, with a different pen: SARA? *'An action done from duty has it's moral worth, not from the results it attains or seeks to attain, but from a formal principle or maxim, the principle of doing one's duty, whatever that may be.'*

The first thing Mayo saw when he went back towards the church was the gleaming maroon Rover of mature years in which the pathologist swanned around. Also adding to what was now promising to be an unprecedented traffic jam in Parson's Place were several more police cars with lights flashing and a van indicating the presence of the Scenes of Crime team. He entered the church and found it humming with subdued activity as the white-overalled SOCOs swarmed over everything, dabbing with Sellotape, crawling over the chancel floor with hand-held vacuum cleaners and amassing their collection of samples in polythene bags. The photographer, Napier, was standing waiting by the rotund figure of the pathologist who was kneeling on one side of the wheelchair with Ison on the other.

The two doctors looked up. Ison nodded and Timpson-

Ludgate, after greeting Mayo in his usual genial manner, said, 'Not much doubt about this one. Plain as the nose on your face. Asphyxiation due to suffocation. The altar cushion, you say? Yes, it's possible.'

Timpson-Ludgate had recently gained a certain amount of fame (or notoriety) by writing a book about his experiences as a Home Office pathologist, the sort of thing for which the general public seemed to have an insatiable appetite. It was written in the racy manner one might have expected, given his personality. Despite the flamboyancy of his approach, Mayo had a great respect for him and his opinions.

'The killers always make the same mistake of thinking their victims are too old and too feeble to struggle but they do,' he went on, 'and he must've struggled hard. See those petechial hæmorrhages? With luck, there'll be skin tissue under sonny boy's nails, if and when you find him. I'm playing golf tomorrow but I know how impatient you always are so I'll have him on the slab before I go, and set your mind at rest. Come on, laddie,' he said to Napier, 'one more shot—here—and then I'm finished.'

The photographer adjusted his lens; the SOCO sergeant, Dexter, had put the altar cushion inside a polythene bag and was waiting to dab Sellotape on to the clothes of the dead man for any contact traces from the killer. Another hour and they'd all gone: the doctors in their cars; the fingerprint men, photographers and plan drawers in the Scenes of Crime van; and the body of the Reverend Cecil Willard in the mortuary van, encased in a green polythene body bag.

Mayo despatched Wainwright home to a belated supper, with a request to be back sharpish in the morning, and leaving one of his men posted outside the church and the rest to await the arrival of the mobile unit, he asked Kite to accompany him on his next call, which he intended to be on Mrs Oliver.

Kite had been gathering more information from Wainwright while Mayo had been otherwise occupied. 'We've drawn up a list of the residents in the square, ready for starting on the house-to-house tomorrow morning. Wainwright knows them all and he's given me some useful gen. Most of them would've known Willard. The Mrs Thorne where Miss Willard is staying teaches languages at the boys' school and her husband's the Director of the Fricker Institute—'

'The Fricker? Where the bomb went off? Hadn't realized that. I only saw his wife when I called earlier.'

The bomb which had been planted wasn't Mayo's investigation, it didn't come under his jurisdiction, but he remembered it and recalled now that the Director of the Institute was a Dr Denzil Thorne. There was no reason why he should have made the connection between the Director and Mrs Thorne before, but now that he had, he felt a sudden prickle of the hairs on the back of his neck. Was it possible that here was the first lead?

It had been assumed, though as far as he knew there had as yet been no claim, four weeks later, that the bomb at the Institute had been the work of animal rights extremists, protesting against the experiments carried out there. He hadn't heard, either officially or otherwise, how the investigation was proceeding and in the absence of any information to the contrary he'd assumed it wasn't complete. The connection with Willard's death might be altogether too tenuous and his suspicions quite unfounded. On the other hand, it might turn out to be a profitable line of inquiry to pursue.

'Who's in charge of the bomb inquiry down at the Fricker?' he asked Kite.

'Uttley, isn't it?' Kite said, after a pause for thought. 'I'm not sure. Somebody in the Hurstfield Division, at any rate. I'll find out. Likely to be some connection?' he asked, his interest sharpening. He'd no stomach for domestic murder and preferred to think there might be some more intriguing motive for what happened, rather than the sordid despatch

of some poor old bugger whose only crime was that he had
lived too long.

'It may be a long shot, but Willard was at loggerheads
with the Rector's wife over—would you believe it—some
badgers who've made his lawn look like a rugby pitch after
an international. Apparently she's one of those people who
are passionate about animals.' He briefly summarized for
Kite's benefit what Wainwright had told him, ending with
his own surmises. First Denzil Thorne, who had escaped
any personal injury in the bombing but who would because
of his work obviously be anathema to the champions of
animal rights. And now Willard, who had been suspected
of instigating a badger-shooting—though he would have
suspected a letter bomb or some such would have been a
more likely method to have been chosen as a means of
despatching him. If indeed seeing Willard's death as a
penalty for shooting the badgers wasn't in any case
altogether too extreme.

'The fact that both men live in the same village is
intriguing, but it proves nothing. Not unless we can find
some other connection.' He added, 'There's the bad lad of
the village we must take into consideration, for one thing,'
and recounted what Wainwright had told him of Danny
Lampeter, though he'd little faith in him being their man.
Even supposing he'd had some differences with Willard,
which there was as yet no reason to believe, a man like
Lampeter seemed unlikely to be the type who would use
that particular method to get rid of an enemy, any more
than animal rights activists would. Shooting badgers, however, might be a very different thing.

CHAPTER 7

The Rectory was the Georgian house with the grey slate roof opposite the church gate, whose front steps led directly off the street. A largish, foursquare house, yet separated from the Thornes' crooked little black and white timbered cottage next door only by a narrow space. It was growing late by the time Mayo got around to seeing Mrs Oliver and the winding-up signature tune to *News at Ten* could be heard from a room at the back as the Rector opened the door to their knock and ushered Mayo and his sergeant into his study. A small, comfortable room at the front of the house, it was lit by a green-shaded lamp on the desk where papers were spread and the Rector had evidently been working.

'We're disturbing you, sir,' Mayo said. 'It's really your wife we'd like to see, now. Would you like us to see her somewhere else?'

'No, no, not at all. Catherine will be along shortly, we've been expecting you.' Previously, the Rector had visibly been out of countenance by what had happened in his church, but his distracted air had now been vanquished by a professional good humour which Mayo guessed was habitual to him.

Almost immediately, Mrs Oliver came in, pushing open the door with her knee and wheeling in a trolley laid with crockery and coffee things. 'I supposed you wouldn't have had time for anything to eat, so I've made a few sandwiches,' she remarked diffidently.

'That's very thoughtful, but you shouldn't have gone to so much trouble, ma'am.' Mayo hadn't the heart to tell her that Atkins had persuaded the landlord of the Drum and Monkey to lay on bacon and eggs for later.

'It's no trouble, we're used to providing hospitality here.'

A smile briefly illuminated her face and when he saw

how vague and sweet it was he was obliged to rearrange
his preconceived notion of her as a bit of a dragon. She
poured out a liquid that didn't promise much from its
pale amber colour, and offered beef sandwiches (dryish,
mustardless and almost meatless, for which even Kite
couldn't show much enthusiasm). She was small and
unremarkable-looking with a meek expression in repose.
Mayo could imagine her being soft about animals, one of
those who put pictures of dewy-eyed kittens on the wall, he
was thinking as he sipped his dire coffee and accepted
another sandwich in the spirit in which it was offered. And
then caught a quizzical gleam in her unexpectedly beautiful
hazel eyes and changed his mind yet again.

The Rector, reaching out for his third sandwich and
munching with every appearance of enjoyment, said, 'Now,
Catherine, I believe the Chief Inspector wishes to ask you
about seeing Cecil Willard.'

'Yes, Lionel, that's why I thought he was here.'

The Rector nodded encouragement to the detectives to
go on, the gentle irony apparently escaping him. Mrs Oliver
waited composedly.

She was evidently one of those women whose mind is on
higher things than the clothes they wear, otherwise she
surely wouldn't have had on that drab jumper and skirt,
garments no doubt practical and tidy but so insignificant
Mayo thought he'd have been hard put to it to remember
them if he closed his eyes for a second. Neither did the
colour do anything but dull her brown and rather weather-
beaten complexion. A dedicated gardener, perhaps, for the
hands which lifted her cup were small and rough-looking
with the nails filed very short. Below her wedding band she
wore an engagement ring which immediately caught the
eye, so out of character with the rest of her did it seem—a
row of five extremely fine diamonds which flashed fire as
her hands moved.

But then, the Rectory had a well-to-do and prosperous
air, none of your brick box on a housing estate type, nor

the draughty unheated Victorian mausoleum whose upkeep is impossible for an impecunious clergyman. It was warmly centrally-heated, tastefully decorated and graciously, even luxuriously furnished: Mayo, whose business it was to know about these things, if not able to envisage ever owning them, had already noted that the tall, breakfront bookcase in the corner of the study was Georgian, the coffee-pot was silver and the table it stood on of polished burr walnut speaking of a couple of hundred years of tender loving care. Pictures in here and in the hall were of the sort he imagined to be of some value.

As Kite led into the questioning, it became clear there was nothing new Mrs Oliver could tell them about seeing Willard going into the church, nothing but what her husband had already told Mayo: she had observed no one else in the vicinity at a minute or two after six when the old man had been propelling his wheelchair up to the church door. 'I remember the time,' she said, 'because I was keeping one eye on the clock. I had to be in Hurstfield by seven.'

'Who was your appointment with, Mrs Oliver?' Kite asked, pencil poised.

'I was due to attend a meeting at a friend's house to discuss raising funds for an animal welfare society I'm concerned with.'

The dedication of people like the Rector's wife to such causes never failed to arouse Mayo's admiration, but at the moment he was more interested in the fanaticism which is sometimes a corollary. It didn't follow that because you loved animals enough to want to alleviate their suffering, you had to go to any lengths to bring this about, however extreme or illogical, yet there were people like that. However, he felt it was going to take an immense effort of will to imagine Mrs Oliver as one of them. With enough of this sort of fanaticism to kill Willard for what he'd done, or for what she imagined he'd done. Even more to imagine her being associated with the acts of mindless terrorism which are indifferent to the killing and maiming of innocent people, such as the bomb attack on the Fricker. He didn't dismiss it as impossible, though. Jack the Ripper might have been a mild-mannered man at home.

He asked her, 'As a close neighbour and presumably a friend, what was your opinion of Mr Willard?'

Mindful of how her husband had reacted to the same question, he expected a similarly cautious assessment from Mrs Oliver but there was neither caution nor hesitation in her response. 'He was no friend of mine! Nor did I want him to be. I know he was a very clever man—much too clever for me, in fact, and too cold, the sort whose head rules his heart. But his attitudes weren't what one expects from a man in his profession and—'

'I'm afraid my wife isn't being very charitable,' the Rector interrupted, throwing her a look of astonishment, rather as if the family pet had suddenly turned round and bitten him.

'I'm only saying what I believe to be the truth, Lionel. I don't want to speak ill of the dead and I know one must make allowances for his age and the state of his health—and I'm very sorry he had to die the way he did. But I didn't like him or his attitudes, nor did I like the way he treated Laura—though that, of course, was none of my business.' She broke off abruptly, then added, 'If you want a champion, don't speak to me, speak to my son Sebastian. He won't hear a word against Mr Willard.'

Sebastian Oliver. The S.O. of Willard's diary? 'Yes, I'd very much like to. Is he in now?' Mayo asked.

'He is, but I don't think now would be a good time to talk to him. He's only just come in and heard the news and he's very upset.'

'Rubbish, Catherine! He's recovered enough to have been running up our telephone bill for the last ten minutes. I'll go and fetch him—if he's not ringing Tokyo or Timbuctoo,' said the Rector, leaving the room with a glance of deep displeasure at his wife and a small silence behind him.

Mayo said, 'Well, Mrs Oliver, while we're waiting, would

you please tell me what you meant about Mr Willard and his daughter?'

She replied with some sharpness, 'I said that was none of my business.'

Then she could only have mentioned it because she wanted him to know, but wasn't prepared to have the accusation of gossip levelled at her, a phenomenon familiar enough but surprising in Mrs Oliver, who so far had given an impression of total honesty. 'Perhaps then we'd better talk about this disagreement you had with Mr Willard over the badgers that were killed.'

'Oh dear. Oh yes, the badgers. I knew someone would've told you about them by now.' While it was evidently upsetting to her, she seemed relieved at the change of subject and took the opportunity to replenish her coffee cup, offering the pot to the others, an offer not taken up. She hadn't, Mayo noticed, eaten one of her own sandwiches. Charitably, he decided she was almost certainly a vegetarian. 'I'm sorry now in view of what's happened that I accused him of instigating the killing,' she went on. 'One doesn't like to feel that any person one knows has died with a mutual bitterness unresolved. But you know, he really was quite obsessed about that lawn of his.'

'I've seen it. It's a mess.'

'But it's only grass! It'll soon grow again. There was no justification for having the poor beasts shot! I don't believe he would have stopped until he'd had them all wiped out, either.'

A small tic twitched at the corner of her mouth. She put her hand to cover it and he saw the hand was trembling. This small, mild-seeming woman had her Achilles heel and the action she believed Willard responsible for had exposed it. Who could say what might have followed?

Fanatics and oddballs were familiar territory, at least you got to meet your share in police work, and soon ceased to be surprised at what small things could trigger them off. But could Mrs Oliver conceivably have become so incensed by the shooting of the badgers that she had deliberately gone into the church after him, taken that velvet cushion from the altar and put it over his face until he could no longer trouble her or take revenge against the animals she doted on? She'd had the opportunity, she had seen him go into the church and it would have been the work of a minute to slip out of the Rectory and in behind him. Another minute or two to do what she had to do and then slip out, perhaps waiting until her husband had emerged from the house and gone round the back of the church to enter through the vestry door. It would have been risky, the timing being so restricted, but so it had been for whoever the killer was.

He realized she was speaking again, but her agitation was now under control. 'One has to keep things in proportion, not be sentimental, Lionel says. But it really was quite horrible. I've been watching the badgers come into the clearing for months. One gets to recognize them, to know their individual characteristics. But however much I deplored what Cecil Willard did, Mr Mayo, I wouldn't have wished any harm to come to him.'

At that point, Lionel Oliver came back into the room, followed by his son.

In his slender build and the slightly quizzical cast of his features Sebastian Oliver resembled his mother, but he had a physical beauty she lacked. That and self-possession, plus a rather conscious charm, immediately suggested itself to Mayo. His thick dark curls were cut close to his shapely head. His eyes were very dark, and they danced when he smiled, but when he didn't they were opaque and shiny, like obsidian. How old was he? Twenty-five?

He perched on the arm of his mother's chair. Kite, who was ready to be prejudiced against anyone who wore pink shirts, thought he looked just the sort of yuppie who *would* be telephoning Tokyo. Besides the pink shirt, he had on a pale grey cashmere sweater and beautifully cut, dark grey slacks and on his feet were soft ox-blood leather moccasins. DC Farrar had nothing on him.

'I find all this fairly incredible, I must say. I've been dining with a friend at the River House in King's Grafton,' he said, naming a currently fashionable, and expensive, establishment in the area. 'We've only just got back and heard the news. I've just rung Philly, Ma, and she's as shattered as I am. Absolutely shattered.'

If he was, or even as upset as his mother had suggested, he was hiding it well enough. Which was more than possible, Mayo owned. Even on such short acquaintance and despite his apparent openness, something about Sebastian Oliver suggested inherent secretiveness, a reluctance ever to give anything away willingly. 'What time did you leave here this evening?' he asked him.

'Oh, just after six.'

'According to your mother, Mr Willard was gong into the church about that time. Did you happen to see him?'

'No, I can't say I did.'

'When *was* the last time you saw him?'

He replied that it had been the previous day, confirming Mayo's surmise that the initials in Willard's diary had been this. 'About half past six it would've been, I suppose, I'd only been here about half an hour. I wanted to see him but he wasn't expecting me and I didn't want to interrupt their supper, so I decided on the spur of the moment to go along and see him before Laura arrived home.'

'He wasn't expecting you? But he had six-thirty, and your name, written in his diary.'

'Had he? Well,' Sebastian said coolly, 'I gave him a ring before I went in, just to see that it was OK, so he must have written it down then. There was no other pre-arrangement to see him, but I usually do make it in my way to pop in when I'm here. I'm afraid I don't have the pleasure of living in Wyvering.' He smiled but nevertheless managed to make it sound as though it was a pleasure he could quite easily forgo and gave an address for Kite to note down in his book which Mayo knew was considered to be one of the more desirable places to live in London. 'I came down with Philly in her car. I thought I'd save myself a lot of hassle—only as you can see from the grey in my hair if you care to take a closer look, it's an experience not to be recommended in any circumstances.' Anticipating the next question, he explained, 'I'm talking about Phyllida Thorne, her parents live next door and that's her MG outside, and I can tell you that driving with her is something else. Have you ever noticed, women reveal more aspects of their character than you'd really like to know about when they get behind the wheel of a car? Yes, well, I'm only here for the weekend. It was a surprise visit and I'll probably leave on Tuesday morning, if, of course I'm allowed to.'

'We have your address, sir,' Mayo said stolidly.

'Seb!' his mother exclaimed. 'Oh dear, I thought you were here for longer, this time—especially since Philly's staying the week. How disappointing!' The Rector said nothing but looked, if anything, rather relieved at the news.

'I thought so too, Ma, but something's come up. I may have to get back. By British Rail, desperate as that is—but better than a ride in Philly's MG, even so. Sorry.' His wide smile had all the confidence of one who fully expects that whatever he does, he will be forgiven for it and Mayo saw from his mother's resigned expression that it would be.

'You appear to have been very friendly with Mr Willard?' Mayo said. 'Unusual, if I may say so, with a such a big difference in your ages.'

'Oh, I've known him for yonks. He used to coach me in history at one time, during the hols. I dare say it says a lot for him that we stayed good friends.'

'What did you talk about when you called to see him yesterday?'

'I really don't remember,' Sebastian replied, rising elegantly from the chair arm and standing with his back to the fire, his hands in his pockets. 'This and that, you know how it is.'

'Did he by any chance mention being bothered by any-thing—or anyone, come to that?'

'Lord no, but then he wouldn't. We didn't meet on those sort of terms. We rarely talked about personal things. In any case, I wasn't there long, fifteen minutes perhaps, no more.'

'Did he strike you as being any different from usual?'

'No.' The young man paused. 'Well, if you call being pretty sharp different then yes, maybe he was. But then, he wasn't exactly renowned for his gentleness, old Willers. Yes-es, I did yet the impression something might have upset him, now you mention it. Perhaps,' he added flippantly, 'his lunch or something hadn't agreed with him.'

Mayo said nothing. Sebastian's grin gradually faded and he began examining his immaculate nails. After a moment he looked up and said, 'People got the wrong impression of him, you know, he wasn't such a bad old stick at all. In fact, I genuinely quite liked him. He was a bit moralistic, but there was no fudging things with him. He told you straight out what he thought so that you always knew where you were with him.'

Mayo had the impression that for the first time, Sebastian Oliver was speaking with genuine feeling and not for effect or evasion. But he was curious about this friendship which had apparently existed between the two, with fifty years between them. Not that he discounted the possibility, he was just interested to know what it was they'd had in common. He continued to watch the young man steadily, without saying anything, and under his silence Sebastian's self-assurance, like many another's, wilted. 'Damn it, you're not suspecting *me*, are you? I *liked* him, I'm hardly likely to have bashed him over the head with a blunt instrument, am I? I wouldn't know how, for one thing . . . I'm so totally cack-handed I'd probably have missed if I'd tried. You ask my pa.'

The Rector made a noise like 'Pshaw!' and Mayo's flash of empathy with young Oliver did a reverse turn.

'It doesn't follow,' he said sharply. 'There's only your word for it that you got on with the old man—and that nothing happened between you yesterday that caused you to kill him today. I'm not saying you did, but where were you at six-fifteen, the time Mr Willard is estimated to have died? King's Grafton isn't more than twelve miles from here. Six o'clock was rather early to be setting off to take dinner there, wasn't it?'

Sebastian looked suddenly pinched round the nostrils, but he said shortly, 'We went for a drive around first. It was a lovely evening and you appreciate the contryside after living in London. I was with Philly and she'll confirm that.'

'In her car? So you pocketed your principles?'

The other acknowledged the irony with a small smile. 'This time I drove.'

Mayo thought about the note in Willard's diary. 'Do you know anyone called Sara—or Sarah, maybe,' he asked, altering the pronunciation to rhyme with 'fairer'.

'No. Should I?' The denial was too quick, too unthinking.

Mrs Oliver put in quickly, 'There's your cousin Sarah.'

'Who lives in deepest Cumbria. And who with any luck might one day fall into Lake Windermere and never be seen again.'

'Seb! That's an appalling thing to say.'

'She's an appalling girl, Ma. The last time I saw her she was fat and spotty and pulled wings off flies.' His eyes were wickedly alive again.

'What nonsense, Sebastian!' said the Rector severely. 'I find exaggerations like that not only uncalled for and unamusing, but in the worst possible taste.'

'Who says I'm exaggerating?'

It was time to leave. Sebastian Oliver had talked a lot of foolishness, making it hard to sort the wheat from the chaff. Most of it was showing off, of course, but it also suggested to Mayo that there was much more tension in him than was apparent on the surface. He thought he might even, in certain circumstances, be a very dangerous and rather cunning young man. That allusion to the method of Willard's death might have been indicative of innocence or might be a bit of would-be clever wool-pulling. Although Mayo was far from convinced that they had got from him all that he knew or thought—it seemed to him that there had been an uncalled for urgency in Sebastian so precipitately rushing off to see Willard as soon as he arrived home, for instance—Mayo was realistic enough to know when he had for the time being lost a witness. At the moment it didn't matter. He could come back to Sebastian.

Contrary to what Miriam Thorne had told Mayo, Laura hadn't taken the pills given her by the doctor, even though she knew she wouldn't sleep without them. She had wanted to keep awake. She had to think what to do, what to say, not to make any mistakes, and sleeping pills made you feel like a zombie. So she was horrified to find she'd slept after all, feeling as though there were something callous and uncaring about being able to, even though it had only been for an hour or two and she knew it was the sleep of emotional as well as physical exhaustion.

She lay in the unfamiliar bed in Miriam's guest room, wearing one of her hostess's nightdresses, a voluminous affair in pink stretch satin, Philly having declared that she hadn't one to lend, nor pyjamas, never having worn either since she was fifteen. Laura couldn't have faced going back to that empty house to fetch her own things.

The sudden glimpse in the wardrobe mirror of the suit she'd taken such care in choosing nearly reduced her to tears again. Now flung anyhow over the back of a chair, the gleam of its rich silk brought back the horror of what had happened. A deep depression washed over her, she lay in such a misery of guilt and fear and horror that she almost cried out. If only one could put the clock back—if David could have been here—if she could beg her father's forgiveness! If only. All memory of the intolerable strain of the last years had gone, leaving only what had been good between herself and her father.

'You didn't know him before his illness,' she'd once tried to explain to David, who thought the stroke no excuse for her father's impossible and sometimes downright unchristian behaviour.

'No.'

The ironic monosyllable had been uncompromising and she'd found she couldn't continue in the face of his apparent unwillingness to try and understand: how much her father had hated the trappings of ill health, his impatience over the necessary preoccupations with the functions of his hitherto taken for granted body, the unacknowledged fear that he might have another, even more incapacitating stroke which would disable him mentally as well as physically.

Laura had feared this as much as her father did. The last one, leaving him as if not only partially paralysed but chronically short-tempered and resentful, had damaged their relationship little by little, much as she had striven for patience. Not that it had ever been a demonstrative relationship, he had always been too dry and detached for that, but there had been respect and affection. His wit, though caustic at times, had made him a sharp and amusing companion and though disappointed in her lack of scholarship, his encouragement to her to read widely had lit a candle in her mind, illuminating corners that might have remained dark and unexplored. She would never cease to be grateful for it.

These were the things she must remember about him, that she must cling to.

From downstairs came the unmistakable jerky ring of the old-fashioned doorbell that Miriam had installed because it was old and 'in keeping', never mind that you could sprain a wrist in the process of twisting it to make it work. Taff's barking and a man's deep voice, not Denzil's, sounded from below. Just for a moment she thought it was David and her heart somersaulted and then she remembered that he was in Brighton and wouldn't be back until late tomorrow. It must be the police again.

She knew she ought to go downstairs and get it over with. No! Instinctively, like a child, she drew the duvet up and buried her head.

It was Mayo's voice that Laura had heard.

As the Rectory door shut behind them, he had noticed that the mobile unit had now arrived and been parked across the square in front of a timbered house that was used as the parish rooms. But there was a crack of light between the curtains in the Thornes' house and he decided it wasn't too late to return Laura Willard's key. Leaving Kite to go across the square, he rang the Thornes' bell.

A salvo of sharp, terrier-like barks came from the back of the house. The door was opened by a scantily-clad young woman who would have been extremely pretty if she hadn't been hiding behind a witch-like make-up, with her dark hair cut very short and spiked like a sea-urchin. She accepted the key with a minimum of thanks and was just about to shut the door when her mother leaned over the half-wall which was all that separated the sitting-room from the tiny hallway, popping up like some outsize ginger-haired Judy, glass in hand.

'Who is it, Philly? Oh, it's you, Chief Inspector.'

'I came to drop Miss Willard's key in, but since you haven't yet gone to bed, would it be incovenient to give me a few minutes of your time?'

'I was just on my way but—oh, all right. Come in.' And to her daughter, 'Bring us some coffee, darling, will you?'

'Not for me, Mrs Thorne, thanks.'

'No? Then not for me, either, Philly. Not such a good idea, perhaps, this time of night. How about a drink instead? No? Oh well, I'll finish mine if it's all the same to you.'

She was wearing a pink towelling bathrobe and slippers which backed up her assertion that she'd been preparing for bed and he assured her again that he wouldn't keep her long. 'Oh, it doesn't matter.' She came round from the back of the screen, still holding what remained of her drink, and opened a door off the hall. 'My husband's study,' she explained. 'He won't be in until very late tonight.'

Watched with what he sensed was silent hostility from the girl Philly, he followed Mrs Thorne towards a small room on the other side of the staircase, where the windows were of old lattice curtained in a cheerful chintz and the low beams black with age. Before stepping inside he looked around for the daughter but she'd disappeared.

The room was so small there was no room in it for anything else other than a set of bookshelves wedged between two of the upright beams, an oak desk and chair and a small chintz-covered easy chair close to the fireplace. It struck him as perverse for a woman of Mrs Thorne's size to choose a house of such miniature proportions, emphasizing the ludicrous contrast with her own, though on reflection he doubted whether that would bother Miriam Thorne overmuch, or even enter her head. She had a humorous face, indicative of good sense but not much imagination. He saw that the preoccupied air she'd worn earlier had been replaced by a purposeful look. She'd made up her mind what she was going to tell him. He pulled out the upright chair before the desk when she asked him to be seated and after kneeling to switch on the electric fire and heaving herself to her feet she subsided into the armchair, watching him with a slightly wary expression.

'I suppose you want to know what I was doing at the time of the murder?' she asked with a wryly lifted eyebrow.

'It's the question we shall be asking everyone, so it'll do to begin with.'

'Well, that's easy. I was here with my feet up and a drink in my hand, if it happened at six-fifteen as Lionel says it did. I teach languages at Uplands House, you know, and we've had an open day today. I stayed on to help with the clearing up in the kitchen. That sort of thing doesn't normally form part of my duties, you understand, but we're very short-staffed at the moment and Richard—Richard Holden, the Headmaster—asked me if I'd help out. I said I didn't mind, all hands to the pump, you know. I was there until ten to six.'

'How long did it take you to get home? Ten minutes?'

'A bit longer than that. I cycled home, no use for a car here.' The vision of Miriam Thorne on a bicycle was too much to dwell on and keep a straight face; he concentrated on getting the facts down. 'As soon as I got home, I had a very dry martini,' she went on. 'And did I need it after four undiluted hours with parents!' Her smile faded and she added soberly, 'God, how awful to think he was being killed while I was here, knocking it back . . . He *was* killed, wasn't he? It wasn't another stroke?'

'We can't know for certain yet,' he replied cautiously, 'but yes, it does look that way.'

'Poor soul. He didn't deserve that, even though he was—' She broke off and finished her drink at one gulp. 'I'm talking too much, probably too many of these,' she said, putting the empty glass down on the floor beside her.

He didn't think she was over the top, just a little loosened up, though the martini probably wasn't her first, or even her second.

'He was what, Mrs Thorne?'

'He was a very dominating man, Laura's father. She should've broken loose, years ago, but Laura's like that, she's too soft. He was making her life a misery—using the fact that he was an invalid as emotional blackmail, being obstructive about her marrying a man who's been divorced —even though it's a wonderful chance for her. David may even be the next Headmaster, there's a fifty-fifty chance, though he wouldn't have been if old Willard had had anything to say about it. But with all his faults Laura loved the old devil. I mean, she was deeply attached to him.'

'Did you see anybody or anything unusual as you came in?'

'Nothing at all. Not a soul, in fact, except Laura coming home in the taxi. Spoke to no one until the Rector brought her here and told me what had happened. Poor darling, her stars can't have been very auspicious today, what with this, and the accident and all.'

'What accident?' he asked sharply.

She darted him a swift, sidelong glance. 'Oh yes, of course, you wouldn't know. She'd been in Lavenstock all day and on the way home she bumped the car. She'd called in at a filling station for petrol and coming out she pulled out into the traffic too soon . . . Another car caught her wing and spun her across to the other side of the road.'

'Where was this?'

When she gave him the name of the filling station, which was just on the outskirts of Lavenstock, one familiar to him, situated on a stretch of fast dual carriageway, he thought Laura Willard had been very lucky indeed to escape without a serious accident.

'She was very shaken up,' Mrs Thorne agreed. 'Someone might easily have been hurt—even killed I suppose. She blames herself, says it was all her fault but I suppose she'd have her mind on other things.'

'What other things?'

'Oh, nothing special,' she said vaguely. 'I dare say she's right, really. I have to say she's not a very good driver.'

'What time did it happen?'

'Late this afternoon, I gather. Apparently it's made a mess of both cars and, as you must know, anything like that takes ages to sort out so she had to get a taxi home because the steering on hers was a bit suspect. That's why she was so much later home than she intended.'

He knew why she was telling him all this. If true—and only a fool would have used such an easily verifiable story as an alibi if it were false—then Laura Willard was likely to be in the clear as far as killing her father was concerned. The timing was too tight, for it was surely stretching credibility to bizarre lengths to believe that she would immediately have rushed headlong to the church after such a grim couple of hours to find her father, and then for some reason have done away with him. Even after a sudden flare-up between them about, say, her damaging the car. All things, however, were possible.

He stood up, and thanked Mrs Thorne, apologizing for keeping her from her bed. 'That's all right. They go to bed early in Wyvering and I've adopted the same habit.'

'Have you lived here long?'

'Twelve years. Since my husband's job brought him to these parts.'

'He's Director of the Fricker Institute, I'm told.'

'My, you have been doing your homework! The Fricker, yes. Where they experiment on animals, not to test cosmetics, but in order to alleviate human suffering. And in case you think otherwise, I wholeheartedly support that.'

'Why not? I'd have thought it a very worthwhile job.'

'Not everyone thinks so. He only just escaped that bomb last month.'

'He was a lucky man, then. I wasn't concerned in the investigation—Hurstfield's not in my bailiwick—but I heard about it,' he told her, and then had to listen while she told him in a forthright and not very complimentary manner what she thought of the police attempts to find the bombers and her opinion of the bombers themselves—'

She stopped abruptly and apologized. 'I'm sorry. I get rather carried away.'

'That's understandable. I suppose it must always be a fear at the back of your mind, but your husband must be used to it, getting threats and so on?'

She looked suddenly rather pinched. 'In his position it's inevitable, isn't it? But there's been nothing lately, that I know of.' And paused. 'I think he would've told me if there had been.'

So there had been something at one time. But what, he saw by the sudden closed look on her face, she wasn't apparently prepared to say. He stood up, ready to leave. 'I'd like to talk to your daughter some time.'

'Philly? She's probably gone to bed by now. She's been out to dinner with Sebastian Oliver and she came back very tired.'

'I didn't mean now, later will do. I've just been talking to him—he's a particular friend of hers, I gather?'

'Yes,' Miriam said, with so little enthusiasm he raised his eyebrows. 'Yes,' she repeated, and sighed. 'Oh, he's all right, I suppose. He's certainly redeemed himself by now but—'

'Redeemed himself?'

'Well, you know, he was expelled from Halsingbury—at least, that's what it amounted to, though his parents—no, you mustn't take any notice. I'm not being fair. He's really quite different now.'

He didn't waste his time trying to make her say any more at this juncture. He could see that she already felt she had said too much.

CHAPTER 8

Mayo finally put his key into the lock of his front door in the early hours of Sunday morning, gritty-eyed and ready only to zonk out. Having reached a point where he'd decided nothing more useful could be accomplished that night except calling a halt and sending everyone off to snatch a few hours' sleep, Cherry had put in an appearance, ready to go through the case so far with his usual thoroughness and not averse to Mayo going through it with him— but then, he hadn't been without sleep for nearly forty-eight hours. Mayo had drunk another mugful of the tongue-stripping coffee that was Spalding's forte, and summoned up a second wind. It wasn't until an hour later that he'd been free to shut up shop.

Moses, the grey cat belonging to Miss Vickers, was sitting as usual on his doormat, waiting for the chance to insinuate himself inside. The familiar moment's struggle for supremacy ensued when Mayo tried to open the door wide enough to get in while at the same time endeavouring to hold the cat back with his foot. He wasn't over-enamoured of this particular feline, which had a wall eye and a frustrated determination to be loved by him. Its plaintive miaouing could be heard through the closed door of the flat, which had its usual desolate look when he came back to it tired and hungry. The daffodils Julie had bought were dying. There was a note from Alex saying the pork chops were in the fridge with the rest of their abandoned meal and they'd better be eaten up a.s.a.p. She reminded him what duty she was on next week and ended with love and kisses, Alex.

Somehow he'd missed out on the eggs and bacon at the Drum and Monkey and he felt ravenous but the thought of cooking the chops was too much. He wondered if the cat might eat them or whether in view of his name he wouldn't consider them kosher. He settled for a corned beef sandwich which he ate propped up at the kitchen counter before dropping into bed.

Once there, he found himself maddeningly wide awake, the events of the case chasing themselves around in his mind. Finally, he gave up the attempt at sleep and began to try to gather up the threads, counting them out as if he were counting sheep:

One, Cecil Willard had been killed for no apparent reason. He hadn't been an altogether pleasant personality but the arguments he had had with people hardly seemed to constitute sufficient grounds for murder.

Two, he was objecting to his daughter's marriage, which was disagreeable for her but hardly insurmountable—killing him to avoid the unpleasantness of opposing him was taking a sledgehammer to crack a walnut.

Three, there had been trouble with Mrs Oliver over the

shooting of some badgers. It had upset her very much but unless the affair had, without anyone being aware, blown up to epic proportions—as admittedly such trifling incidents had been known to do—it didn't at the moment seem to be of such paramount importance that he was prepared to give it much credence.

Four, what seemed more important was that Willard's death had come at a time when he might have been troubled in his conscience about some unspecified moral issue he had come across, very likely to do with someone called Sara. Was it coincidence that the name had appeared in close conjunction with that of Sebastian Oliver, the smooth young man with the sharp edge who had visited Willard the day before his death but claimed to know nothing about any Sara? He was adamant that his relations with the old man had been friendly. There was no reason to believe otherwise and he had an alibi for the time of death. This depended upon Phyllida Thorne—and hers upon him for that matter. Mayo was not easy in his mind about either of them, though he'd yet to speak to her—and to Laura Willard, if it came to that.

Five, six, seven and so on . . . there was more than enough to occupy him before he need start reaching for conclusions.

Having decided this, he turned over and fell dreamlessly asleep until he woke at seven, fully awake to the exigencies of the day before him which included, first thing because of Timpson-Ludgate's golf commitments, attendance at the post-mortem. For reasons not too far to seek, he decided to skip breakfast.

The events of Saturday night produced on the following morning an interest in the church at Wyvering normally not granted to it. Half the village seemed to have found urgent and compelling reasons to be out and about in the direction of Parson's Place and a great deal of confusion was occasioned in the narrow confines of Dobbs Lane, owing to cars being refused entry into the square and having to reverse out.

Lionel Oliver, dismayed at the unwonted intrusion but unable to do anything about it, finally gave up and went back into the Rectory, looking decidedly upset at such distasteful behaviour, envisaging the quiet decorum of his church disappearing in a welter of chocolate wrappers and Coke tins. 'I hesitate to believe such ghouls can be our own village people, gawping and staring at the scene of a murder! Not that there's anything to see, as I have repeatedly told them. I explained, in so far as I could, why it had been necessary to cordon off the churchyard and to limit vehicle access into the square and I endeavoured to suggest—quite reasonably in my opinion—that they were being no help at all to the police in hanging around. But I don't think they were really listening.'

Catherine wasn't surprised. Lionel's orotund utterances frequently had that effect on people. 'Well, at least it meant we had a good turn out at eight o'clock,' she reminded him briskly.

He had pinned up a notice from the vicar of St Peter's in the neighbouring village of Stapley, inviting the faithful to join his own Sunday flock for Matins and Evensong, but Holy Communion had been celebrated here in the parish rooms. There had been twice the usual number of communicants but this evidently hadn't pleased Lionel.

'Hardly a matter for congratulation, having them to do the right thing for the wrong reason,' he answered Catherine's cheerful remark with pained reproof, yet feeling for some reason—and not for the first time lately—that it was he who was in the wrong.

This unusual state of affairs was very unsettling to him. In fact, he was feeling thoroughly upset—and much of this, he was sorry to have to admit, was due to his wife. He was seeing her with new eyes, ever since she had blurted out her confession to him. Which she had done with trepidation, obviously afraid he would be disturbed by what she had to tell him, as well she might be, after having been so secretive.

Well, he certainly was disturbed, not only by the fact that she had deemed it necessary to keep from him that she had written a book, but also that it was about to be published.

Was he then such an ogre? he asked himself. Would he not have been delighted to hear of it? The answer was no, in both cases. No, he was not an ogre—he was a very approachable man, as everyone knew, and he rarely lost his temper, though that did not mean he wasn't entitled to show his displeasure when the occasion warranted it. And no, he was certainly *not* delighted to hear about her book. The idea of his wife seeking notoriety was repugnant to him.

'Notoriety? What rubbish, Lionel! It'll be a nine days' wonder, if it's noticed at all—which I doubt very much indeed.'

'Not when you're sponsoring an organization which supports violence for its own ends.'

'You know me better than that,' she said, but avoiding his eyes. He had the feeling she wanted to tell him something else but didn't know how to begin. He waited but when nothing happened he sighed and turned away.

Yes, he was upset. For the first time in nearly thirty years of what he had always regarded as mutually supportive work and marriage, he felt he didn't know how to deal with Catherine. He was shattered, as his son would have put it. Oh dear, Sebastian! Another worry. That business rearing its ugly head again, after all these years! Lionel was very much afraid that, much as he disliked the idea, he was going to have to try again to resolve that situation, this time once and for all.

Lionel Oliver was God-fearing, upright, and would never knowingly hurt anyone, but these were attributes which came naturally to him, without effort. He had never had to fight any tendency to personal sin. Nor felt any great need for introspection or self-examination. But now he had to ask himself why there were things going on in his own house, within his own family, about which he had been told nothing. That he would most certainly have put a stop to them was one reason, he admitted that. But were his loved ones, in fact, also *afraid* of him?

After the PM, and the essential briefing of his team at Milford Road station, a session with Atkins who would from now on be in charge of the incident room at Lavenstock, and a quick run through the papers and documents which continually piled up on his desk as inexorably as sand round the Pyramids, Mayo had a senior level discussion with Cherry and the ACC, concentrating mainly on what information should be released to the media and how to keep it as low-key as possible. By the time he was clear, it was mid-morning. Kite had already left for Wyvering and Mayo followed, driving himself. Leaving his car in the Drum and Monkey car park, he walked up Dobbs Lane. By the time he reached Parson's Place there was no sign of the house-to-house inquiries so presumably they had finished knocking on doors there and moved on elsewhere to find out the whereabouts of everyone in the village on the previous day.

'The posh school included?' DC Deeley had asked at the briefing.

'Everyone,' repeated Kite. 'And if any strangers were noticed anywhere in the village. Which shouldn't stretch you too much. Village like this, they won't have missed a thing—casual comings and goings by outsiders, unusual behaviour, anything.'

It was a hazy, fitfully sunny day, cool for May, but warm when the sun came out. Mayo walked slowly so as to take a better look at the square, seen previously in the dark, liking what he saw even better in daylight. The little precinct had a timeless feeling about it and, despite the jarring police presence, a slumbrous sense of history to which the violent death which had occurred there would in time add its own dispassionate contribution. There were pink flowering cherry trees in the churchyard, lightening the gloom created by the large number of yews, unclipped, with great sweeping branches; he counted thirteen houses, every one charming and no single one like any other in the square, before completing his circuit. One or two were in fact no longer houses. Apart from a largish timbered one, now the parish rooms, he saw that one erstwhile cottage announced itself in its window as a knitwear cooperative, and spotted another of Georgian vintage which had become a solicitor's office.

He was looking for an entry Kite had spoken about, and found it opposite the back of the church. A high wooden gate marked PRIVATE, it nevertheless stood wide open, wedged with a stone. He walked down a narrow space between two houses to the top of an overgrown pathway between the two gardens flanking it, where it ceased to bear any semblance to a real path and plunged downwards. It was now little more than a slippery gully between rocks and overgrown clumps of gorse and bramble, likely to appeal to reckless children out playing but no one else. The reason for the gate being propped open was evident. Someone had been tipping garden rubbish, lawn mowings and hedge clippings, now littering the path either side. With some difficulty, he descended a few yards until he could see that it ended at the river bank, then he scrambled back, dusting the loose red soil from his hands and knees and continued on his way.

He was so busy thinking about the entry that he almost missed the building in the corner. Wedged in between two taller ones, it was a tiny house with a tall chimney, no more than one room and a door wide, one storey high, which had been turned into a shop. The window had been shuttered the previous night and he saw now something he had missed then, a modest signboard above the door which read: M. SMITH, ANTIQUES.

Feeling under no immediate obligation to hurry, he stopped to look in the window. It was very small, the original window to the house, with a consequent lack of room for anything other than a pretty little display of Victorian trinkets, some glassware and china, odds and ends of bric-à-brac. A lamp had been placed at the back of the display and shone on some small pieces of antique jewellery—and there, set out on black velvet, was a pair of cameo earrings which he knew instantly would solve the problem of Alex's next birthday present. It wasn't her birthday until September and by then, the small thought niggled, who knew where she would be? On the other hand, if he waited they might have gone.

But the shop would be closed for Sunday. He was about to turn away, half-relieved that the problem had resolved itself, but on second thoughts tried the door. Unexpectedly, it opened to a jingling bell and he pitched forward into a dark interior, missing the step down and only just saving himself. As he regained his balance and his wits, his eyes adjusted to the dimness and he saw a face he recognized.

She'd been Macey then, an ambiguous name: he'd never been quite sure whether it was her Christian or surname, or just conveniently taken over from the ancient sign, MACEY'S MARKET, above her junk shop premises, which were situated in a ratty, half-hidden corner in one of Lavenstock's less salubrious districts near the canal.

At one time she'd been a familiar figure around the station, but although he'd never actually had occasion to question her himself, she must have known who he was. For reasons of her own she didn't let on that she did. When he inquired about the earrings, she named a sum that made him wince. It was three times what he'd expected and he shook his head.

'They're stone cameos, none of ᵗ our shell. Perfectly matched faces.'

'Too much, I'm afraid.'

'I could drop the price a bit if you're really interested.'

She was anxious to sell. He guessed she hadn't been here long and wondered who'd buy from her, how many customers she could hope to expect, apart from the odd tourist or two who came visiting the church. His glance round the shop showed there wasn't much stock, but not bad, what there was of it. No tat. Going up in the world, Macey, and going straight this time, he hoped, though she'd always been too fly to have anything pinned on her. No definite proof, just a strong suspicion.

He thought the story of her gipsy origins might be true. She had the fierce, dark looks and the wily cunning to make it believable, at any rate. Though no longer young, she was still handsome, with a proud nose and a hypnotic eye. It would be wiser to keep on the right side of Macey if you could—cross her palm with silver, ward off the evil eye. He wasn't altogether joking.

He decided to call her bluff. 'Come on, Macey, you know I'm just a poor copper. I can't afford that sort of money.'

'Oh, so you're one of *them*!' Her head jerked in the direction of the mobile unit and the police cars, keeping up the pretence that she didn't know him. 'What about something else, then?'

A small tray of jewellery stood on a table near the door which led to the back premises but when he moved towards it she said, 'Oh, that's rubbish, I haven't had time to sort it yet,' and swept it aside.

She's up to her old tricks, he thought, making a mental note to warn Wainwright what sort of customer he'd got on his patch, but finding nothing further to arouse his suspicions, nor anything else he thought likely to appeal to Alex, he said maybe he'd look in again later. What were her opening and closing times?

'Here, I've told your lot once.'

'So tell me again.'

With a sigh she informed him that she only opened a couple of days in the week and at the weekends. Just until she got going, as you might say. She was new to Castle Wyvering but you had to diversify these days, she added grandly. She'd closed at six yesterday and opened again at ten this morning.

He went to the window and stood looking out. Small as

the aperture was, he was able to see most of the lychgate and the churchyard path, as well as the houses opposite. 'I don't suppose you get away bang on time,' he remarked, 'you'll have things to do after you close.' Though he couldn't imagine what, frankly. No cashing up to speak of, no sorting the stock out or anything of that sort—there'd be all day to do that.

'There's the locking up to see to,' she agreed, as if the tiny premises required security measures at least equal to those of the Bank of England. 'But I'd left by twenty past six—as I told your mates. I'd been hanging on, see, waiting for my son to pick me up in his van.'

Mayo knew all about Tigger Smith, the origins of whose nickname were shrouded in the mists of time, but for sure hadn't come out of Winnie the Pooh. If Tigger had shown his weasel face in the vicinity it meant trouble, most likely of the sticky-fingered variety. Most *unlikely* that he'd stepped out of line and killed somebody. Villains, like union members, tended to stay within their demarcation lines. It was, however, one more fact to file away for reference.

No, Macey answered his next question, she hadn't particularly noticed who'd been in and out of the church all day. 'Why should I, I wasn't nosey-parkering about, I'd other things to do, hadn't I? Except I saw a woman go in with some flowers and the parson once or twice.' Which seemed to Mayo a pretty good score, considering she hadn't been watching much.

'Which parson?'

'The one they call the Rector. Not that old one in his wheelchair—him as copped it, poor old bloke. Seen him before but not yesterday,' she said, picking up a feather duster which he couldn't imagine being put to use for long if he knew Macey, indicating this was the limit of the information she was prepared to impart. 'What about them earrings?'

'I'll think about it.'

'Special price to you,' she wheedled.

'I'll think about it,' he repeated. 'Don't worry, I'll be back, I promise you.' And before he left her to make what she could of that, he added, 'I'd get a warning put up about that step, if I were you. Somebody could kill themselves before they've had a chance to buy anything!'

CHAPTER 9

The house was as full of her father's presence as if he were still there, sitting in his wheelchair, and not for the world could Laura have touched anything that had belonged to him. It would have to be done, all the grisly clearing away of the remnants of a life, but not yet. Before that she had to get over the present hurdle of being questioned by the police: this tall, lanky sergeant who had an easy manner but a quick, shrewd glance—and the other, the older man with the Yorkshire accent, who didn't smile much at all and whose eyes never left her face. She listened, ashen-faced, while he told her the results of the post-mortem, and how her father had been killed. She had partly expected it. Dr Hameed, when Laura had been unable to believe her father's death was unnatural, had indicated how it might have happened. But the altar cushion! She wished he had been spared that last profanity.

She said, her voice not quite under control with nerves, 'I suppose you want to ask me all sorts of questions and I'll do my best to answer, but I can't promise to be very bright. I feel absolutely exhausted and yet my mind won't seem to let go.'

She was very relieved to hear the Chief Inspector say that he wasn't going to trouble her overmuch at this stage but alarmed at the implication that there would be later, perhaps more difficult, stages. 'Thank you,' she said, 'you're very kind. I haven't really taken it in yet, the whole of yesterday seems like a dream, the accident and—and everything. Miriam says she told you about that.' She was talking too much, it would be wiser to say nothing, just answer their questions. She tried desperately to pull herself together, while the Sergeant said yes, they had heard, and asked her when she had arrived home after it.

'It was quite late. My father had already left for church.' Asked to be more specific, she thought it must have been about twenty past six. The rector had arrived about ten minutes later to tell her what had happened, just as she was about to change and start preparing supper. The supper they were destined never to eat. As this occurred to her she was suddenly overcome. Her voice faltered and finally broke. She groped for a handkerchief. 'I'm so sorry!' She was desperately ashamed of herself, but she couldn't help it. Tears came easily to her.

'Take your time, Miss Willard.' He spoke kindly, the Chief Inspector, there had been compassion in the way he'd told her about her father, but his eyes were no less watchful. He seemed perfectly content to wait until she felt herself sufficiently recovered to put away the handkerchief before he remarked, 'So you were out shopping most of the day. Was your father alone?'

'Yes, but I'd left him a cold lunch. I knew he'd be on his own all day and that was why I was so anxious to get back.' Oh damn! she thought, feeling herself flush up in a defensive way that must be telling him more about her guilt feelings than the tears had done. 'I telephoned him and told him I'd been held up, though I didn't tell him why.'

'What I really meant,' he said mildly, 'was whether your father was expecting any visitors?'

'No, I don't think so. He was going to take things very quietly. A friend came to see him on Friday and it seemed to have tired him out more than usual. And he'd only made tea for himself. The things were still on the tray.'

'This friend would have been Mr Quentin?'

'Professor Quentin, yes,' she answered quickly, to hide the sharp stab of dismay she felt. How did he know that?

Then realized that of course, he must have read her father's diary. Trying not to sound agitated at the mention of his name, she explained that Quentin was a Fellow of her father's old college in Cambridge, that they had kept in touch. 'He looked forward to seeing him more than anyone else. He didn't come too often, and he was younger than my father, but they had things in common, a lot to talk and argue about. It was guaranteed to cheer him up as a rule.'

'But not on Friday?'

'No.' She explained about Quentin's shortly-to-be-published book and her father's unfinished one. 'I think that must have depressed him much more than he admitted.'

'That confirms Mr Oliver's—Sebastian Oliver's—impression that he wasn't quite himself.'

She was taken aback. 'Sebastian? He's at home, is he? When did he see my father?'

'On Friday, just before you came home, I believe.'

'That's funny, Father never said anything. How peculiar, he was always specially pleased to see Seb—in fact, he never failed to mention if anyone had been in to see him. It was something to talk about, over supper, you see,' she said simply, not knowing that her words conjured up for Mayo a sudden brief vision of long, silent evenings stretching into the future, the unremitting boredom of spending them with someone whose interests you didn't share and with whom you'd long since ceased to have anything new to say.

He seemed curious about the relationship which had existed between Seb and her father, evidently thinking it a strange friendship for two so disparate in age and temperament. How did she account for it?

She'd often wondered, herself. 'Well, I suppose Seb cheered him up, amused him—though he used to get exasperated with him sometimes and say any fool can make money, it's a clever man who knows what money's for. He thought Seb was wasting a good brain. I don't know exactly what he thought he should be doing with it. They just got on together as some people do. I know that for some reason, Seb used to take advice from my father where he wouldn't from his own.'

Mayo looked amused. 'That's about par for the course where parents and children are concerned.'

He might have a sense of humour, despite appearances to the contrary. She wondered if he was married, with children. She was surprised to see how much the smile lightened and gave character to his serious, anonymous face, made him look years younger and much more attractive. It was the sort of attraction she could appreciate—conventionally handsome men had never had any appeal for her. It was the whole picture, the entire personality which mattered.

'So it would seem as though he'd no reason to have borne your father a grudge, then,' he was saying.

She blinked, then almost laughed. 'Seb? Good gracious, no!'

'But perhaps you can think of someone else—of anyone in fact who might have had cause to wish your father out of the way?'

'No, of course I can't, that's preposterous! I know he wasn't an easy man, and I can think of one or two people who've been at odds with him from time to time—but mostly, it was something and nothing, it quickly blew over. Surely he must have disturbed someone who meant to steal from the church . . . there can't be any other explanation.'

'Possibly.' His voice was deliberately neutral and she guessed it wasn't a solution that appealed to him. 'Tell me about your gardener,' he said suddenly. 'Lampeter, isn't it?'

'Danny?' She frowned. 'Oh. I see you've already been told about the badger incident. You know, I'm really getting awfully sick of those wretched badgers. My father made a lot of fuss about them ruining his lawn and Mrs Oliver encouraging them, and she over-reacted but that's all there

was to it. There's no way my father could have shot one—
and anyway, however angry he was, he'd never have been
deliberately cruel.'

He asked what her father's attitude had been to the bomb
at the Fricker Institute. 'Well, he was shocked, naturally,
and had some very hard things to say about the sort of
people who are prepared to do such things. He believed all
this concern about animals might be better transferred to
the plight of some human beings.'

'Need the two be mutually exclusive?'

'No, but they often are.'

He leaned back in his chair against the old worn velvet,
seeming quite at home and at ease and in no hurry to carry
on. At last he said, 'So—Danny Lampeter. You'd discount
the possibility of him being responsible for shooting the
badgers?'

She thought for a moment or two. 'He might have for all
I know, he's probably capable of it, but it wasn't at my
father's instigation, I'd swear. For one thing, Danny wasn't
exactly my father's favourite person and he certainly
wouldn't have put himself under an obligation to him.'

'Pardon me, ma'am, but in that case, why did he employ
him? If he had something against him?'

'It wasn't anything specific,' she said carefully. 'And it
was through me Danny came to work here. His sister and
I used to be great friends, we went to school together. We
haven't seen so much of one another lately, but Danny's
been having a hard time since he came out of the army and
I thought the least I could do would be to offer him some
work, though it wasn't much, just a few hours a week. My
father thought he was lazy and insolent, but he's all right
if you handle him the right way . . . Surely you can't suspect
him? I—' She stopped suddenly, remembering something
she had totally forgotten in the present crisis. How could
she have forgotten it?

'Yes, Miss Willard?'

'Oh, it's nothing.'

'Better let me judge that.'

'No. No, really, it was just something unimportant that occurred to me.' She couldn't tell him what was going through her mind until she'd had time to consider what it might mean.

He gave her a steady look but made no further comment, and proceeded to his next point. 'There was an entry in your father's diary that puzzled me.' He felt in his inside pocket for his notebook, opened it and read the words he'd copied out: ' "*An action done from duty has its moral worth, not from the results it attains or seeks to attain, but from a formal principle or maxim, the principle of doing one's duty, whatever that may be.*" ' He looked up. 'I take it to be some sort of quotation?'

She recognized it immediately and for a moment or two she was silent, reliving the pain of Friday night, when her father had spoken of finding himself faced with a moral problem. His words, she realized now, had practically been a paraphrase of that quotation. She felt again the coldness that had come over her as he spoke, knowing what it meant. David had said, when she'd told him later that night, that Quentin was a discreet and honourable man; if he had told her father what he knew about David it would have been because he assumed the same qualities in his friend. If so, they both knew he had miscalculated. Her father would never have hesitated to use anything in his vendetta against David.

'It's from Kant. Father was always quoting him,' she said with an attempt to shrug it off. 'It was his habit to jot down things that took his fancy as he was reading. It won't mean anything.'

He accepted this without further comment and asked, 'Who do you know called Sara, or Sarah? Or rather, who did your father know of that name?'

She hesitated a split second. 'I'm not aware that he knew anyone called that—I certainly don't.'

As she spoke a car was heard to draw up outside, at the

front of the house. Its door slammed. Shock and pleasure combined to give her a rush of blood to the head, render her momentarily immobile. 'It's David,' she said, astonished and delighted that he should be here.

He gave her no chance to get to the door, but pushed it open and walked straight into the house without ringing, indicative to her as nothing else could be of how different things were going to be from now on. Nevertheless, he paused in the doorway of the sitting-room before he came in—the room where he had been so unwelcome that he had seldom been invited to enter—as if her father might still speak and show his displeasure. There was tension, too, in his hunched shoulders, the way his hands were thrust deep into his pockets. He was a tall untidy man, thin and long-legged, like a heron, with a shock of un-disciplined dark hair, a beak of a nose and a fierce glance the heavy bar of his dark spectacles did nothing to mitigate.

'Laura.'

She forgot her own worries in the protective need to smooth away the defensive aggression never far from the surface. Regardless of the others in the room, she threw herself at him, and he held her for an all too brief moment in his awkward, brusque way. 'Don't grieve too much,' he murmured against her hair, so quietly she wondered if she'd imagined it, especially when he released himself almost roughly from her clinging arms. She was conscious of her father's last, hurtful words about her being led into marriage with David because she was afraid that life was passing her by. But no. She had known she was marrying a difficult man who found it hard to accept what had happened to him but she also knew that he needed her as much as she needed him, she knew his tenderness when they were alone—and his determination that her father should not be allowed to ruin her life.

'How did you—?' she began.

'Miriam telephoned me, first thing. You should have let

me know, Laura,' he said shortly. Then: 'Aren't you going to introduce me?'

Her father's death was for her a horror and an obscenity, the more so because she had, however subliminally, wished for it, but she could see that for David, there could only be insincerity in a pretence of sorrow: it had solved most of his problems at one stroke, there would be no unpleasantness over their marriage—and perhaps more importantly for him, without her father's opposition he would believe that now nothing could stop him becoming Headmaster. She wouldn't have expected him to utter platitudes which he patently didn't believe in, about a man he had never liked. Always a reserved man, intensely private, in times of stress he tended to maintain a neutral silence—or worse, become uptight and sarcastic, either of which could so easily be misconstrued. She could see how the police might view his uncompromising attitudes and at this moment she passionately hoped he was going to make the effort to unbend a little. Total honesty at all times could be a disaster.

She made the necessary introductions and he said, 'Is there some coffee, by any chance? I left before breakfast, straight after Miriam rang.'

'Breakfast, then?'

'A sandwich will do.'

She hesitated, reluctant to leave him alone with the police.

'Carry on, Miss Willard, don't mind us,' said the Chief Inspector easily. 'I've only a few questions to put to Mr Illingworth. We'll be gone by the time you get back, so I'll say good morning to you.'

Mayo had watched the interchange between Laura Willard and her young man with interest. On the surface, he could see no compatibility between the two—Laura, who in normal circumstances he guessed would be a warm-hearted, sociable woman and Illingworth, cool and withdrawn, not a man to suffer fools gladly. His expression now clearly said that questioning him would be a waste of time. A sense of his own intellectual superiority emanated from him, an impatience with lesser mortals. As a prospective head-master, which Miriam Thorne had indicated he might be, he would not have impressed Mayo. He said suddenly, 'What do you want of me? I can see you have to know the whereabouts of everyone concerned, but how does that affect me? I was nowhere near Wyvering when Laura's father died.'

'That's not my immediate concern either, sir. I'm more interested to start with in what you can tell me about Mr Willard—what sort of man he was, what your relations with him were, that sort of thing.'

Illingworth smiled, not kindly. 'Don't expect me to white-wash him. If I pretended I was sorry he was dead I'd be a hypocrite. I'd no time for him and there's plenty who'd be ready to tell you so. He disliked me and was doing his best to screw up Laura's chances of being happy with me because of his outmoded principles. He'd done it to her once before and I wasn't prepared to let her stand for it again.'

'Hard words that might be better left unsaid in the cir-cumstances, Mr Illingworth.'

'I was far enough away at the time he was killed for that not to worry me.'

'Near Brighton, I believe?'

'Yes, it was a weekend conference. I skipped the first session on Friday night to help get ready a computer exhi-bition we were having at the school but I left here first thing yesterday morning.'

'What exactly was the trouble between you and Mr Willard?'

'My first marriage ended in divorce and there are certain sections of the established church who hold the time-honoured view that marriage is for life and re-marriage an unforgivable sin. He held rigidly to that. He'd never heard of compromise.'

Mayo wondered what Illingworth—who was not giving the impression of being a person to give way on anything, any more than Willard apparently had been—meant by compromise in the circumstances. Did he mean living together? Marriage wasn't regarded as a strict prerequisite for moving in with someone these days, though Mayo guessed with Laura Willard it might be. Her father's influence had been strong, by all accounts. From Illingworth's own point of view, living together without the benefit of clergy might not be such a good thing either: you could hardly expect a school, however progressive, to risk upsetting parents on that score—even if the parents were not always themselves like Cæsar's wife, beyond reproach. With the coveted Headship within his grasp, he wouldn't want to put a foot wrong.

'I believe Mr Willard also opposed your consideration for the position as Headmaster at Hillside?'

'He supported Jonathan Reece, which isn't quite the same thing, but he wasn't the only governor. I'm confident that even with his vote, Reece wouldn't have been appointed.'

Too clever by half, Mayo summed up Illingworth. The man was, like himself, from north of the Wash: Derbyshire or South Yorkshire at a guess. Beneath the veneer of educated university-speak Mayo recognized the broad northern vowels and something of the bluntness, the bloody-minded determination that sometimes characterized his own actions. This might make him easier to deal with, or trickier —for how completely do we ever understand ourselves?

'How did he strike you, Martin?' he asked as they left.

'Never been easy in my mind with his sort—he's a type, isn't he? Always ready to take a rise—but the first to back down if you stand up to 'em.'

'Very perceptive of you—though I didn't see any signs of Illingworth backing down. Not the sort to endear himself as a prospective son-in-law, was he? What would you have done if Sheila's father had tried to stop you marrying her?'

'What, him? Couldn't get her off his hands fast enough —she was costing him too much in telephone calls!' Kite grinned. 'But if he had I'd have told him to take a running jump. We've come a long way since Queen Victoria.'

'That's what I thought you'd say.'

And similarly, Mayo didn't see even Laura Willard knuckling under to her father's domination for ever, nor Illingworth giving a damn what Willard felt about their marriage—though his career prospects might have been another matter. If, despite what he said, Illingworth had believed Willard had had the power to put a spoke in the wheel in that direction, could he have killed Willard? Was he a killer? It was a pointless question. Mayo believed anyone was capable of killing, given the right circumstances and motivation. Even a motive that might be so slight as to be non-existent in the minds of everyone except the murderer's.

'Anyway, if he was in Brighton he's covered for the time of the murder. Have him checked all the same, Martin,' he reminded Kite as they came to the mobile unit. 'See what time he arrived. Meanwhile, let's have a word with Danny Lampeter. He's beginning to interest me. According to Wainwright, he lives at the post office with his sister.'

'Want me to go and see him?'

Mayo looked at his notes and considered. 'We'll both go.'

'The sister should be free as well. The shop shuts at eleven-thirty.'

George Atkins looked up from a plan of the village spread before him, squinting through the foul fog of his pipe smoke. One of these days, Mayo promised himself, he'd do something about getting rid of that damned pipe. Or George. On second thoughts, it would have to be the pipe, George was much too valuable, though he could be equally irritating. A dedicated workhorse, completely unflappable but a law unto himself, he knew inside out the division, the men working it and the criminal element therein. He jabbed with the pipe-stem at the plan of the village. On the plan had been superimposed a grid, with each square being allocated to one pair of officers. 'They're working along the main street now,' he said, jabbing again. A globule of tobacco juice landed on the plan. Atkins rubbed it off with his coat sleeve.

'It'll save them a bit of time, then, if we take the post office,' Mayo said, with difficulty restraining himself from making some caustic remark. 'I want to see Danny boy myself.'

'By the way,' Atkins said, 'know who we've got here? In Castle Wyvering? We've got Macey, haven't we, our gyppo friend from Lavenstock.'

'I know, I've seen her,' Mayo said, and stealing his thunder, he added, 'Tigger was around yesterday as well. Keep your eye on her, she's up to something, I shouldn't wonder. At any rate, she was mighty anxious I shouldn't go poking around.'

CHAPTER 10

Ruth Lampeter was just closing the shop. She opened on Sunday mornings for a few hours, ostensibly for the sale of newspapers, sweets and tobacco. But since it was the only shop of any account in the village, she also did a useful trade in other goods that people had run out of or forgotten on their weekly shopping forays to the supermarkets in Lavenstock, with scant regard for any petty restrictions against Sunday trading. It was with obvious reluctance that she unlocked the door and let them in, and then only after Kite had shown his warrant card through the glass and stated their business.

The sub-post office occupied a few glassed-in square feet

in one corner of the available space. The rest of the shop was devoted, floor to ceiling, to the varying needs of a small community. She led them on safari into the back premises, through the crowded stacks of tinned and packet goods and the frozen food counter, skirting the piles of wire baskets and a roundabout containing paperbacks. Past brightly-coloured woolly hats and socks for children occupying part of a shelf, and one-size, one-colour tights and a selection of ladies' underwear in peach or pale blue stacked on another, with wellingtons in all sizes lolling beneath the shelves.

After the overflowing cornucopia of the shop, the living-room felt spacious, though it was small enough to be crowded by a beige moquette three-piece suite, a dining table, a sideboard and four upright chairs. It was obsessively clean. A fire smouldered in the grate, yet it felt cold and at the time stuffy and airless. It made you want to throw the windows wide to the spring breeze.

'I hope this isn't an incovenient time, Miss Lampeter?'

Her indifferent shrug implied there was no time which could conceivably be convenient, but she indicated where they might sit. Kite chose one armchair and Mayo settled his bulk in the other, and though the settee remained unoccupied Ruth Lampeter chose to perch herself on the edge of one of the hard, upright, leatherette-covered dining chairs, her back rigid and her feet and knees pressed tightly and virginally together.

A small woman with a figure that was curiously asexual and a prim, narrow, buttoned-up face devoid of make-up, she might have been any age between thirty-five and fifty. Her dead-straight brown hair was parted at the side and held in place with a tortoiseshell slide. She wore a shapeless grey skirt that was much too long, and a neutral coloured jumper with a V-neck, apparently hand-knitted. The whole effect, Mayo realized after a moment or two, was of a bizarre throwback to the nineteen-thirties. It was dowdy and ageing, but he doubted if Ruth Lampeter was aware of that, or even cared.

'We're making inquiries into the death of the Reverend Mr Willard, which you've probably heard about, Miss Lampeter.'

'Of course I've heard, they've been talking about nothing else all morning, but I don't know why you've come to me. I never had anything to do with him, except sometimes to sell him a few stamps.'

Mayo noticed how precisely she spoke, articulating the syllables in an old-maidish way, with no trace of the local accent. He sensed an obstinate nature that would defeat any attempts to get her to cooperate. She was like a blank slate that would resist all attempts to write upon it. He pitied her schoolteachers. And wished he'd brought Jenny Platt along with him—although on second thoughts, perhaps not. He didn't think it was in Ruth Lampeter to be communicative with anyone, man or woman.

'We're not singling you out, Miss Lampeter,' he said. 'We're talking to everyone in the village, asking them where they were yesterday.'

'Well, I was here in the shop, as anyone in Wyvering could tell you.'

'What time did you close?' Kite asked.

'Half past five, the same time I always close on Saturdays. After cashing up, we tidied the shop. I stayed in all evening and went to bed at ten.'

'We, you said. You've an assistant?'

'I meant my brother,' she answered reluctantly.

'Danny?' She nodded. 'Maybe we could speak to him as well?'

Perhaps because of that inadvertent 'we' she became, if possible, even more close-lipped. 'No, you can't. He's gone away for a few days.'

'He has, has he? That's interesting. When did he go? And where?'

'He went as soon as we'd finished yesterday. Well before six, at any rate. He didn't stay for supper.'

'You're sure about that?'

'Positive. And I don't know where he's gone. Why should I? He doesn't have to tell me everything.' Her words implied indifference but the cool precise voice had sharpened a semi-tone. 'What do you want to see him for anyway? He's done nothing, he was here with me all afternoon.'

This woman, as unattractive as the claustrophobic little room where they sat, depressed Mayo. He tried to imagine her singing, or laughing, or in bed with a man, and failed in every dimension. 'If he's done nothing, he's nothing to worry about—which makes me wonder why he's disappeared.'

'I didn't say he'd disappeared. He'll be back.' An ugly colour suddenly suffused her face and neck before receding and leaving her paler than ever. 'You can't leave him alone, can you? It was just the same over those badgers. It's horrible to think of anyone killing them—horrible! And Danny wouldn't have, I know he wouldn't! He told Wainwright he didn't have a gun but it made no difference. Now everyone in the village,' she said bitterly, 'is convinced he shot them, and they'll think the same about old Willard.'

There was more here than the hostility and uncertainty engendered in even the most law-abiding people when being questioned by the police. She was afraid, too, and yet he didn't think she would easily be frightened—not for herself, that is. 'You've no idea where he's gone? What about a girlfriend?'

'He doesn't have any.' Not that you know about, said Kite's look as he wrote down 'No known girlfriends'.

'Does he often go away like this?'

'He does as he pleases. I'm not his keeper.'

'You're sure you don't know where he's gone? Think again.'

'I've told you, no.'

'In that case, we may have to put a call out for him.' She drew in an almost imperceptible breath. Her hands were already tightly clenched, as they had been throughout the interview. 'Please give the sergeant here the details he needs.'

Kite flashed her his Robert Redford smile, intended to put her at her ease as he asked her questions about Danny's motorbike. A waste of time, smiling, Mayo could have told him. Sexy or otherwise, it would cut no ice with Ruth Lampeter.

'Did your brother enjoy working for Mr Willard?' he asked when Kite had finished writing.

She shrugged. 'It was a job. He hadn't been there long.'

'How did he come to work for him?'

'I know Laura. I went to school with her. We used to be friends.'

It wasn't easy to imagine Laura Willard with her warm brown eyes and emotional nature and this reserved, unresponsive woman having anything to say to each other, much less being friends. He noted the past tense and remembered Laura Willard had also used it.

'Do you have a photograph of your brother?' Kite asked.

With a mixture of pride and defiance she produced a snapshot from a drawer, taken, she replied when asked, only the week before. Danny wore his hair long, but slicked straight back from his face into a pony-tail. He appeared to be in his mid-twenties, a muscular figure hard-packed into tight jeans and T-shirt. On one forearm a snake entwined itself around a naked, busty female form, on the other a wreathed death's head was tattooed. He had light, downward-slanting eyes under heavy brows and a heavy square chin. He looked as if he wanted trouble.

When they had gone, Ruth took a pile of papers from the cupboard where they were hidden and put them on to the fire with an extra shovelful of coal, pulling open the damper so that the flames roared up the chimney. Impassively, she stood watching and only when she was sure there was nothing left did she move away.

Selecting a few ingredients for an unimaginative salad

from the fridge, she proceeded to prepare an early lunch. She never ate breakfast and had been up early, marking the Sunday papers for delivery and then dealing with the usual regular stream of customers, with barely time for a cup of tea. When the salad was assembled she went into the shop and chose two pots of chocolate mousse from the keep-cold cabinet to follow. She had a very sweet tooth.

Having first spread a spotless cloth on the corner of the table in the living-room and poured herself a glass of water, she switched the radio on for *Desert Island Discs* while she ate her meal. But the castaway this week was a comedian with a manic sense of humour who couldn't resist making jokes and trying to put Sue Lawley off her stroke, and his choice of music was incomprehensible to Ruth, so she switched it off and ate in silence.

Shrewd as he normally was in his assessment of character, in his judgement of Ruth Lampeter Mayo had been very much mistaken. Far from being the despair of her teachers, she had once been one of the bright hopes at the High School, but experience had taught her to keep her ideas and dreams and most of what she thought to herself. He would have been amazed at the richness of her inner life. She could lose herself in music and books, especially poetry. And while she served the customers in the shop and let their trivial conversation wash over and around her, she was sustained by the thought of the evenings and weekends to come, when she could draw the curtains and be alone to work, or leaf through holiday brochures while she decided where to take her next fortnight off. Not for Ruth the sun-soaked beaches of Greece and the Costa del Sol. She had once been to Greece, it was true, on a tour which had included Athens, Delphi, Epidaurus and Corinth. She had soaked up culture like a sponge, but it had been too crowded and too hot for her to really enjoy it. She preferred to go off-season to the museums, churches and art galleries of Florence, Venice and Rome, to wander at leisure round places like the Prado and the Louvre. Planning her next fortnight off was one of the greatest pleasures of her life, second only to the beliefs that sustained her.

Until recently.

Ruth passionately loved her brother Danny, while being fully aware of his faults. But loving him and having him to live with her all the time was not the same thing. In fact, since she had bought him out of the army after succumbing to the pressures of his endless moaning about his life there, fear had entered her life. For Danny and, to a lesser extent, for herself.

She stood up quickly and began to clear the table. She wouldn't think of it. It was better that way.

She had barely washed up her lunch things when there was a knock on the door.

The two women stood looking at each other for several seconds. 'You'd better come in,' Ruth said.

Laura went in to the once-familiar living-room, which she hadn't entered for years. Nothing had changed. The same beige and green patterned wallpaper, even the crotcheted chairbacks from Ruth's mother's time still adorned the three-piece suite. The photograph of Mrs Lampeter, which might easily have been Ruth, still sat on the mantelpiece.

'I'll make some coffee,' Ruth said, after her first awkward condolences to Laura had been offered and accepted.

'It's Danny I really want to talk to, Ruth.'

'He's not here—he's gone away for a few days.'

'Where was he yesterday? He never turned up to do the garden.'

'Didn't he?'

Ruth didn't look at Laura as she spoke and Laura said, 'No, he didn't. Or if he did, he didn't do any work.'

Filling the kettle, spooning instant coffee granules into mugs, Ruth gave no answer. 'Has he packed the job in?' Laura asked. 'Naturally, I'd like to know, one way or the other.'

'I don't know, I'm not his keeper,' Ruth answered sharply, which seemed to be a phrase that sprang easily to

her lips these days. Translated, Laura guessed that meant:
I wouldn't tell you if I did know, either.

They'd quarrelled about Danny before, or had words
about him. At any rate, disagreement about him had always
hovered on the edge of their friendship. It was in all prob-
ability the reason why they were no longer as intimate as
they'd once been.

Of the same age, they had gone together to the Princess
Mary school in Lavenstock, the only girls from Wyvering
at that time. Laura went as a paying pupil while Ruth, a
clever, self-contained girl, went on scholarship. They
became firm friends. Then, instead of staying on and pursuing the brilliant future her school career so far had indicated
as likely, Ruth left school at seventeen and thereafter they
had gone their separate ways. What else could she have
done? Her divorced mother had just been diagnosed as
having contracted the progressive disease which was ultimately to kill her, and Danny, a postscript to their parents'
unhappy marriage, was then only six years old. The income
from the post office was a necessity, and so she'd left school
to take her mother's place, much to Laura's disgust.
Women, Laura argued, should not be expected to sacrifice
their lives, etcetera, etcetera, accepting and quoting the
received wisdom of the sixth form without much considering whether it was right or wrong. Not being an original
thinker, however, she found the argument difficult to sustain in view of the circumstances.

And presumably, reflected Ruth, had found it no easier
later: when faced with a not dissimilar situation herself,
Laura had reacted in precisely the same way as she herself
had done. Where were her advanced opinions now?

For nine years, until her mother died, Ruth kept things
going and afterwards took over the post office and the responsibility for Danny. He had been a difficult child, a worse
teenager. It was a relief when he finally decided to make a
career of the army. His enthusiasm for the life hadn't lasted
long, and when he found himself posted to Northern Ireland

he was soon begging Ruth to buy him out which, after considerable misgivings, she finally did.

'I saw him yesterday, Ruth,' Laura said. 'I had an accident with my car on the Hurstfield road and came home in a taxi. He passed us going down the hill on his motorbike. Have the police asked about him?'

Ruth watched her in cold silence. 'What are you implying?' she asked finally.

Laura took a deep breath. 'I haven't told the police this, but I think you ought to know. It's not easy to say—but for quite a while now, we've been missing things from the house. I have to say my father was sure it was Danny who took them. It wasn't anything much until yesterday, when I found a gold brooch missing, and some other bits of jewellery as well. My father told me he was going to confront Danny with it.'

Ruth listened to what Laura had to say without speaking. 'Somebody has killed my father, Ruth,' Laura went on. 'I'm not saying it was Danny, good heavens, but you must see I'm going to have to tell the police I saw him. He won't have anything to fear if he hasn't.'

'You have a better view of the police than I have,' Ruth replied.

There was a defiant look in her eyes. It wasn't new, when talking of Danny. She wasn't shocked, she didn't deny the possibility of him being a thief, but suddenly, she said, 'I don't know why he didn't do your garden, but he was here all afternoon. The reason he left was nothing to do with anybody else . . . In fact . . . Well, you might as well know, we—we had a quarrel. He just stormed out and I don't know where he's gone.'

And suddenly her unresponsive face crumpled like a piece of used tissue paper. To Laura's horror, slow, heavy tears began to course down her cheeks, painful and somehow shocking. 'I'll never forgive him. He's betrayed me.'

'*Betrayed* you?'

'That's what it looks like from where I stand.'

'How? What can you mean?' Keeping her face averted, Ruth only shook her head. 'You'll make it up,' Laura said after a long, awkward silence, wanting to comfort her, knowing better than to try.

Ruth raised a ravaged face, changed almost beyond recognition. 'You don't know what he's done.'

'Ruth. What are you trying to say? What has he done?' Laura asked fearfully.

'Don't ask me! How could I possibly tell anyone? Just don't ask me.'

'Don't get into such a panic,' Philly said. 'She's not due home for at least another ten minutes. There's plenty of time.'

'Ten *minutes*?' Galvanized, Sebastian swung his legs off the bed and began to scramble into his clothes. 'Jesus, Philly!'

'What's the matter with you? You're never like this in London.'

But this wasn't London, and Philly's mother coming home from church and catching him in the sack with her daughter wasn't part of the scenario Philly had outlined. It occurred to Sebastian that she'd probably left that part out on purpose. She relished a spice of danger in whatever she did, even more, if possible, than he. Putting her head into the dragon's mouth positively turned her on.

'Anyway, she never comes into my room.'

She lay naked on the bed, in 'Grande Odalisque' pose, her skin tones as golden and tender as ever any Ingres painted, though her body lacked such voluptuous curves. She was slender and so light that when he held her in his arms he sometimes felt as though he might crush her with his passion, snap the delicate wrists and ankles if he held her too tight. She was in fact as tough as old boots. Violence roused her from a kitten to a tigress. The rougher he was, the more she wanted. Which was just as well, because he loved her to the point where all sense had left him.

'You'd better get dressed,' he said.

Propped on her elbow, chin on her hand, she stayed where she was, watching through half-closed lids as he finished pulling on his jeans, a secret smile on her face, like a cat replete with cream. He could only guess her thoughts. She wouldn't tell him what they were, even if he asked her. It was all part of the secrecy that surrounded her movements, not always through necessity but because she liked it that way. She became prickly, surrounding herself with barbed wire defences if he wanted to know too much. She had never let him know, for instance, how deeply she was involved until she'd spoken up last night. Another of the no-go areas in her life which had been closed to him.

But then, he didn't tell her everything, either.

Yet suddenly, in the relaxation that came after making love, and sensing that she, too, was more soft and receptive than she normally was, he knew he must tell her. He had to share it with someone, get it all off his chest, confess to her about old Willers. It was dangerous, might turn her against him. But past experience told him that was unlikely.

He blinked and came from a long way back as the roar of an engine was heard from outside. Looking out of the window, he was in time to see a car emerge from St Kenelm's Walk and slow for the turn into Dobbs Lane. 'Whose car's that?'

'Which car?'

'A red 1965 Super Minx, with Laura Willard in the passenger seat.'

'It'll be David Illingworth, Laura's boyfriend.'

'I saw it in Lavenstock on Saturday afternoon.'

'You couldn't have. He's been down in Brighton since— oh, sod it! I've just remembered—'

'I don't make mistakes about cars. Especially ones like that. It must be a collector's piece by now.'

'Never mind about that. Mum's going to be furious with me. I was supposed to go and ask them to have lunch with us.'

Seb stayed by the window, watching until the car had

gone, then turned back to Philly. 'If your mother's going to be mad at you, you'd better get out of her way. Get dressed and we'll go out in the car,' he ordered. 'Somewhere we won't be disturbed. I've something to tell you.'

She heard the dominating note in his voice and suddenly she looked guarded. 'I'm not sure I want to know.'

He stared down at her. 'Do you love me, Philly?'

It was a question he'd asked, phrased in various ways, dozens of times and it might have been better not asked now, but she only replied scornfully, as she always had before, 'Oh, *love!*'

But this time, he thought he detected something subtly different about the way she spoke the words. Perhaps because she knew there was a finality in the question, perhaps she was tired of prevarication and procrastination, perhaps because she really had made her mind up at last. As the thought came to him, he found his breathing was becoming difficult. So far, she had insisted on keeping their relationship secret—which was fine with him, if it wasn't going to be permanent. He'd no wish to be the object of sympathy when it ended, either with his parents, or with hers for that matter. But if there was a chance it might be more than that . . .

'How far would you go for me, Philly?'

She uncurled herself from the bed and came towards him. 'Now that, if ever I heard one, is a leading question.'

CHAPTER 11

Driving down the hill towards Uplands House School, Mayo sat hunched in a deep silence which Kite knew better than to interrupt.

The interviews with Ruth Lampeter on the one hand and Laura Willard and Illingworth on the other hand had both, in their different ways, set up unsettling questions in

Mayo's mind. He knew that Danny Lampeter's sister was hiding more than just knowing where her brother was, but then, a murder investigation which didn't turn up at least a few stones revealing nasty things beneath which had nothing to do with the inquiry was something he'd yet to encounter. He knew also that he must beware of allowing his dislike of the type of woman she was to colour his judgement. Likewise with Illingworth. As investigating officers, they weren't supposed to have private likes and dislikes, but contrary to opinion in some quarters, police officers were human beings and it was hard not to have them sometimes, especially in the case of someone like Illingworth.

Maybe the man hadn't meant to be boorish, but he didn't seem to have gone out of his way to contradict the impression that he was. On the other hand, it could be he was trying on a double bluff, on the premise that no one who was guilty would deliberately present himself in so objectionable a light to the police. He was a tricky enough customer, either way—and the only one so far to emerge with any sort of motive. Or alibi. His story would be checked, of course, but with a hundred and twenty miles between here and Brighton and any number of conference delegates to say he was there, it was unlikely to have been fudged.

And Laura Willard, jumpy as a cat, what was he to make of her?

Gina Holden looked longingly at the garden after she'd put the telephone down, glanced at her disgraceful jeans and grubby hands and decided they wouldn't pass muster, it wasn't what was expected of a headmaster's wife. Abandoning her precious Sunday morning with barely a sigh, she moved quickly and had changed and was just finishing making coffee when the doorbell rang. She crossed the hall with her usual swift stride, now tidily dressed in navy trousers and a cream silk shirt, showing no signs of her former dishevelment.

'Hope we're not disturbing you, Mrs Holden,' Mayo

said, 'I thought we'd better ring before we came . . . school timetable and so on.'

'No problem.' Smiling, she took them through to the drawing-room, offered them coffee and then left them while she went to bring it in.

'Nice room.' Kite looked around appreciatively. 'Bit untidy, like,' he added, in case he should seem to be denying his Leftist tendencies by being too appreciative of a room containing a grand piano and a Chinese carpet.

Mayo, who was in no position to make judgements on anyone's tidiness, grunted an ambiguous reply. The sunlight showed a light film of dust and the less than well polished windows and emphasized the rumpled cushions and covers, but he, like Kite, found it attractive, a room for living in and not for show. Decorated in soft shades of apricot and buff, sparely furnished, an arrangement of copper-coloured leaves and cream flowers in the empty grate, plenty of books, the small grand piano. When Gina Holden came back she found Kite admiring the garden and Mayo bending a covetous eye on the brass timepiece standing on the mantel. She asked him whether he was specially interested in clocks.

Old ones, yes, he told her. 'It's a long time since I saw a lantern clock in as good nick as this. My dad used to have one, years ago. He sold it to buy an old second-hand car and regretted it ever after.'

She laughed, showing beautiful teeth and rather a lot of gum. 'This one wouldn't buy a second-hand bike. It hasn't gone properly for months.'

Mayo could find nothing at all to say to this heresy. If the clock had been his, he'd have had it spread out on the table in bits and fiddled about with it until it did go. It hurt him physically to see a clock neglected or not correctly adjusted; a stopped clock was like a bereavement in the house. He almost toyed with the idea of offering to repair it for free but thought better of it.

Mrs Holden suggested that since the sun had at last

emerged from the clouds they might like to go and sit in the garden while they talked. Nothing loath, Kite took the tray from her as she led the way through the open french window, across a flagged terrace to a sitting-out area outside an old thatched summerhouse. Chairs faced the lawn and a small pond, with a table between them.

'Not too draughty for you here?' she inquired. 'I like to take every opportunity to sit outside when there's some sun about.'

'Don't blame you, when you've such a beautiful garden,' Kite said. It was no empty compliment. Unlike the house, the garden was immaculate. Kite enjoyed pottering in his own when he had the chance. He was reminded that he'd intended putting out his bedding plants today. He hoped Sheila would remember and make a start—and not mistake the petunias for the nemesia, or let the cat scratch them up, or accidentally water them with weedkiller, or anything else his dearly beloved but accident-prone wife was only too apt to do.

The terrace looked out over a long, quiet lawn flanked by a stone-flagged path and a wide herbaceous border, beyond which could be seen the playing fields and the main school buildings. 'Very peaceful,' remarked Mayo, no gardener himself but knowing what he liked.

'It is, isn't it? I do most of it myself and I can't bear the thought of leaving it to someone else's tender mercies when we go. My husband's retiring at the end of the school year.'

'Perhaps the new head or his wife will enjoy gardening as much as you do.'

She smiled ruefully. 'Depends on who gets the job— he hasn't been appointed yet. There was to have been a governors' meeting on Monday. We hoped it would've been decided then but of course it's been cancelled. We really can't make proper plans until we're sure. We're going to live near Antibes.' A shadow crossed her face but was quickly dispelled as she went on in her easy, talkative way, 'Well, Richard loves it there, we'll make other friends, no doubt everything will turn out for the best. He had a slight heart attack, you see, and though he's fit enough now, it was a warning to take things more easily, they said. Running a school like this can be rather hectic at times.'

Gina Holden had been a surprise. An energetic woman with a bright, alert face, an engagingly tip-tilted nose and short curly hair, she was much younger than Mayo had expected, mid-thirties, but still younger than he'd assumed the wife of a man presently retiring would be. Perhaps, though, she wasn't, if he was retiring through illness.

They drank their coffee and ate some delicious crunchy biscuits which Mayo welcomed in view of having missed breakfast. There was a few minutes' pleasant chat about holidays in the south of France and the differences in climate and gardening out there, which brought him neatly round to the flower arrangements in the church. He complimented Mrs Holden on them, bringing a pleased look to her face, and asked what time she had arrived to do them.

She replied that it had been nearly five o'clock. 'I was running late. We'd had a sort of open day for parents and prospective parents—really to show them what use we're making of modern technology, computers and so on, and a lot of the parents were so interested they just wouldn't go. I'd forgotten until yesterday morning that it was my turn to do the flowers—I've a memory like a sieve! I tried to swap turns with someone else but everyone seemed to have something they couldn't put off. Mrs Oliver would've done them, I suppose, but she always gets landed with things other people mess up, poor thing, so I didn't ask her.'

'Was the church door locked when you arrived?' Mayo asked, when he could get a word in edgeways. She nodded. 'And you locked it again when you left?'

'Yes, I picked the key up from the Rectory and I'm sure I locked it because I was carrying some sheet music Jon Reece had left in church earlier and wanted for choir practice here—he stands in for the church organist occasionally

—and it was difficult to stop it slipping while I locked the door.'

'How long would you say you were in the church?'

'Nearly an hour, including clearing up. Throwing out the old flowers on the altar—plus the ones from the window-sills and the ends of the pews from the wedding last week. Such a pity . . . they were so pretty. But they don't last, of course.'

'So no one could have been in the church without you being aware of it?'

'Oh, absolutely not.' She stared at him. 'Goodness, you don't mean you thought someone might have been—well, hiding?'

Mayo sighed. 'No, Mrs Holden, it doesn't seem likely from what you've said.'

Whoever had killed Willard must have waited until he had unlocked the door and then followed him into church, though nobody so far had admitted to having seen who it was—and in view of the number of people in and around Parson's Place at six o'clock Mayo was beginning to think this nothing short of miraculous. He returned to something Mrs Holden had been saying earlier that had reminded him of one of the entries in Willard's diary. 'You mentioned a school governors' meeting—'

'To decide on the next Head, that's right. It'll probably be one of the masters here, Jon Reece or David Illingworth. I suppose you know David's engaged—practically engaged —to Laura Willard? I imagine that's why you're here,' she finished abruptly, her smile vanishing, 'to ask about Laura —and her father.'

'Partly, yes. He used to be headmaster here, I gather?'

'Before my husband. I don't know what I can tell you about him, though. He was a school governor but I didn't know him well, not in the same way as I know Laura. Richard had more to do with him. He'll be able to tell you what you want to know when he gets back from his walk, I dare say, which should be any time now. Since his illness, he's been advised to take a moderate amount of exercise each day.'

'Let's talk about Miss Willard then, for a start. She's a particular friend of yours?'

'Oh yes. We see each other most days with her working here. We've become very close . . . poor Laura, what a frightful shock. But . . .' She hesitated. 'Well, I'm sorry it had to happen this way, but let's face it, at least she'll be free now—no more of this stupid business of not approving of David as a husband just because he's been divorced. Her father would much rather she'd married Jon Reece, you know, which was stupid really, because anyone with one eye could see they were neither of them really interested.' There was a momentary silence while she watched Kite as he took all this down in his large, sprawling hand. 'It's Jon without the "h". Jonathan actually. And Reece as in fleece.'

'Oh, sorry.' Kite smiled his thanks and made the alteration.

'And she—Miss Willard—went along with this?' Mayo asked.

'Sounds unbelievable, this day and age, doesn't it? But you see, it had happened once before—Laura'd met someone her father didn't find acceptable and he managed to interfere so that in the end she called it off. Her father was right, as it happened. The chap turned out to be a real rotten egg. But still it was a hideous and unforgivable thing to do, and I suppose it shook Laura's faith in her own judgement. She's rather easily—well, she always believes the best of anyone. Not like her father. He used to make me absolutely furious,' she said, leaning over her chair and tugging at a harmless daisy which had seeded itself in a crack in the paving until at last it conceded defeat. Rubbing her grubby fingers on her trousers, she looked up and added soberly, 'All the same, I think you should probably forget what I've just said. I've made him sound like a monster and he wasn't really—'

'Merely a clergyman of the old school, with very fixed

ideas,' came an amused voice from behind her chair.

Gina Holden swung round, the expression on her face one of relief when she saw who it was. 'Richard, you made me jump! Thank heavens it's only you—one day I might learn to keep my opinions to myself.'

'Or make sure the wrong person isn't listening first, Gina my love.' The man who'd walked unseen across the grass behind them smiled and dropped a kiss on her head, released the dog from its lead and shooed it off. A large unruly retriever-type dog answering to the name of Rory, it galloped off kitchenwards, where loud slurping noises presently indicated it had found its water bowl. Gina Holden had immediately jumped up and while introducing Mayo and his sergeant, pulled a chair round for her husband, poured and sugared coffee for him. 'You've had a long walk, darling. Not overdone it, have you?'

It seemed to Mayo she was a little too anxious, a trifle over-demonstrative, and apparently Holden thought so, too, from the way in which he good-temperedly waved away her solicitous inquiries. 'Do sit down, Gina, and don't fuss.'

The Headmaster had a quiet but authoritative way of speaking. He was a man of medium height and slight build, with a witty, mobile face and two wings of grey hair either side of a bald one, whom Mayo guessed to be nearly twenty years older than his wife. He gave the impression of being a man with a tolerant outlook on life, a calmly efficient headmaster, but underlying that he seemed tired, with a deep inner exhaustion that was more than the physical results of an over-long walk. As though Antibes, with its long, lazy, sun-soaked days beckoned.

The dog came back, flopped heavily beside its master and rested its slobbering chops on Mayo's shoe. Holden gently moved the dog's head with his foot, stirred his coffee and said, 'We were all very shocked to hear about poor Willard. I suppose it's certain—that he was killed, I mean? After all, he wasn't well, and an old man like that, it was always on the cards . . .'

'The post-mortem this morning proved otherwise.' Deep cyanotic congestion of the lungs and other organs had been found, and led to the conclusion that Cecil Willard had died by asphyxiation in conditions consistent with some soft object having obstructed the nose and mouth. Mayo told his listeners in plainer language what the result was, omitting to say what the means had been. There was a silence. Gina Holden looked horrified, her husband grave and thoughtful. 'So at the moment we're concentrating on finding out what everyone in the village was doing yesterday.'

'And that includes us, here?' Holden said. 'Well, we were having an open day and all the staff were here until late afternoon—except for Gina, who had to rush off to do her thing with the church flowers—'

'I've told them about that, Richard.'

'—and Illingworth, who's at a conference near Brighton.'

'No, he's not,' his wife said. 'He should be back here by now. Miriam Thorne rang him first thing this morning and told him what had happened and he was going to set off immediately.' When Mayo told her they had already seen Illingworth, she seemed pleased. 'That's good. Laura's going to need all the support she can get.'

Holden frowned. 'I can't see the course organizers being overjoyed about that. It was very much over-subscribed and they weren't too happy about him opting out of the Friday night session.'

'Oh, surely, in a case like this—' his wife was beginning, when at that moment the doorbell extension sounded. Hastily excusing herself to answer it, she crossed the lawn, the dog leaping and bounding in front of her. Her husband's eyes followed her graceful stride.

Mayo said, 'Will you give me the names of your staff, Mr Holden? All of them, I think, although for the moment we're only concerned with those who were here yesterday.'

'Not the boys, I hope?'

'Not unless I have to—nor the parents who were here either, at this stage.'

If the investigation warranted it, they would certainly have to be questioned, but for now he was restricting any interviewing to those members of the staff who were present yesterday.

Holden gave the requisite names, which included most of the masters, Miriam Thorne and the matron, and some of the wives who were helping out on this occasion by superintending the serving of tea and sandwiches provided by the kitchen staff, all of whom lived in the village. Holden smiled as he confirmed what Miriam Thorne had told Mayo. 'That's right, we do try to be flexible about duties here.'

From the house came the sound of a piano. It was Rachmaninov, the melodic theme from his second piano concerto, played competently but, to Mayo's ears, with more verve than sensitivity. They listened in silence for a minute or two, until Holden remarked that if Mayo wished to talk to the staff, he was welcome to do so. 'That sounds like one of them now—Jon Reece, our geography master. It's rather a nice piano Gina has and she lets him use it whenever he wants.' He smiled slightly. 'Women seem to fall over themselves to do things for Jon.'

'Which has to be useful for a headmaster,' remarked Mayo. It was a gift some men seemed to have, he'd noticed —headmasters and clergyman in particular—of having a string of excellent and willing women at their beck and call.

'Headmaster? Hm. I suppose Gina's been telling you he's a candidate. It's very much on her mind at the moment. It is unsettling . . . ought really to have been decided some time since, there's been far too much shilly-shallying. We had several very worthy applicants but we've now got it down to a short list of two from our own staff and I think, unless this unfortunate business delays things further— Willard was one of our governors, you know—we should settle it fairly quickly.'

'It would help if I could build up a picture of what the dead man was like. From the general opinion so far, I've gathered that he wasn't much liked. What did you think, Mr Holden?'

Holden said thoughtfully, 'It's true that he was a difficult man to get on with in many ways, more so since his stroke, but that can't be a complete judgement. He was an exceptional teacher and he inspired great loyalty in the boys he taught, so he couldn't have been all bad.'

Sebastian Oliver had also been coached by Willard and had apparently felt the same, Mayo reflected.

'His problem was that he tended to judge everyone by his own high standards—and as his faith, it always seemed to me, sprang from reason rather than the heart, he gave the impression of coldness. He told me that he entered the Church because he'd always been intended for it by his clergyman father. But I fancy he believed what he often preached—that he saw Christian principles as the only rational extension of a thoughtful and disciplined life. He was a parish priest only briefly. Teaching history, research, publishing the occasional monograph was much more congenial to him.'

'As far as appointing the new Headmaster, which candidate did Mr Willard favour, Mr Holden?'

'Oh come, you can't expect me to know that!'

'Or to tell me if you did?'

Holden smiled slightly. 'As a matter of fact, it's been a difficult decision for everyone. Neither one stands out above the other. David Illingworth, our senior science master, has a brilliant academic record, he held a research fellowship at Cambridge before he came here and I've no doubts about his administrative capabilities. The boys respect him but I sometimes wonder if they don't stand rather too much in awe of him. He's not inclined to suffer fools gladly. Perhaps he'll mellow when he marries Laura. Whereas Jon Reece . . . He's very popular with the boys, especially with the younger ones, and he's been here longer. Teaches geography and sometimes takes games, but he's willing to involve himself with a lot of after-school activities as well. Full of enthusiasm and drive. So, it's wide open. The choice is very important to me, as you might guess. I've worked as Head of this school for eight years and it's been my life. I had hoped for longer, but . . .' He shrugged philosophically, though it was evidently a subject painful to him. 'Uplands House isn't yet in the top league but its reputation is growing and I need to know it's in the right hands when I go.'

Mayo had the impression that he was struggling too hard to be honest and impartial, trying not to show where his own sympathies lay. 'Is Mr Reece married?' he asked.

'No. My wife says there was talk of him and Laura at one time, but if so it never came to anything,' Holden said absently, still following his own train of thought as he went on, 'I'll be frank with you—I shall heave a sigh of relief when this is all over. I dislike very much the rivalry and lobbying that's been going on. Two factions have developed, both within the school and the governing body and frankly, I haven't enough energy to spare for coping with it.'

The music had stopped. He stood up. 'Would you like to talk to Reece now?'

They were bending together over the piano as the three men entered the house, Gina Holden laughing at something Jon Reece had said. Very tall and athletically loose-limbed, looking extremely healthy, wearing tracksuit and trainers, he swung round on the piano stool as they came in and Holden introduced them. Mayo found himself towered over, his hand gripped until it felt numb. When it was free he waved it at as much to get the circulation going again as to invite Reece to reseat himself.

The geography master's fair hair was slightly damp and there came from him a faintly sweaty odour, as though he'd recently been undertaking some form of violent exercise. He responded to the questions put to him in a manner that was likeable and open. He had a lock of hair which fell boyishly over his eye.

When told they were trying to establish where everyone was between 6.0 and 6.30 the previous day and asked what time he had been free of his obligations he replied with a grin that he'd scarpered thankfully as soon as the last parent had departed, which would be at about—'What, ten to six?' he asked, looking at Holden for confirmation.

'Quarter to. We left the main building together and I came straight back here to wait for Gina.'

'That's right, we did. Then I went straight back to my flat, intending to have a quick shower and a drink before supper duty at half past six. I don't live in the main building,' he explained, 'I'm lucky enough to have a flat over the old stables.'

'Good, that takes care of times then, for both of you,' Mayo said. 'Mr Reece, as you'll appreciate, we're interested in anybody Mr Willard happened to know. Have much to do with him, did you?'

'I suppose I knew him fairly well, yes. We actually taught at the same school for a short spell, years ago.'

'What were your relations with him?'

'My—?' Reece looked startled. 'Oh, friendly. But then, I try to make a point of getting on with most people. Life's too short for anything else.'

'Agreed. But from all accounts, he was a difficult man to get on with.'

'He could be an awkward old cuss, sure, but I found him OK. He'd a sardonic humour that appealed to me. And a passion for Mah Jong, which I used to play with him on a fairly regular basis. We also shared the same tastes in music.'

'Wagner,' said Mrs Holden, 'which Jon plays so loud he can't hear the doorbell.'

'One of the reasons I like living apart from the main building. I like my music loud, especially when I'm having a shower. Actually, I did hear, Gina, but by the time I'd grabbed a bathrobe you'd gone. I found the music on the mat, thanks. I'd left some sheet-music in church at lunch-time,' he explained lightly.

'You were in the church at lunch-time yesterday, Mr Reece?'

'Yes, but I wasn't skiving off my duties here, if that's what you're thinking. I skipped lunch in order to run through a solo in a new anthem with one of the choirboys —intended for today, though of course we shan't be doing it now.' With a faint smile he watched Kite noting this down. 'If you've any doubts you can ask the boy in question —he's Simon Rushton, lives in the village.' His eyes were of a vivid blue, like chips of lapis lazuli, reflecting the sky blue of the tracksuit he wore. You could see why women liked him. And not only for his good looks. There was a warmth and spontaneity about him that anyone might be expected to find attractive. Mayo wondered why *he* didn't. Perhaps he was too obvious. Perhaps there was a lack of depth. But Reece's next words didn't indicate that.

'I'm damn sorry the old man's dead,' he said suddenly, 'and even sorrier for poor Laura.' His face was momentarily bleak and Mayo felt the force of something dark and secret, an undercurrent he didn't understand. Had the previous attachment to Laura Willard which Holden had mentioned been more serious then he'd imagined? Had it left its scars? The quirky smile returned. 'Also, I must admit, quite sorry for myself. I do have very personal reasons for wanting him still alive.'

'Maybe you'd like to elaborate on that?'

Reece tossed back his wayward lock of hair and looked questioningly at Holden. 'Go ahead, Jon,' said the Head-master, who seemed to have an easy and informal relation-ship with his staff.

'Well,' said Reece, 'I'm sure you've already been told I'm in line for the Headmastership when Richard leaves and that it's going to be a damn close-run thing. There are those who'll vote for Illingworth because they're impressed

by his Cambridge background and think how good his
Ph.D. would look on the school prospectus. However, let's
hope there are others with whom good sense will prevail. I
shall need them—now that Willard is dead, I've lost one
of my strongest backers.'

'Oh come on, Jon!' Gina Holden protested, 'you're doing
yourself an injustice.'

'You're still young,' Holden commented drily. 'There *is*
life beyond Uplands House.'

'Oh, I've no patience with that! If I can't have Uplands,
I'm not sure I want a Headship anywhere else. But what
the hell, it's not worth getting worked up about. I'm not
going to lose any sleep over it. May the best man win, as
they say.'

He spoke with a conviction that inclined Mayo to believe
him. If only because Reece struck him on the whole as the
rather immature sort who would demand gratification, if
not instantly, then quite soon. What did surprise him, for
more reasons than that, was that Holden should see him as
a future Headmaster of Uplands House.

Something else also struck him: if Reece had indeed lost
his strongest supporter as he claimed—then the opposite
was also true, and Illingworth had lost his strongest op-
ponent. He thought more about Illingworth. A Cambridge
background? he was asking himself as they got into the
car, and why had Illingworth abandoned it? Senior science
master at Uplands House was a far cry from a research
fellowship at Cambridge. No wonder the appointment was
so important to him.

CHAPTER 12

A more interesting, not to say surprising, alternative to pork
pie presented itself on the menu at the Drum and Monkey,
where something described as *carbonade de bœuf* was on offer.

A brave man, the landlord. Enterprising, to challenge the sacrosanct Sunday roast. Kite was suspicious of such foreign muck but he was tempted by the prospect of a hot meal and on being told it was only a kind of stew, ordered for them both. With rice for Mayo and chips, unrepentantly, for himself. It was advertised as being available at all times but was a long time coming, raising Mayo's hopes that it might not, after all, be a microwaved mush, *carbonade de bœuf* in name only.

He had elected to sit in the snug after glimpsing some of his own people eating in the bar lounge—Farrar, Deeley and pretty Jenny Platt, the latter a welcome addition to CID since being transferred from the uniformed branch. They were in good spirits, sharing a joke. He'd been a DC himself once and knew the constraints the nearby presence of a senior officer could impose, so he walked past and into the public bar, to which he wasn't averse anyway, away from the red plush and the hunting prints.

A real spit and sawdust place, he saw as he pushed open the door, stone-flagged, overheated by a great roaring fire and full of noise which abated somewhat when they entered but immediately began again. Not a man there hadn't had to answer personal questions from the police about his movements. Not one person in the village had escaped being touched by the murder; it had affected all their lives. But none of them were going to be inhibited by it.

The customers were all men, ranging from a couple of teenage darts throwers to two ancients playing dominoes. As Kite brought their drinks to the corner Mayo had selected, glances were cast from time to time in their direction, remarks were obviously being made, no prizes for guessing the subject. It wasn't possible to hear what was being said until one old man in a cloth cap joined in, speaking in the over-loud voice of the hard of hearing, heavy with the local accent. 'Bloody parsons,' he informed the bar in general, 'no damn better'n nobody else and I'd say that if it was the Pope himself what had been murdered.'

Did the noise suddenly become louder? Or was it just the altercation which had arisen between the darts players? The old chap who had spoken took no notice of any of it. 'Interfering old bugger he were, and what I say is, if he's got hisself killed he's got nobody but hisself to blame.'

'Come on, Sam.' The landlord was a thin man with a melancholy look underlined by the long sideboards he wore. 'Drink up and have another on the house.'

'You won the pools or summat, Arnold?' But the old man downed what was left in his glass in one long swallow and upon the promised pint being actually drawn, thereafter kept his voice down. Mayo, however, his ears now attuned, caught the name 'Lampeter' once or twice.

The place grew quieter as one o'clock Sunday dinner-time approached. Most of the customers gradually left for home, leaving as the sole occupants only old Sam propping up the bar, with one of the domino players still in his corner. Mayo went to replenish his and Kite's drinks. 'My name's Mayo,' he said to Sam, signalling the landlord to give the two old men the same again. 'My colleague and I are investigating Mr Willard's murder.'

'Oh ar.'

'You happen to know Danny Lampeter?'

Sam's seamed old face took on a gratified expression as the second unsolicited pint of the morning arrived at his elbow. But there wasn't much in this life that hadn't to be paid for, one way or another, and he prepared to do so. 'Good cause to, haven't I?' he began. 'Got that grand-daughter o'mine, Tracey, in the family way and then wouldn't own up to it. Bad lot, that's what he is. Ask any-body. Good 'ealth.'

Drinking deep, he wiped his mouth with the back of his hand. The domino player echoed, 'Good 'ealth.'

'Is that right?' Mayo prompted.

'What I said.' Sam communed with his beer while Mayo waited patiently and was presently rewarded. 'Summat else —did me outa that there gardening job with the old Reverend, he did. Soon's he heard from my granddaughter I were prepared to do a few hours to supplement me pension, off he goes and gets the job hisself—stands to reason he would, don't it, considering his age and mine?'

That hadn't been Laura Willard's version as Mayo remembered it, but if Sam thought that was how it had happened, it would explain his antagonism to both Lampeter and Willard.

'What was that you said earlier about Mr Willard interfering? Have you something specific in mind?'

He received a wary look. 'Not specially. He were just an old killjoy.'

'Nothing that might have given someone a grudge against him?' A shrug. 'Well then, what about Lampeter's sister?'

'Oh, Ruth's all right,' Sam said surprisingly. 'Her's had it rough, poor wench, one way or t'other.'

At that moment a middle-aged woman in a crossover apron and bedroom slippers appeared in the bar entrance, holding the door open. 'You going to be here all day, Dad?' she shrilled at the old man. ' 'Cos if y'are, might as well throw yer dinner on the fireback for all the good'll it be.'

'All right, our Doreen, I'm coming as soon as I've finished me beer.'

'Well, don't be more'n five minutes or it'll be five minutes too late,' was her parting shot.

'You get back to your Yorkshire pudding,' Sam muttered to the closed door, but his confiding mood had been broken and he rose to follow her, nodding good day to Mayo, who rejoined Kite for the *carbonade* which had at last been brought in by the landlord's wife.

'Lampeter again,' Kite said, liberally dredging his chips with salt and vinegar. 'Keeps cropping up, doesn't he? Willard seems to have specialized in getting up people's noses, mebbe he just went too far with Lampeter, and that's why he's skipped.'

'We don't know that he has skipped, he might be back tonight.'

Mayo considered what Kite had said, however, turning the idea round in his mind but feeling it was too easy an explanation. He never felt comfortable with explanations handed to him on a plate; maybe it was some perversity in his nature that made him feel uneasy unless he'd had to work his socks off to achieve anything. 'In any case, whether he has or not, we've nothing on him other than his taking off at a singularly appropriate moment. We're trying to find a murderer, not chasing all the petty criminals in Wyvering.' He lapsed into silence, studying his meal while he ate it as though cracking the secrets of its composition would give him the solution he was looking for. Finally, he pushed away his plate with most of the soggy rice untouched. The rest had been OK.

'You should've had the chips,' Kite said.

'I'm going for a walk. That'll do me more good than chips.'

'Sounds a good idea.'

'Not you, lad, you've enough on. Me, I've taken a fancy to see something of the village.'

Kite shrugged and conceded the point. Apart from what he still had to do here in Wyvering, there were his dreaded reports to write back at the office, and he didn't know how he was going to get through all he had to do and be home before cock-crow, though he fully intended to be. In any case, if he knew Mayo, the walk wouldn't be just for the good of his health.

'Let the old chap have his dinner and then get somebody to find out from him or his daughter where this Tracey lives, for the record,' Mayo said.

As they were leaving, the landlord looked up from polishing glasses behind the bar. 'I wouldn't take too much notice of what old Sam Biggs says, he's prejudiced. It's true his granddaughter got herself in the club, but it don't necessarily mean Lampeter was the father. She's well known for putting it about a bit, that Tracey. Didn't seem to make much difference to her, having the baby. Left it with her mother when it was a few weeks old and took herself off, nice as ninepence.'

'Where'd she go to? Any idea?'

'God knows. Mebbe her mother can tell you, but I wouldn't bank on it.'

At the end of St Kenelm's Walk, the railed footpath, affording a scenic view of the river valley, led behind Main Street to the castle, or what was left of it: the stump of a square tower, a few tumbledown walls and a now dry moat. Within the walls rose the motte, on which stood a stone cairn with a plaque attached. It said the castle dated from Saxon times, that Owen Glendower had been repelled here, and pointed the direction to look if you wanted to see clear into Wales, towards the Wrekin and the Rotunda in Birmingham. Whether or not these extravagant claims could be supported there was no way of telling today. Visibility was hampered by the haze which the breeze up here had failed to disperse. The sun which had been so warm in the Holdens' garden had disappeared and it had turned distinctly chilly and overcast, in the shivery way only the month of May can. Leaning over the safety railings, Mayo couldn't see much further than Uplands House School below and to the right, and the church tower on his left.

The location was evidently a favourite Sunday afternoon venue. Dogs were being walked, prams wheeled, children played on bikes or skateboards. A father and his young son were attempting to fly a kite within the somewhat restricted confines of the bailey. And somewhere in this quiet, ordinary hilltop village was someone who had murder on his conscience.

In the course of his admittedly quick walk round it, it had seemed to Mayo that Wyvering, outwardly so united, fell into three self-contained parts: the somewhat rarefied world of church precincts and private school; Main Street with its old-fashioned, square little houses and square little gardens crammed with bright flowers; and Elm Tree

Crescent, a little transplant of suburbia where grass was neatly mown, roses pruned and hedges trimmed. Neat as Noddyland, the twenty or so bungalows built on to that side of the hill with the less favoured view were as alike as two pins, distinguishable from one another only by their own touches of individuality: a white-painted trellis where clematis would later climb, an outcrop of rockery on a lawn, the chosen style of their net curtains.

He wondered to what extent the three sections mixed and interacted. How far would the net have to stretch to take in the murderer? Or did he come, as Mayo intuitively felt he must, from within Willard's own small circle?

His thoughts were interrupted by a stumpy-legged Welsh corgi trotting fussily up to him and beginning to sniff around in an alert, foxy-faced way. Funny how fashions changed, even in dog-ownership. A few years ago you couldn't move without falling over corgis, but you didn't see so many around now, the fashion was all for big macho dogs that cost as much as a man to feed. A misunderstanding arose when Mayo, who should have known better, bent to pat the corgi, whereupon the ungrateful animal, apparently mistaking his motives, began to growl and snap at his ankles in a decidedly threatening way. He was hoping he wasn't going to have to boot it away when it was called to heel.

'Here, Taff!' The owner was approaching, a man clad in green Barbour jacket and a red woolly hat with a pompom on it, assuring Mayo in the manner of all doting pet-owners that the dog was all right, it was his way of being friendly, wouldn't harm a fly, really, though not until it had been called to heel several times did it obey. 'May I introduce myself?' he went on breezily. 'I'm Denzil Thorne. I believe you're the detective i/c the case here.'

Mayo acknowledged that he was, meeting an eager, bright-eyed smile and an outstretched hand. 'Dr Thorne. I was hoping to call and see you this afternoon.' He gave his own name and his hand was gripped hard.

'I've been expecting someone to come round. Why don't we walk back together?'

'If you wish.' Mayo turned in the direction he'd come.

'Not that way.' Thorne indicated a track leading downwards. 'This way's quicker and I can let Taff off the lead. It joins the path above the river bank and we can get into my garden from there. It's a bit muddy but we'll manage.' He strode off without waiting for a reply, rubber-booted, followed by Mayo, whose own gumboots were back in the car and who was annoyed to find himself having to pick his way around deep puddles like some latter-day Hercule Poirot.

The footpath itself, which joined a track leading from the school, was overgrown and Denzil Thorne shouted over his shoulder by way of explanation that it wasn't much used except by the residents of the houses on St Kenelm's Walk and Parson's Place, whose garden boundaries it skirted. As they progressed, Mayo saw that the gardens did not, as he had supposed, end at the river bank, but levelled out for some twenty or thirty yards before their boundary hedges which separated them from the river footpath. Then again, beyond the footpath was another stretch of ground, irregular in contour where the course of the river, several feet below it, had made erratic inroads into the soil, forming small scrub-covered islands and peninsulas. It was on one of these peninsulas, further downriver, he was presently to learn, that the badgers had their sett.

Mrs Thorne was weeding at the bottom of the garden, kneeling on the grass, clad in an anorak with her substantial rear end in the air and a trug full of tangled white roots beside her, attacking ground elder as though it were a personal enemy to be vanquished.

'Got to root out every last little bit,' she announced, digging her fork in with venom. 'Leave so much as an inch and it'll take advantage and start a dynasty before you can say Jack Robinson!' With obvious regret at having to abandon such an enjoyable task, she heaved herself to her feet. 'I'll be right with you but excuse me for a minute, will you, I must take this little tyke and clean him up. He's too near the ground to keep clear of the mud. Heel, Taff!' With much more docility and obedience than he'd shown with his master, Taff obeyed.

'No hurry, Mrs Thorne,' Mayo said. 'I don't think there's anything more I want of you at the moment—'

'It's my turn now for the old inquisition, eh?' interrupted Denzil brightly. The idea of being questioned seemed to amuse him, as if the activities of the real-life police were a parody of some detective novel or telly-drama, as if Mayo were some sort of stage policeman, and he the innocent victim. But it was an attitude Mayo had come across many times before and he took no notice.

'If you'd be so kind, Dr Thorne,' he said patiently as Miriam Thorne, followed by the dog, disappeared through an archway cut into a clipped Leylandii hedge which led to the next, higher, part of the garden.

'No problem about *my* whereabouts. I was at the Institute all day. Stayed until nearly eleven, in fact.'

'A long day, sir.'

'Not unusually so. The sort of work I do means I often stay late. I'd some important work to finish and I wanted to see an experiment through. I'd already lost time because of a top level meeting—which was actually with some of your own people, I might add. Because of the bomb we had there, you know. They seem to think our safety precautions have been slipping and need stepping up, though I have to say,' he added with a hint of umbrage, 'it's what they themselves laid down in the first place.'

Mayo disregarded the invitation to comment on a situation with which he was only too familiar. It happened all the time. Tight security to begin with, everyone conscious of it, then familiarity and a gradual relaxing of vigilance. Finally, slackness and downright negligence . . . until disaster occurred and too late, every stable door in spitting distance was being locked and barred within an inch of its life. Had he been in Denzil Thorne's position, responsible for an organization as vulnerable as that, he'd have kept quiet on the subject.

'The meeting,' added Denzil, 'was at half past four and lasted for a couple of hours.'

And you couldn't have a much better alibi than that, closeted with senior police officers.

'So—that's all I can give you. Not much, but I hope it's been of help.'

Mayo said it had but there was one thing more which he'd like to know about the security at the Institute—Thorne looked wary—had he ever received threats of a personal nature?

'From time to time, but nothing I couldn't handle.' His caution was obvious, in the same way, the previous evening, that his wife's had been. What, Mayo wondered, had made them so cagey?

'One expects that from cranks,' Thorne continued, more easily. 'And from people who just can't see straight—though they must think they have a legitimate point of view, I suppose,' he added, smiling his Boy Scout smile, striving so hard to be fair it must have hurt him. 'But I don't understand what that has to do with Willard's death.'

Mayo was saved from explaining his theory about the connection between Willard and possible animal rights extremists by the return of Mrs Thorne who, having dealt with the dog, was now quite prepared to deal with the constabulary. 'Well, what are you doing about finding Danny Lampeter, Mr Mayo?' she demanded as soon as she came through the gate. 'I hear he's pushed off.'

The village grapevine hadn't been slow. Mayo murmured something non-committal about having no reason at the moment to try and find Lampeter.

'No reason? Only that a pound to a penny he shot those badgers,' she returned, as though that immediately made him the prime suspect for smothering Willard, too.

'Miriam, that's pure guesswork,' her husband protested, but mildly.

'No use pussyfooting around! Everybody knows it must've been him. He's always been in trouble one way or another, even before he went into the army, and I've seen nothing to show that he's changed. Bad blood there, y'know. The father was the same—upped and left them when the mother was diagnosed as having multiple sclerosis. Didn't want the responsibility, not even for Danny. Left it all to Ruth.'

Mayo thought of what old Sam Biggs had said to him about Ruth Lampeter having had a rough time. Maybe he ought to look more kindly on that uptight young woman, it was beginning to sound as though maybe she had plenty of reason for being the way she was.

'Why d'you think Lampeter would want to shoot the animals?'

'Danny?' She laughed shortly. 'People like him don't need a reason for causing trouble. They just enjoy mindless violence.'

This wildly outrageous generality, unsubstantiated by any evidence, needed no comment from him, Mayo felt. But there was a grain of truth in it. The shrinks might not agree—would certainly trump up some connection between Lampeter's anti-social behaviour and the missing father, he was sure. In his own opinion violence was as inbred in some men as blue eyes or short stature—bad blood, as Miriam Thorne had it. What she'd said threw a little more light on Lampeter's character—or at any rate his reputation. There was always at least one scapegoat family in any village and sometimes they actually were responsible for the things they were blamed for. It was interesting to speculate on, but of doubtful use in the present circumstances.

Unless Danny had misinterpreted Willard's wishes in wanting to be rid of the badgers in too zealous a manner . . .

'Have you seen the badger sett?' Mrs Thorne asked abruptly.

Mayo had to say he hadn't.

'You should. Come on, I'll show you.' And zipping up her anorak to her chin, the lady opened the garden gate and prepared to set off down the path.

Mayo felt he'd already been told more about badgers than he wanted to know, and that he'd better things to do —like solving a murder—than spending all his time on Sunday afternoon walks. Further, he didn't want to be bossed around by Miriam Thorne. Still, at the back of his mind the thought persisted that in some way as yet unfathomable, the truth about Willard's death might lie in clearing up the mystery of the badger-shooting. If nothing else, it would eliminate at least one useless line of inquiry. Meekly, he followed the determined figure and carrotty head of Miriam Thorne along the river bank, with her husband bringing up the rear.

The sett was in a sheltered beech coppice about a hundred yards downriver from the houses in Parson's Place, where the high plateau on which Wyvering stood gave way to rocky slopes and the river began to swing out. There was little to see, however, except a criss-cross of well-worn tracks in the soft red earth, wandering between low scrub and bracken and a great spread of yellow gorse. The water was so clear you could see the pebbles lying in the shallows and watch the minnows darting. Blue dragonflies skimmed the surface and a moorhen paddled quietly across to the far bank. In the soft haze of the day it was very quiet, with a slight melancholy hanging over the place, like some sentimental Victorian painting.

Denzil Thorne pointed to a thick clump of holly and thorn growing at the foot of an old beech tree. 'See that?' he asked, lowering his voice to a sibilant stage whisper. 'It completely obscures the entrance to the sett. You have to know where to look, but I don't think we should go any further in case they catch our scent. It's not right to disturb them.'

The footpath, though considerably less muddy here than

the first stretch, had degenerated first of all into a mere track and had now disappeared altogether, and Mayo was not averse to the suggestion of calling a halt. 'So anyone wanting to get to the sett would have to come from Wyvering,' he commented.

'That's right. The river's not navigable from here. Much too shallow and weedy.'

'Unless they walked up from that direction?' Mayo waved towards a church spire which could be seen in the distance.

'From Stapley? No way! It's a good four or five miles and no proper path. You'd be mud to the eyes.' Returning to his theme, Thorne said, 'It was just here, outside the sett, where they found the bodies of the badgers.'

'They? Who were they?'

'Couple of ten-year-olds. Cycled down that track over there.'

'Cycled?' Mayo looked back, following Thorne's pointing finger to a track that was steep as a house-side and slippery with loose red earth and stones, recognizing it immediately as the one leading from Parson's Place and seeing its appeal to small boys.

'Well might you ask!' Miriam said. 'We—the parish council, that is—put a gate across the top and a notice forbidding entry, but that doesn't stop the kids. They dare one another to ride down on their bikes and I can't tell you the number of broken arms and legs we've had, not to mention one concussion. Good job he didn't end up in the river, which I might say one or two of the little monsters have nearly done. We can't keep it locked, it's a right of way.'

And a useful rubbish tip, thought Mayo, recalling the propped-open gate.

'All the same,' said Denzil, 'those lads knew it was illegal to kill badgers from all these wildlife programmes they watch and went back and told Jack Wainwright straight away. There's a lot of talk about kids watching too much television but I'm all for it if they understand that sort of thing.'

'I could see Willard's point,' Miriam said as they trudged back along the river bank, having seen all there was to see and leaving the badgers sleeping in their dark secret world under the earth. 'Much as I disagreed with him. Must've been infuriating that his garden—and old Mrs Crawshaw's next door to him—are the only ones affected. The badgers have never dug anyone else's lawn up, but you can't expect the poor creatures to tell the difference—it's their instinct to go where they know they'll get food. You couldn't tell him that, though. Couldn't tell him anything in fact, he never listened to a word anyone else said, once he'd made up his mind.'

'He should've put food out for them like Catherine Oliver does,' Thorne said, 'then they mightn't have bothered with his lawn.'

'Oh, phooey!'

'I don't know that's so crazy. But as a matter of fact,' he said to Mayo, 'I've got a bit of a conscience about this business. For suggesting it to Willard, I mean. The thing is, he hadn't known what Mrs Oliver was doing until I told him, though of course I hadn't realized that. Mentioned it quite casually in conversation and he nearly hit the roof. Called her a sentimental fool of a woman and sent her a very stiff note, then complained to Constable Wainwright and caused no end of fuss. Poor Catherine was very upset about it. Better to have kept my mouth shut.'

'Don't be such a clot, Denzil! No use beating your breast at this late stage. You might've known that's how he'd take it. And you could've told him it's not sentiment with Catherine. She encourages them because she wants to draw them, Mr Mayo. She's just written a book that's to be published and illustrated with her drawings—not only badgers of course but other nocturnal animals. Enchanting. She draws the most beautiful owls. Philly—my daughter

—works for a publisher and she's heard on the grapevine that the book's likely to be a success. Not that it's any secret.' She added obscurely, 'Even Lionel knows now.'

They had reached the garden gate where Mayo had stopped, intending to go back the way he had come, until he heard voices somewhere ahead of them in the garden which made him change his mind about going back into the town by way of the castle walk. 'Is that your daughter I hear? If so, I'll take the opportunity to see her.'

'Yes, that's Philly.' Mayo had a moment to wonder why the reluctance, why the worried line that suddenly appeared between Denzil's brows before he pushed open the gate, with a hearty 'Be my guest.' But then, recollecting his glimpse of Phyllida Thorne the previous evening, remembering her attitude and what she had looked like, Mayo thought of several things her father might have cause to be worried about.

Thorne and his wife followed Mayo through the archway in the hedge which he now saw led on to the first of a series of crazy-paved terraces, bright with aubretia and alyssum. Two people were there, sitting close together on a low wall: the Thornes' daughter, Phyllida, and Sebastian Oliver. The air between them vibrated like a plucked violin string.

The girl shrugged indifferently when Mayo told her he'd like to ask her a few questions. 'I suppose. I'm not going anywhere. But Seb was, weren't you, Seb?'

Her right hand was rhythmically stroking a malevolent-looking Persian with rusty black fur which Mayo vaguely remembered seeing wandering around Parson's Place and which now lay on the low stone wall, watching him with slitted eyes, its tail dripping over the edge.

'That's all right,' he said, 'Mr Oliver and I have already spoken.'

Her mother and father, having made their farewells to Mayo, had already gone forward into the house. Sebastian, however, showed no signs of following them. He kept his black eyes on Phyllida. He was another Sebastian from the smooth, flippant young man Mayo had seen before, his face now set and rather pale. As for Phyllida, she was flushed and her eyes sparkled, but with temper rather than excitement. Mayo saw that he had interrupted, not a love scene as he had first thought, but a battle. Which could, on second thoughts, amount to the same thing.

He availed himself of the seat which the girl had offered with a casual wave of the hand. He wondered for a moment whether to let Sebastian go, though he seemed in no hurry to leave. The feeling that he had had when they first met returned, the certainty that Sebastian Oliver was in some specific way central to the mystery. In what way this could be so remained to be seen, and he decided that meanwhile he would do better to see Phyllida Thorne alone. He looked at Sebastian until that young man finally got the message, came reluctantly to his feet in one graceful movement and for a moment remained standing, looking down at Phyllida, his hands in his pockets, his face unreadable. Then he said abruptly, 'See you, Philly,' and went.

She didn't turn her head, but sat up very straight. Mayo waited until the young man, with his quick, light strides, had disappeared up the garden path before asking the girl, 'Who else was here with you? Who was it just left?'

'There wasn't anyone,' she answered coolly. 'You must've been mistaken.'

Mayo knew he wasn't. He'd heard another voice. Moreover, one he'd heard somewhere before, and though he hadn't yet placed it he knew he would, given time.

'OK. I don't mind answering questions,' she said suddenly, 'though you can put your handcuffs away, you've no reason for arresting me.'

Not unless it's for being indecently dressed, he thought.

She was wearing jeans so tight he wondered how she could sit, and a sleeveless top striped like a pirate's jersey, fairly obviously nothing at all underneath. Isn't she frozen? he thought, but there wasn't a single goose bump on her smooth, brown young arms. Minus the thick make-up of the previous evening, he could see that her face was lightly tanned also, and against the tan her eyes were a startling blue-green. Her mouth was stubborn.

'Nothing so interesting,' he said, assuming the deliberately avuncular expression he could when he chose. 'Just a few minutes' chat.'

She shrugged in an offhand manner that didn't hide the fact she was nervous. Not as cool and sophisticated as she was trying to make out, Miss Phyllida Thorne.

He sat back as easily as the uncomfortable seat, digging into the backs of his knees, would allow, refusing to be provoked. 'I expect it was quite a shock when you heard about Mr Willard being dead.'

Her hand reached out again to caress the cat with long, slow strokes; the cat responded with a purr like an engine. 'Nothing to be shocked about, was there? He was old and anyway, I didn't know him, I don't suppose I've spoken more than twenty words to him in my life.'

'But his daughter's a friend of your mother's.'

'Well, I'm sorry for Laura, but she's not the one who's dead.'

She was like one those seeds, lupins or some such, the sort that put him off gardening. With a coating so hard it had to be chipped or soaked before it would germinate and flower. This flower, when it bloomed, might be spectacular, a prize-winning exotica; or it might turn out to be a miserable specimen, withered and atrophied through some unseen canker within.

He was growing fanciful. He said, 'Tell me what happened since you got here on Friday night.'

She had stayed in, talking to her mother, she said, looking bored, done a little shopping the next morning for her at the village store, worked on some papers she'd brought with her until six o'clock, when Sebastian had called for her. From then on, her version of events tallied with his, which was neither more nor less than Mayo had expected: Sebastian, he recalled, had telephoned her that evening as soon as he arrived home and heard that Willard was dead—or had been found, which was not quite the same thing. And if they hadn't agreed what to say then, they'd had plenty of time since.

'Where did your drive take you?'

'As far as Denver Bridge.' He ignored the exaggerated patience she assumed, knowing it was deliberately designed to be disagreeable. 'We got out and walked in the woods for a while, then drove on to the River House. I can't remember what time we arrived there, but I'm sure they'll be able to tell you. What we ate and drank as well, and how long I spent in the bloody loo, I dare say.'

'That won't be necessary,' he said mildly. He thought she was shockingly spoiled. Probably never had so much as her hand slapped when she was a child, more's the pity. 'You must appreciate the countryside, living in London. Mr Oliver says he does.'

'Mr Oliver will say anything for effect,' she said, mocking, but her eyes were a flame of aquamarine at the mention of his name.

I was right, he thought, there is something between them. For a while he let himself play with the question of what linked them together. Sex, yes. She was an open invitation. But it was more than that. Beneath her casually immature rudeness, he sensed something older, essentially tough and implacable, perhaps a passion for the unattainable, certainly a contempt for compromise. Sebastian might find this an irresistible combination but Mayo knew that women like her spelled trouble with a capital T. Of the two he'd rather deal with Sebastian Oliver any day.

'See much of him, do you? In London?'

'We're friends. Naturally, both coming from Wyvering.'

The opposite might more probably be the case, he thought, but didn't say. Was it correct, he asked, that their visit here this weekend was unscheduled?

'If you mean we came on the spur of the moment, yes. I

hadn't seen my parents for months and thought it was time I made the effort.'

A few spots of rain fell and suddenly the cat, lightly for one of its weight and age, leaped on to her knee and draped itself against her shoulder. She held it to her, looking at him from over its head, running her hands through the thick fur. 'Florence doesn't like rain,' she said. 'Me neither,' and stood up.

The drops came slowly at first, then in a drenching downpour that had them running for the house, scrambling up steps, brushing against the purple and white lilacs that overhung the hedge from the Rectory garden next door and releasing their heavy, cloying scent on the air.

CHAPTER 13

By the time he finished what he had to do in Wyvering, however, the downpour had eased off and finally stopped.

Following a train of thought set up when standing near the badger sett, Mayo made the decision on his way home to turn off the main road and have a look at Stapley, the village a few miles along the river from Castle Wyvering. He discovered it to be little more than a hamlet: a few houses clustered round the bridge over the river, a pub, a shop-cum-post office and the church whose steeple could be seen from Wyvering. He drew to a halt at the far side of the river, wide at this point, and walked to the ancient packhorse bridge, so narrow that foot travellers in days gone by had been obliged to take refuge from a single coach or cart by pressing themselves into recessed bays at either side.

Standing in one of these, looking at the water, he felt the wind, stronger now, with a colder edge to it. Rain threatened again. It was an altogether unpleasant late afternoon, grown dark too early, and the fortunate inhabitants of

Stapley were all indoors before the fire, lights from their houses already glowing, while outside the air smelt of woodsmoke and wet grass and drenched May blossom. Mayo leaned over the parapet, looked upriver and thought about possibilities. Nothing very interesting occurred to him. Alongside the river the footpath was indeed as bad as Thorne had suggested and seemingly disappeared altogether a few hundred yards further along in a sea of mud. The river certainly wasn't navigable, either: the water at the edges was clear and as shallow as it had been near the badgers' sett. Only in the middle was it deeper, but there it was choked by a thick growth of rank weed.

He saw the map of the area clearly before his mind's eye: the country road off the bypass winding up to Castle Wyvering, past the school, along the crest of the hill through the village and down the other side where it rejoined the bypass. And another narrow road off, leading eventually through Stapley, arriving at the point where he was now standing, thus completing the circle.

Having found nothing profitable after all in his diversion, he was turning back to his car when he heard children's voices and a gaggle of small boys appeared down this same road, clad in running gear, their faces hot, red and sweaty. Straggling untidily in twos and threes, they staggered to the bridge, collapsing against it in attitudes of exaggerated exhaustion, with many dramatic utterances to the same effect. Mayo, who regarded this type of exercise as a form of masochism anyone could do without, watched them with every sympathy from the shelter of a large chestnut tree. He began to be less worried for their survival when one lad, tiring of the histrionics and looking round for some more interesting way to pass the time, presently descended to the path and began chucking boulders into the water, so starting a general movement towards the bank. Competition to see who could make the biggest splash soon became fierce, water and mud flew, until down the road came the rest of the contingent, Jon Reece in his blue tracksuit jollying along the forlorn hope.

Not wishing to be seen, Mayo drew back further into the shadows, while a clamour of voices immediately assailed the schoolmaster, the gist of which seemed to be a plea to be allowed to return to Wyvering via the river bank.

'Certainly not,' said Reece.

'Oh, *sir!*' twenty boys chorused. Additional pleas to the effect that they were soaking already, that it would wash the mud off, that it was boring going the same way back fell on deaf ears. The enterprising one added, 'I think I've sprained my ankle, sir.'

'Tough,' Reece returned. 'And bored you'll have to be, the lot of you. Hungry too, if you don't get a move on. It's bangers and beans tonight.'

A few token groans, some *sotto voce* grumbles, but Reece's bracing strictures and the promise of supper soon had them starting at a brisk trot back up the road whence they had come, sprained ankles and faint hearts miraculously mended.

As he watched Reece sprinting after them, Mayo reflected that Holden seemed to have been correct in his judgement of Reece's popularity with the boys—whether or not this was a necessary or even a desirable trait in a headmaster. He walked back to his car and slid thoughtfully behind the wheel again. An idea had come to him as he had stood there unobserved, watching the stones being thrown into the water, seeing Reece and hearing his voice call to the children, and seeing something else he'd seen before, without knowing he'd seen it. He understood now what had puzzled him about Reece. Why the hell didn't I make the connection before? he asked himself. And what does it mean, anyway?

'If you want to know about the bomb at the Fricker, it's DCI Uttley you want to see at Hurstfield. Fred Uttley,' Kite was informing him over the telephone half an hour later. 'He's not in for the next couple of days but he says if it's convenient to you, he'll be there first thing Wednesday morning. I okayed that, but I can change it if it's not suitable.'

'No, don't do that. I want to see him as soon as possible.' Mayo spoke absently, thinking that if Kite, who had left Wyvering before him to return to the station, was still there, they could take the opportunity to discuss the day's proceedings and compare notes. Kite, however, was not.

'Matter of fact, I got a move on and finished sooner than I expected and I'm at home now,' he said. 'In Sheila's good books for once. But look, if you want us to talk, why don't you come around here and have something to eat with us first? There'll be more than enough. Sheila always cooks enough for the five thousand.'

'*I* shan't be in her good books if I butt in on your one and only evening together.'

Mayo could imagine the frantic gesticulating going on at the other end, Sheila wondering how she could spin out the meal to include an extra one and cursing him for ruining their evening. The thought he imputed to her reflected his own disinclinations. Being sociable with Kite's wife, much as he liked her, and talking to his boys, was the last thing he wanted tonight, but he'd warded off enough similar invitations to make him feel he was being boorish and standoffish by refusing yet again. It was all very kindly meant —they imagined he must be miserable, alone in his flat, preparing and eating a solitary meal—and suddenly, seeing it that way, the thought of company other than his own appealed. Kite then clinched it by adding, 'Farrar handed me his report just before I left and I think you'd like to see it.'

Mayo gave in. 'Thank you very much, I will come round, but I'll eat first and join you for coffee afterwards, if that's all right with you.'

It was a compromise, and Kite recognized it as such. The kids would be in bed by then, he said, and they could

go and talk in the conservatory afterwards, dignifying with
the name his latest DIY project, an extension to the back
of the house which he'd recently managed to finish against
all the odds, and which he was anxious to show off.

It was a very creditable job, Mayo had to admit when
he saw it. And agree that it hadn't taken too much off the
garden, had extended the scope of the house. And admire
Kite's plants, one or two already large and handsome, most
as yet immature but hopeful. And approve the furnishings
Sheila had chosen. And pay her the deserved compliment
of having as light a touch with the décor of her house as
with the delicious cake he was sampling with his coffee.
Sheila, not being one of those women who see every man
living on his own as being liable to go to the dogs without
a woman's tender loving care, and not susceptible to flattery
either, regarded the slice of walnut cake reposing on her
own plate with surprise. 'It's not bad, is it? Afraid my cakes
are a matter of luck. I'm much better with casseroles and
things like that, where you just bung everything in.'

'I'll second that,' Kite teased, offering another slice to
Mayo and helping himself to one.

She made a face, but laughed and poured more coffee.
They had an easy, natural, uncomplicated partnership that
Mayo sometimes envied. She was an uncomplicated and
cheerful woman, Sheila, coping without fuss with a responsible job of her own, her home and family. Putting up with
Kite's unsocial hours with only the routine amount of com-
plaining, as far as Mayo could gather. Contrary to what
Mayo had thought, she was evidently delighted that he had
consented to drop in and he felt ungracious in hoping he
hadn't started something he didn't want to continue. Never
a man to socialize much with his colleagues, he preferred
to keep his private and professional life in separate compart-
ments, though he knew this gave rise to speculations about
him down at the station, and no doubt about Alex, too. He
knew his reticence helped to fuel their curiosity, but he
couldn't help that, it was the way he was made.

With commendable tact, Sheila found an excuse to leave them alone when the coffee was drunk. Kite produced whisky.

'Well,' Mayo said, as a glass was set at his elbow and Kite had poured one for himself, 'what did you get from Tracey's mum?'

'She's fed up to the back teeth with Tracey, landing the baby on her. But I reckon she thought the poor little beggar would stand a better chance with her than with a daughter who doesn't want it. Tracey's living here in Lavenstock and her mum thinks it's ten to one Lampeter is with her—or at any rate that she'll know where he is. Seems the landlord at the Drum and Monkey was nearer the mark than her grandad, whether Danny's the kid's father or not. It wasn't just Danny refusing to marry her, the feeling was apparently mutual, though they're still good friends.'

'And what did Farrar have to say?'

'Ah,' said Kite. 'This is interesting. He couldn't find anybody at the conference centre who remembers speaking to Illingworth before nine o'clock Saturday night.'

'Nobody?'

'Which, of course, doesn't rule out that he was there. Place is like a rabbit warren, Farrar says, an old converted country house with five or six acres of grounds. Apparently there's about two hundred delegates milling around this weekend, and Illingworth may or may not have been among them.'

Anyone, it appeared, could arrive at Thornaby and not be noticed, possibly not for some considerable time. All the necessary papers, with room allocations, were sent out by post beforehand, cutting out the requirement for a registration desk and the need to book in. No occasion to pick up one's room key even, since there were no locks on the doors. 'It's owned by a religious organization and all run on communal lines—self-service meals, make your own beds, that sort of thing.'

'Sounds like one big security headache to me,' Mayo commented.

'They don't seem to think so. Mutual trust seems to be the order of the day.'

'Trust my backside! Still, that's their pigeon.'

Kite now threw a copy of Farrar's report down on the coffee table. 'It's all there. Chap by the name of Peter Collins had a drink in the bar with him at nine, and after that one or two folks either saw or spoke to him—but nobody before then.'

'Well,' Mayo reflected, 'if he did decide to do for Willard, he could have got himself down to Brighton by nine, easily. There's also a way he could have made his way into the church without being seen. I called in at Stapley on my way home, that's about four miles downstream from Wyvering. Nothing to stop him walking up the river from there.'

'Jesus!' said Kite, not inappropriately.

'You look at the river and you'll see how shallow it is at the edges. If it's like that all the way to Wyvering, and I suspect it is, all he'd need would be a pair of gumboots or waders with him. Anybody saw him, he could've made out he was fishing, though it's unlikely anybody else would be wallowing through all that mud. Then up that path that comes out in Parson's Place.'

It took a few minutes to convince Kite that it was possible, but when he saw that it was he agreed to have a man try it out the following day. 'I'll put Spalding on to it, he's the athletic type, that slope'll be nothing to him. He'll need to have a pair of trainers or something in his pocket, though, never get up it in gumboots.'

Kite was convincing himself of the feasibility of the idea as he spoke. Yes, he agreed, it would have taken no time at all for the killer to dodge from the entry and through the back gate of the churchyard, after which he'd have had cover from the trees. Much less likelihood of him being seen than if he'd entered Parson's Place from either Dobbs Lane or St Kenelm's Walk. 'It's possible,' he admitted. 'Mind you, he was still taking some risk of being seen, but as we've already said, that applies to whoever followed Willard into the church, that way or any other.'

'Better not get too sold on Illingworth, all the same. Not at this stage.'

'Well, yes, there's still time for someone to turn up at Thornaby who remembers seeing him earlier in the day. Some of the delegates had already left for home when Farrar got there. He got names and addresses,' Kite added, though Farrar, of all people, wouldn't have forgotten.

'Well, leaving aside Illingworth for the moment,' Mayo said, 'let's look at it another way. At Willard himself. We've been concentrating on who he saw on Friday, but what about yesterday? He was supposed to have spent it alone, but did he in fact? Did something happen during the day that sparked off the murder? What have we got? It was the day for the nurse who used to attend to him. She calls early, about half past eight according to Laura Willard, who waited until the nurse had gone before she went out herself, leaving her father a ham salad which he ate for his lunch. At some time during the afternoon he had some tea and a piece of fruit cake. Laura Willard feels that if anyone had called—anyone he knew, that is—he'd have made them a cup of tea. But there was no sign of that—only one cup, saucer and plate. He left the house, presumably at six. At any rate Mrs Oliver says that it was just after six when he arrived at the church and went in, and it could only have taken a few minutes to get his chair round there. Mrs Holden had locked the church door at five-thirty and no one else had keys, apart from the churchwardens, Brigadier Finlay and George Washburn.'

Kite agreed with this. 'Washburn took his wife shopping in Lavenstock and afterwards to a meal at that Italian place, Gino's, in Sheep Street, and they didn't get back until about nine. Brigadier Finlay's daughter and her family were visiting him, so he was in all day but nobody approached him for the key.'

'What do Willard's neighbours say? Did they notice anyone coming or going at the house?'

'There's that high brick wall opposite, the backyards of
the houses on Main Street, so it's not surprising nobody
saw or heard anything. The people at the first house in
St Kenelm's Walk are away on holiday and his next-door
neighbour on the other side, an elderly woman called Mrs
Crawshaw, is in Lavenstock General with a suspected
thrombosis. I'll have a WPC go and see her, if you think
it's necessary.'

'That was the woman I saw being taken away in the
ambulance when I went round with Wainwright to Willard's house. If she's feeling up to it, you can send Jenny
along, but don't let anyone bother the old girl if not,' he
said. 'She's had enough to put up with, and if she was
feeling that bad, she wouldn't have been peering through
the lace curtains at Willard's visitors anyway.'

Mayo swished the ice round in his glass, leaning back
and following the progress of an enormous cheese plant,
apparently on its way to heaven. 'We've rather lost sight of
Sara in all this, haven't we? Nobody turned up of that
name, I suppose?'

'There's a baby called Sarah—with an aitch—in Elm
Tree Crescent, but that's all. Who the devil is she?'

'I'll swear young Oliver knows, for one, but he's not
saying. I don't trust him, still less that girlfriend of his, any
further than I can throw either of them.'

'You think he might've had a problem with someone
called Sara and gone to Willard to ask his advice?'

'Martin, I haven't one damn clue what to think.' He
shook his head regretfully at the offer of another drink and
moved to the edge of his chair, saying, 'Had my limit,
thanks. Must be off anyway, and say my goodbyes to Sheila.
Thank you for everything, Martin.' But he didn't move.

'You know who it is, don't you?' Kite asked abruptly. It
depressed him slightly how quickly Mayo, an unimaginative man—or so he professed himself—could make a

quantum leap and reach a point way ahead of Kite, who knew himself to be sharp and intuitive.

'No,' Mayo said after a moment. 'I don't know. It's just a vague idea I've had. Something that occurred to me that probably has nothing to do with anything. I'm not holding out on you—it's just so nebulous I haven't been able to form it in my own mind yet. You know what it's like, Martin,' he added, conscious of not being fair to Kite but feeling that the various threads he was trying to knit together were as yet insubstantial as the threads of a spider's web, 'talk an idea over too soon and it disappears like smoke up a chimney.'

CHAPTER 14

Uplands House School was a former country house, once-prosperous but fallen upon evil times until being bought and renovated as a school in the nineteen-twenties. Built of warm sandstone in the Strawberry Hill Gothick tradition, it was an imposing pile, castellated and pinnacled, with a great mullioned window in the centre of the creeper-covered south front and towers terminating each end. Little had been done to alter the original structure, apart from the building of a chapel which had been tacked on as an after-thought to the side. The science block was another addition but was housed in a series of Terrapin huts round the back of the school, out of sight.

As one of the unmarried masters, Illingworth lived in the school building, in a set of rooms housed in the upper storey of one of the towers whose entrance, Mayo and Kite dis-covered when they arrived at the school, was obscured by a network of tubular steel scaffolding, with ladders resting on platforms set at intervals to the height of the roof.

'What's all this, then?' Kite asked a workman who was

perched on a pile of planks, reading his newspaper and
drinking tea out of a pint pot.

'Roof repairs, mate. Damage from the gales last winter,'
the man informed them, laying down his paper. 'Blew the
capping from one of the unused chimneys and broke near
a hundred tiles, didn't it? Be a long job, this. Weeks,
maybe,' he added with satisfaction, digging into his pocket
and lighting up a cigarette of the more pungent variety.
'Brought this joker down with it besides.' He indicated an
enormous stone finial, its point broken off, which lay against
a pile of scaffolding clamps on the ground. Knobbly with
what had once been sharply-carved acanthus leaves, it
looked now, smoothed by the weathering of time and
impaled on its steel support, uncannily like some grisly
severed head mysteriously resurrected and transported
from the medieval gate of the Tower of London. 'Need more
than an aspirin if that trapped your toe, I can tell you.'

'Must weigh half a hundredweight,' Mayo speculated.

'And the rest.' A small shower of grit descended from
above. 'I should use the main entrance if I was you while
we're messing about here.'

They were directed in through the front door, past the
vast, mullioned-windowed room which was now the library,
and up on to the main landing, from which led a short flight
of steps with a door bearing Illingworth's name at the top.

Mayo had decided to interview him in his rooms, mainly
because he wanted to see him alone. He wasn't, therefore,
at nine o'clock on Monday morning, best pleased to find
Laura Willard already installed on the sofa when he and
Kite entered. He suspected Illingworth had arranged this
purposely and was of a mind to ask him to accompany him
somewhere else while he was questioned, until it occurred
to him he might be able to use Laura's presence to turn the
situation to his own advantage.

The main door had opened straight into a large, comfortable sitting-room, with a glimpse through an open door of
a bedroom beyond. They were typical bachelor's quarters,

not particularly tidy, with books stacked wherever happened to be convenient, and a large oak desk in front of the window, covered with piles of exercise books and what looked like exam papers. But Mayo thought he detected the hand of Gina Holden rather than Illingworth himself in the furnishings—the chintz-covered chairs, walls colourwashed in palest green, two fringed oriental-type rugs lying on a gleaming expanse of wood flooring, a small television set. However, a couple of flower vases on the stone window-sills stood empty, and one cool modern seascape and a framed photograph of Laura Willard on the oak mantelpiece were the only concessions to ornamentation.

Laura in person was a different creature from when he'd last seen her. Then she'd been nervy and tense, but gone now was the feverish urge to talk, the inclination to tears. The inquest, after which the coroner would release the body and the funeral could take place, and which Mayo would also be attending, was scheduled for that afternoon. She was apparently already dressed for it. Black wasn't her colour; it robbed her skin tones of the warmth they needed, but it undoubtedly gave her an elegance she had previously lacked, emphasized by the way she was wearing her hair today, richly coiled into a knot at the back of her head instead of tumbling down to her shoulders. She sat with her hands folded calmly on her lap, listening quietly as Illingworth was asked whether he'd like to reconsider the statement he had made regarding his movements on Saturday.

Illingworth was as truculent as ever. 'I see no reason to change anything I said,' he answered shortly, looking taller and thinner and not so much like a heron as some scrawny cormorant this morning, his black gown hunched on his shoulders, the sleeves hanging like folded wings, hands deep in pockets, head thrust downwards ready to swoop on his prey. And not disposed to be any more amenable when he was informed of the checks made at the Thornaby Conference Centre and that no one there actually remembered speaking to him until nine o'clock that evening. His answer to that was a sharp reply to the effect that it was hardly surprising no one should remember, since he hadn't actually spoken to anyone until after dinner.

'You were there all day and spoke to nobody,' Mayo repeated flatly.

'That wasn't what I said.' He wasn't bothering to hide his impatience with what he evidently considered time-wasting preliminaries and thick policemen, and pounced in a pedantic and donnish fashion which Mayo found extremely irritating. Giving him the benefit of the doubt, he decided Illingworth was probably the type who is his own worst enemy and likely had no idea of the impression he was making. All the same . . .

'What I actually said was, if you recall,' he was continuing, 'that I left Wyvering at about half past eight. Now look here, I can see you have to know the whereabouts of everybody concerned, but what the hell does it matter where I was and what time I got there? I was nowhere near Wyvering when Laura's father was killed.' He shot his cuff to look at his watch. 'And if that's all, I have my first lesson in ten minutes.'

Maybe I should've been a teacher, Mayo thought sourly. Clocking on at half past nine and off at four.

Kite had stopped writing and was waiting with interest to see what was going to happen. Hadn't Illingworth realized he was on course for getting his ears chewed off? Better men than he had been taken apart for much less. Sergeants and DCs, even, never mind nerds like Illingworth. Kite had a poor opinion of the intelligentsia.

But at that point Laura Willard intervened by speaking Illingworth's name, though in a voice so low it was barely audible. He heard, all the same, and swung round to look at her. What passed between them was some communication between them alone but after a moment he shrugged and turned back to Mayo. 'All right, all right, I didn't actually arrive at Thornaby until five. I had a walk round the grounds to stretch my legs, then fell asleep on my bed and missed dinner. I woke and went into the bar at just before nine, which was when I saw Collins. Will that do?'

'And where,' Mayo asked austerely, 'were you between eight-thirty a.m. and five p.m.?'

'I don't see that's any business of yours.'

'Maybe you don't, but I'd like an answer, all the same. Where were you?'

'I had another engagement.'

'It must have been important for you to have missed out on the day's proceedings, as well as the previous evening's.'

A long silence. Laura got up and opened the window behind her and stood apparently breathing in the scents of early summer. In front of her the scaffolding, the diagonal slash of the ladders across the windows, made a surrealist landscape of the view and after a moment she turned away and resumed her seat, watching Illingworth, her eyes wide and watchful, deeply brown.

'If I tell you,' Illingworth said at last, 'I must ask you not to divulge it.'

'I'm sorry, there's no way I can agree to conditions.'

Laura said into the silence that followed, 'There's no reason why he shouldn't know, David.'

'Except that Richard should be told, first.'

'Another half-hour isn't going to make any difference.'

Suddenly, Illingworth smiled. It was a smile of great charm, all the more surprising after his previous ill-temper, giving a whole new dimension to the dark planes of his face. For the first time Mayo saw what his attraction might be for Laura. He threw out his hands in a gesture of surrender and she said steadily, 'David was with me in Lavenstock, Mr Mayo. We had an appointment at the register office and then we went on for a rather special lunch. He left me round about three o'clock.'

Mayo sat back. He was too much in command of himself to show the surprise he felt but it took him a moment or two to digest it. She smiled very slightly and confirmed what he thought he'd heard. 'We were married on Saturday, Mr Mayo.'

'Married?'

'People do,' said Illingworth.

Through the open window a motor-mower could be heard in the distance. The rich, yeasty smell of newly-cut grass came into the room.

'I think David's told you how my father felt about our marriage. I did my best to talk him round but he couldn't be moved—so we decided to marry regardless.' Despite her newfound confidence Laura's voice was not quite under control.

'Don't be sorry,' Illingworth said, 'God knows, you've a right to a life of your own.' There was a hard, gritty edge to his voice.

'I'm not *sorry*! It just seems so—oh, I don't know. But I couldn't simply walk out and leave him, not in his state of health! So I looked round for a live-in housekeeper and finally found exactly the right person, someone I felt I could really trust and who I was sure wouldn't let him browbeat her. For rather complicated personal reasons—her previous employers suddenly decided to go abroad—she needed to start immediately. That was all right, but if I hadn't moved out when she moved in, there wouldn't have been much point to the whole thing. So we just got married. It had to be a *fait accompli*, you see, before my father could raise objections.'

Mayo thought she might really be saying, before she lost her nerve. Or that Illingworth had given her an ultimatum.

'It was obvious we couldn't have the sort of wedding I'd always wanted, in church with all our friends and relatives to wish us well. My father would have refused to attend, never mind officiate, and I couldn't have gone through with it in those circumstances. Which meant the register office.'

OK. These were Laura's reasons. But Illingworth's? Mayo wondered briefly if congratulations were in order, but decided against it as being inappropriate in the circumstances. He thought a glass or two of celebratory champagne at lunch might well have had something to do with Laura's accident.

'So you say now you left around three, Mr Illingworth, and reached Thornaby at five.'

'Not only *say* I got there at five, I did!'

'It would be better if there was somebody else who could say so as well.'

Illingworth shoved his hands in his pockets impatiently. 'Are you seriously suggesting that I married Laura, then went straight back and killed her father? That's obscene!'

Mayo suddenly lost patience with him. 'Since you've mentioned it, sir, don't let's lose sight of the fact that it's quite possible, obscene or not. You left Miss Willard at three. Her father wasn't killed until six-fifteen. Plenty of time for you to get over to Wyvering and then drive down to Brighton before nine.'

'And how do you suggest I did all this without being seen?'

'That I don't know at the moment. But if you did, I shall find out.'

He noticed the fine film of sweat on Illingworth's forehead and thought: Good, let him sweat. It'll do him no harm. He didn't like the man, much less his attitudes and had been inclined to feel sorry for Laura, thinking her gullible and easily manipulated until he saw how Illingworth appeared to take notice of her. He still felt sorry for her, but there was no accounting for how women felt.

He became aware that she was speaking again, rapidly, as though she wanted to get over what she had to say quickly. 'There's something else that perhaps you ought to know, Chief Inspector.'

She took a deep breath and Mayo thought: Here it is. When anyone said this to him, addressing him as Chief Inspector, it was usually worth listening to carefully.

'It's about Danny Lampeter.' Her colour was suddenly high and the explanation came out in a rush. 'Yesterday morning I went to look for a brooch to wear on my suit. It was a Victorian one in the shape of a lovers' knot, gold. I don't care for Victorian jewellery on the whole and I hardly ever wore it but it had belonged to my mother and I wanted to wear it for my wedding. I couldn't find it. I feel almost certain Danny Lampeter took it. There were one or two more bits and pieces gone, too, some jet and a cameo brooch.'

Well, well. 'Presumably you had reasons for believing he'd taken them?'

It all came out then, about her father's suspicion that Lampeter had for some time been pilfering things from the house, and how she'd managed to stop Willard from accusing him before because there'd been no proof. 'It was never anything much,' she said, 'a bottle of whisky, some money left out for the window-cleaners, that sort of thing. But when I told my father about the brooch, he said that was it, Danny would have to go. As I was coming home on Saturday, I passed him on his motorbike going very fast down the hill—but then the Rector came and told me about Father and—well, I forgot all about Danny. It wasn't until later that I began to wonder if . . .'

He helped out her embarrassment. 'To wonder if your father had confronted him with the thefts and Danny had lost his temper?'

'It wouldn't be the first time that had happened,' she said unhappily, 'Danny's pretty handy with his fists.'

Had she forgotten that hadn't been the way of it at all? That her father's life had been snuffed out in a very different way? He wondered, watching her, how much else she'd 'forgotten'. She hadn't deemed it necessary to tell him about Danny until she thought suspicion might be falling on Illingworth, whereupon Danny Lampeter, the village scapegoat, had conveniently emerged and she had found it her duty to tell what she knew about him.

Duty. A word that kept cropping up. Mayo tried to pic-ture the diary page where Willard had written the quotation. '*The principle of doing one's duty, whatever that may be.*' Yes, that was it. And into his mind also came the name written above it, Professor Quentin, a man who had seen Willard the day before his death—a professor at Cambridge, what was more, where David Illingworth had been a research fellow. Had it been the same college? Mayo decided then and there to check, and if so that a trip to that venerable city was indicated. He was suddenly, perhaps irrationally, but never mind that, convinced that the key to Illingworth's actions lay there.

As for Danny Lampeter . . . The story Laura Willard had told provided a likely explanation for Danny's disappearance. Hearing of the old man's murder and knowing what he'd done, escape would have been the first thing he would think of. In any case, Ruth Lampeter had lied. If Danny had left before 6.0, as she swore he had, he couldn't have passed Laura Willard coming up the hill in the taxi at 6.20. Mayo decided to leave that bit of business with Kite, knowing he'd ferret it out, if only for his own satisfaction.

CHAPTER 15

After the drive across the flat, empty fenlands, parking convenient to the college in Cambridge presented difficulties. Hampered by incessant traffic, tourists on foot, undergraduates on cycles and the usual fiendish one-way system, Kite eventually settled for a space in a multi-storey car park above a new shopping centre. From this they walked straight into a maze of narrow busy streets, where shops and markets rubbed shoulders with churches and college buildings of grey stone and ancient brick. Glimpses of quadrangles with creeper-hung walls and of quiet college gardens were vouchsafed through open gates, and the traffic noise receded as they made their way through the Backs towards Quentin's college. A young man and two girls in a punt were tailed by a pair of floating swans . . .

'Got it made, haven't they?' Kite asked, casting his eyes up. 'I'd been on the beat three or four years by the time I was their age.'

'Good luck to 'em.'

'Chance is a fine thing. I don't know that many from Lavenstock Grammar ever made it,' Kite answered belligerently, looking prepared to argue about privileged beginnings and head starts.

'Must admit it's a bit rarefied for me, too,' Mayo answered, more pacific than truthful, but Kite was mollified and said no more, while Mayo thought of the city's sense of timelessness and the beauty of its lucid architecture and didn't see how anyone could fail to feel a sense of uplift.

Professor Quentin met them at the porter's lodge and welcomed them with formal courtesy, offering them tea and scones when they had negotiated the narrow stone staircase to his rooms. He was very short and bald, a man in his fifties, of kindly if contradictory appearance, suggesting a certain impatience with sartorial details. He was wearing a conventionally tailored suit, pristine white shirt and blue-spotted bow tie, and with it a Fair Isle pullover which had all too obviously not well survived its too-vigorous washings. Walking before them up the stairs with small, precise steps, he revealed beneath his neatly-pressed navy-blue trousers, thick, gaudily patterned socks and a pair of scruffy, down-at-heel brown shoes in want of a lick of polish.

He had been saddened to hear of the death of his old friend, he said, unspeakably shocked at the manner of it. Over tea, he described his visit to Castle Wyvering the previous Friday and what he and Willard had talked about at some length, inclined to reminisce about their friendship and the correspondence they had conducted for many years. No mention of Illingworth and eventually it was Mayo who had to broach the subject. A shade of reserve crossed the other man's face as soon as his name was mentioned. 'Yes,

I remember him. Always spoken of as a man to be watched.
I mean, of course, in the academic sense.'

'Did you know he was teaching at Uplands House School
in Castle Wyvering?'

'I was aware of it, yes.'

'And that he was engaged to Mr Willard's daughter? Is
in fact married to her now?'

The thin Spode cup stayed half way to their host's lips,
then he drank and put the cup down precisely on the saucer.
'No,' he said carefully, 'that I did not know.'

Seconds passed while the Professor absorbed the implica-
tions of this news. Mayo drank his tea and waited. The
dark old room was used to silent thought. It reflected the
same unself-conscious contradictions of its owner's person:
a lovely rosewood table gleamed under the open window,
choice watercolours in gold frames hung against the dark
panelling, yet the chairs, though exceedingly comfortable,
were disreputable and the frayed rugs apt to trip the
unwary. A gas fire, simulating coal, stood incongruously in
the sixteenth-century fireplace. Apart from that, the room
was in a considerable state of confusion, with articles of
clothing and piles of papers strewn all over the place.

Eventually Quentin said, 'This is why you were here, of
course. You wish to know the circumstances of his leaving
here.'

'Whatever you can tell us, sir.'

'I can give you the facts, but about Illingworth himself
I knew comparatively little. Few people did, I imagine. But
very well, I'll do what I can.' He stood up and walked to the
empty fireplace, sat down on the club fender and clasped his
hands round his knee, an elderly, sharp-witted little gnome
gazing at them through this thick spectacles. 'He never
entered into the swim of things here, you know. Not un-
remarkable in itself—we have our share of individualists,
not to say eccentrics, here. He was married, but his wife
didn't mix with the other faculty wives, either.' He paused
thoughtfully. 'May I speak plainly, without prejudice?'

'Please do.'

'Then I will say that I am sorry to hear that Illingworth has married again. In my view, he should never have married in the first place. There are men, and I include myself among them, who do better for various reasons to remain single.' A dry, objective assessment from a man who, Mayo suspected, had never been stirred by passions. 'In Illingworth's case . . . well, for one thing, he was consumed by his work. Not that I am in any way against total dedication, quite the reverse, but simply of the opinion that it cannot combine with family life—unless the wife is singularly self-sufficient in one way or another—which Sarah Illingworth plainly was not. She struck me, the few times I met her, as beautiful but not in the least clever. Self-absorbed to a degree. As a consequence, she was unhappy with the other dons' wives, many of whom are academics themselves or have satisfying and demanding careers. There were all sorts of rumours. Not to put too fine a point on it, she was highly promiscuous, and had a drink problem, too. I was not in the least surprised to hear that they had divorced, especially after what happened to the boy.'

'They had children?'

'One son. He should have been sent away to school. There at least he might have found some sort of stable background, some code of ethics, the right sort of companionship, standards to live up to. As it was, he was sent to the local comprehensive, which might have been all very well if Illingworth hadn't been too absorbed in his work and his problem with his wife to suspect what was happening to the boy, and the mother too selfish to care how he passed his time or what company he kept as long as he kept himself out of her way. I dare say Illingworth did his best in difficult circumstances but it was the usual story. The boy was fourteen when he died.'

An exuberant yellow rose had climbed the wall outside and thrust its head throught the open lattice; suddenly the room was filled with its exquisite fragrance.

'Drugs?' Mayo asked.

'What else?' There was no doubt about Quentin's compassion. His gnomish face looked inexpressibly saddened.

'It's not always easy to tell until it's too late.'

'No. Though there was a good deal of talk within the college—there is never any shortage of people ready to apportion blame, and it was clear that what had happened had done his prospects no good at all. A man's private life is not his own if he chooses to set his sights on academic advancement. Eventually he left.'

But he had left quietly. Nothing had been forced upon him, no scandal had followed him to his next appointment at Uplands House. Quentin managed to convey, without actually saying so, that scandal within the hallowed precincts of Cambridge would have been as damaging to the college as to Illingworth, and that having to bury himself in an obscure place like Wyvering was punishment enough.

'Presumably Mr Willard knew of all this?'

'Not from me, certainly, though Illingworth's name was mentioned on Friday and I was not aware that Willard would have liked to discuss the circumstances of his relinquishing his Fellowship here. However, in the course of my life, I've learned that nothing is so easy to damage as a man's reputation. His career had had one irremediable setback and I saw no reason to add to that. I have only spoken now because I see where your questions are leading.'

'Perhaps you don't know that Illingworth is being considered for the position of Headmaster? Do you believe if his background was known, it would prevent his appointment?'

'That's a question I prefer not to answer. You must draw your own conclusions.' Quentin suddenly became the vague, mild-mannered academic again. 'Dear me, is that the time? I'm very much afraid . . .'

Mayo stood up, sliding his notebook into his inside pocket.

'When is the funeral? Friday? I have written to Miss Willard but I shall not be attending,' said the Professor.

'I'm leaving tomorrow for a short lecture tour of the United States. I was in fact just packing when you arrived,' he added, waving his hands in a helpless gesture as though hopeful of the scattered belongings picking themselves up and putting themselves into suitcases.

'Then we'd better leave you to it, sir. Thank you for your help.'

'Sarah,' said Kite as soon as they were out of the college. 'Did you hear that? Illingworth's wife was called Sarah.'

'Pronounced with the aitch, though.'

'He's old-fashioned, he'd have pronounced it Sarah whichever way it was spelt.'

'Even is she herself pronounced it the other way? All right, granted, I think he probably would. And that means Willard knew about her, and probably about the boy as well. Which might easily have stymied Illingworth's chances if Willard was prepared to use it against him.'

'Well, you'd think twice about appointing a man like that, wouldn't you?' Kite said. 'A man who can't keep his own son out of trouble isn't going to be the best bet for looking after other folks', is he?'

'Maybe he would be, just because of that. Maybe better, having learned the hard way. But what a price to pay! Poor devil,' Mayo said, surprised to find himself in sympathy with Illingworth, 'with a wife like that, he had problems.'

WDC Jenny Platt was on her way out of the station and did a double take when she saw Mayo and Kite approaching the door from the car park. 'Too late, too late!' she muttered. 'And nearly made it this time.'

'Hi, Jenny,' Kite said. 'Managed to get over to the hospital and see Mrs Crawshaw, did you?'

Jenny swore, not very politely, to herself. She was already late for her date with a self-aware Scotsman called Duncan who wasn't the sort to wait around for police women who put their jobs before an evening out with him. 'Yes, Sarge.

I've left a report on your desk, sir,' she said to Mayo who had just followed Kite in.

'Maybe you'd better come upstairs then till I've read it.'

'I've typed it out, sir.'

'All the same.'

Jenny rolled her eyes at the desk sergeant and followed in their wake.

'Sit down, Jenny,' Mayo said when they got upstairs, and quickly scanned her report, while Jenny hoped there were fewer spelling mistakes than last time. Mayo reckoned he couldn't abide spelling mistakes, so there was competition in the department to spot his own errors—which had been known to happen.

'How was the old lady?' Kite asked, as Mayo read.

Jenny smiled. 'Feeling much better and bad-tempered with it. She's only in for observation and they've put her in the geriatric ward, which she doesn't like, being only seventy-three. But she's bright enough. She remembered what she overheard quite clearly.'

'She seems to think it was a quarrel,' Mayo remarked, throwing her report down on the desk and sitting back.

'She's certain it was, sir. She'd gone upstairs to have a bit of a lie-down because she was just beginning to feel poorly. She had the window open and the voices came up from Willard's garden—his and another man's. She couldn't recognize that one, couldn't make out what they were quarrelling about, but she heard the name Sara mentioned.' Jenny didn't pronounce the name to rhyme with 'fairer'.

'And she's sure of the time? Just after twelve?' Jenny said certainly, Mrs Crawshaw had been absolutely sure. 'All right then, Jenny, you can leave it with me. Thanks very much.'

'Sir.' Jenny slid out smartly, before anyone else could find her anything to do, though she'd long since given up hope of darling Duncan still being there.

'Just after twelve?' Mayo said, as the door closed behind

her. 'If she's sure of that, Illingworth's covered, for that time at least. He was in the register office getting married then.'

The moment Mayo pushed open the door of his flat he knew Julie was home again by the delicious smell of cooking wafting towards him. From the kitchen a cheerful voice called, 'I'm home, Dad!' His heart plummeted.

He was feeling more than a little frayed around the edges. He'd have liked a quiet evening, talking the case over with Alex perhaps, valuing her no-nonsense approach, her professional opinion. The next-best thing would have been a simple meal, a quiet drink, some music, tinkering with his clocks. The last thing he wanted was a re-hash of Julie's problems. She threw down her wooden spoon as he came into the kitchen and met him with a great hug, and immediately in a rush of love he forgave her.

'Gran thrown you out?' he teased. 'I thought you were going to stay with her for another two weeks.'

'Let me finish the cooking and then we can talk. I rang to ask Alex to join us but she's just come off duty and she's whacked. That's how I knew you were on the way, she said she'd spoken to you.'

He thought this might be Alex being tactful. Julie, he imagined, knew by now how things stood between them, since she had stopped asking him why they didn't get married. There was a strong bond between the two women, a deep, shared affection, Alex in fact having been Julie's friend before his. Years before, his wife Lynne and Alex had been at school together, and Alex had helped Julie through the crisis of her mother's death better than he'd been able to do.

'Have I time for a quick shower?' he asked.

'Fifteen minutes?'

'Less.' On his way to the door, he stopped. 'What was that noise?'

'What noise? I didn't hear anything,' Julie said, bending over the cooker to taste her recipe.

She was cooking halibut—*au poivre*. One of his favourite dishes, spicy with peppercorns, rich with brandy, port and a little cream. He was evidently being got round. But he was glad to see that her scruples against eating her fellow-creatures didn't extend to fish. He listened. 'There it is again, a sort of screech. I'd better see what it is,' he said, thinking of Miss Vickers's Moses and imagining dire possibilities.

'No, I'll go,' Julie said hastily. 'You go and shower.'

She's up to something, he thought, and stayed where he was, waiting. When she came back into the kitchen, she was almost obscured by a huge birdcage. In the cage was a parrot.

'What's all this?'

'He's called Bert, short for Flaubert . . . Flaubert's Parrot, association of ideas, get it? Oh well, never mind. Isn't he beautiful?' The bird was deep crimson with black markings on his wings, blue wing-tips and tail. Handsome, as parrots went, certainly. He had a fierce beak and a beady black eye that reminded Mayo of Macey. 'He's a parakeet, not a parrot, and he doesn't take any looking after. He's very good.'

'But not quiet,' Mayo said, when he could speak above Bert's shrill cacophony.

'That's because he's in strange surroundings. He'll soon get used to them.'

'Oh no he won't,' Mayo said. 'Not these surroundings, anyway. What am I going to do with a flaming parrot?'

'He'll be company for you. Oh Dad, don't be a spoilsport! John brought him for me—' John, he thought; well, it was a reassuringly ordinary name—'and when we leave he'll be homeless and won't have anywhere to go.' Her eyes were huge. She used to look like that when she was a kid, just before she cried. 'Dad? Please?'

A bloody parrot, he thought, as he shaved and showered. That's all I need.

Later, after they'd eaten, he learned why he'd been selected as the recipient of this great favour, though by then it came as no surprise. She had come home only long enough to pack a toothbrush. She was leaving before six the next morning, next stop Dijon, and promised to keep in regular contact. He wasn't to be worried about her—Gran wasn't, she thought it would give Julie a chance to get her act together. Had given the enterprise her blessing, especially after meeting John and his girlfriend.

His girlfriend?

'You weren't listening when I told you, were you? She's French, her name's Marie-Solange, you can't possibly have forgotten.'

'Oh, *that* Marie-Solange,' he said.

No reason, really, why he should feel so much better. But he did, and said goodbye to her the next morning with a cheerful face and what he hoped was a good grace.

While Mayo was digesting his dinner and a *fait accompli* he could do nothing about, and being given instructions on how to feed his new flatmate, Sebastian Oliver was walking quickly along the high path towards the castle ruins. His light, springy steps made no sound. He was wearing black trainers, his dark roll-neck sweater and navy-blue jeans, and he kept his hands shoved into the pockets. Only his face showed white and set where the light caught it.

Reaching the castle ruins, he stood by the safety railings on the path, under the shade of the horse chestnut trees with their white candles gleaming in the darkness, facing the shadowed sweep of the valley. It was the dark of the moon and windy and the night was full of echoes; small things stirred in the grass-grown moat. He had never before felt the ruins to be sinister, but as he looked and saw them black against the dark sky, he felt a sense of the inimical, a tremble akin to that his Welsh ancestors must have felt in the minutes before the raids over the border to storm just such a fortress as this.

He was keyed-up, aware that his life had reached some kind of crisis. If things went the way he intended tonight, he would cut out, make a clean break with the past, perhaps never come to Wyvering again. What was it about the place that induced this uneasiness with himself, the feeling that there was something lacking in his successful lifestyle? Perhaps old Willers had been right and pursuit of the purely materialistic was not and never could be enough. Thinking of the old man, however, remembering him as he'd last seen him, was hardly to be borne.

Since Willard's death Sebastian's conscience, never before a thing to trouble him much, wouldn't now leave him alone. The chance for revenge—a chance he'd waited for —had come, his quick mind had put two and two together and he had seen the advantage for himself and had acted without stopping to think it through. Too late, he deeply regretted it. Revenge was sweet, but remorse was bitter medicine that he was afraid he might be swallowing for the rest of his life.

He heard a footfall and as he turned towards it a figure materialized out of the darkness, approaching him. 'You took your time,' he said as he stepped out of the shadows.

CHAPTER 16

Having despatched Kite to see what he could make of Danny's girlfriend Tracey, Mayo went along first thing the next morning to see the man handling the bomb case at the Fricker Institute, Detective Chief Inspector Uttley, who worked from Hurstfield.

Hurstfield's police station was a replica of the Divisional Headquarters at Lavenstock, standard county constabulary architecture, a collection of concrete and brick units constructed on the Lego principle, but not half as cheerful, especially on a depressing wet morning. Rain was slashing down as he parked his car and ran, head ducked against the wind, for the station entrance.

'What have you got for us, Gil?' Uttley was ready for him, a large placid-looking man with a big hard stomach tightly straining against his trousers. 'Have some tea, help yourself to sugar. Don't take it? Wish I didn't.' He drank his own tea from a pint pot with 'Grandad' written on it above a picture of a benevolent old codger in a rocking-chair with a pipe. He had a proven reputation for being sharp, shrewd and ruthless.

'I was thinking it might be the other way round,' Mayo said, 'but help might be mutual. I've an idea your bomb at the Fricker Institute and this death at Castle Wyvering just may be connected.'

Uttley's little blue eyes flickered but otherwise he showed no surprise. 'I suppose you know that's where the director of the Fricker lives?'

'The fact that Thorne lives there may simply be a coincidence. I don't know yet. I'm still feeling my way.'

'Hm.' Uttley clasped his hands across the mound of his stomach, his chins settling one on the other. 'You'd better tell me your side of it first—then I can tell you what I've got that may be relevant.'

He listened without comment to the facts of the Wyvering murder, staring into space. The silence continued when Mayo had finished what he had to say. Then Uttley blinked, refilled his visitor's teacup and focused his attention again. 'Remember that theft from the furriers in Hurstfield a couple of months ago?'

Mayo cast his mind about, remembering it without being able to recall specific details.

'All right, no reason why you should, I suppose. Not on your patch, and it wasn't a big job. But you might remember the nicked furs being subsequently set fire to on the lawn in front of the golf club when there was a dinner-dance being held there.'

Mayo did remember that.

'It was a big do,' Uttley went on, 'car park full of Jags and BMWs, a Merc or two and the odd Roller, and I suppose it was predictable a lot of the women present would own furs and be wearing 'em. At any rate, that seems to have been the supposition. We'd no leads on who the fire raisers were—scarpered before the fire was discovered. They'd made their protest and it got them a paragraph in the local rag, which was presumably what they wanted, though at that point no special group claimed responsibility. But then we got lucky and had a tip-off and subsequently we've been keeping an eye on two women here in Hurstfield: Sylvia Patman and Theresa Quinn. Patman used to work at the Fricker Institute as a typist until about a year ago and Quinn has two brothers in the IRA. There's reason to believe both women are heavily involved in an animal liberation group which may have been at the bottom of the fur job—and which, incidentally, has now got itself a name. Calls itself the Sorority Against Research on Animals, if you please.'

There was silence. 'Bloody silly name,' Uttley added.

'S-A-R-A,' Mayo repeated, enunciating the letters separately. SARA, as Willard had written it. He wanted to kick himself, hard. Not a girl's name, not even the name of Illingworth's wife, but an acronym made from the initials of an organization.

'It rings a bell?'

'It rings several.' He thought further. 'Christ, Fred, IRA connections?'

Uttley thought not. 'Apart from a bit of know-how from Quinn's brothers and a streak of inherited violence, I should doubt it. One of these tinpot little outfits that keep mushrooming everywhere. It was a homemade bomb at the Fricker—capable of doing a fair bit of damage, mind—the poor sod who copped it was probably killed accidentally, if that's any consolation to his widow. Between the fur job and the bomb, the members seem to have confined themselves to protests at hunt meetings, letters to the papers and MPs and so on, none of it actually concerning animal research, I might add, but I suppose it's all one to them. After the bomb there was complete silence, which seems to support the theory that they'd gone a bit further than they intended. Until last week, when they claimed responsibility through a telephone call to the editor of the local paper. He's a rare bird—a journalist with a sense of responsibility —and realizing this was a lot more serious than burning a few furs, he contacted us before doing anything about it. He agreed with us to hold back publishing their claim, since that's all they want, publicity.' He added sourly, 'But they'll go to someone else eventually who won't be so high-minded, local radio or TV probably.'

Mayo was still thinking about those initials. 'Sorority? Does that mean they're all women?'

'Sorority, sisterhood, I wouldn't put anything past women these days,' Uttley said, with a regretful glance back at the days when women knew their place. 'But yes, I think so, originally, though they seem to have enlisted the help of a few men recently. Probably need their help if their activities are becoming more militant. Anyway, since the Fricker incident, we've kept as much of an eye on Patman and Quinn as we can spare the manpower for. There was some sort of meeting on Saturday evening at the terraced house here in Hurstfield where they live.'

'Last Saturday?'

'Right, the nineteenth. And this is what might interest you—a couple who were followed back to their car when they left. It was an MG coupé and it was subsequently traced to a Phyllida Thorne. Don't have to spell out who she is, do I?'

'Good God.'

But the shock was merely an initial one. It needed no effort of the imagination, as far as Mayo was concerned, to see Phyllida Thorne as a member of such a group and to be convinced that if she were she would be at its militant centre. He didn't share Uttley's view that men had been needed in SARA to run the group's militant activities. In his opinion, she for one would be more than capable of orchestrating the violence and any men who joined would be subject to her will.

'You don't think she could've been organizing a cell in Hurstfield of some bigger organization? It would account for her being involved here, when she lives and works in London.'

'Distinct possibility, yes. One we're working on. It's a name we've heard before, by the way,' Uttley said.

'What, SARA?'

'No, Phyllida Thorne. About seven or eight years ago she was one of a gang of sixth-formers who made a protest sit-in outside the gates of the Fricker—causing us the usual amount of bother, wasting God knows how much taxpayers' money. Set fire to an effigy and nearly had the gatehouse on fire into the bargain.' Uttley paused. 'An effigy of the Director. Her own father,' he added, in case Mayo hadn't taken his point.

Mayo understood now what the Thornes had been so evasive about. Why Denzil Thorne had been so uneasy in the garden on Sunday. Did they suspect their daughter's involvement with SARA? And if so, how would they feel about that? How would he feel himself if Julie had transferred her half-baked ideas into something like this? The kind of hopeless despair, he imagined, that all parents must feel when their offspring are intent on pursuing a life-denying, wrong-headed course that can lead only to self-destruction. How far had Phyllida Thorne's involvement with SARA taken her? To the point where her own father had almost been destroyed by her fanatical ideals? As far as Cecil Willard's melancholy end?

'Does the name Sebastian Oliver mean anything to you?' Uttley asked.

'Yes, I know him. I take it he was the one who visited the house with her?'

'That's right. Parson's son, I hear. You wouldn't credit it, would you? Every advantage and they screw up their chances, getting involved in tacky little schemes like this. They were followed after they left the house. Went straight out to that new place in King's Grafton, what's it called, the River House? Had dinner there and then drove back to Wyvering.'

'That's what they told me—only they omitted to say where they'd been first. D'you know who else was at this meeting?'

Uttley drew a list of names from his desk drawer and pushed it across, followed by a file. Mayo ran his eye down the list, then flicked through the photographs in the file— crowd snapshots and individual ones bearing the name of the subject beneath, with biographical details. Most of those in the crowd snaps had not been identified. One face he wouldn't have been surprised to see was not there— that of the Rector's wife—but there was another which did surprise him.

'Sebastian Oliver and his girlfriend aren't the only ones who've been lying to me,' he remarked.

'Someone else in your case?'

Mayo stabbed his finger at a snapshot of a woman caught in a milling crowd, struggling to hold up a banner. If, when trying to envisage something which would have animated her, he had tried hatred, he would have succeeded. The face that looked straight into the camera was alight with fanaticism.

'This one,' he said. 'Her name's Ruth Lampeter.'

Things had suddenly begun to look different. SARA was explained, and offered some positive connection with Willard's murder. In some way Willard must have learned of the organization and it was this which had posed his moral dilemma—whether to inform the authorities and implicate his young friend Sebastian Oliver, or to remain silent, with further risk to human life. It could not, Mayo thought, have been a dilemma unresolved for long, as far as someone like Willard was concerned. Only he had not been given time to resolve anything.

The case building against Illingworth was collapsing. It was nothing, after all, to do with what had happened to him at Cambridge. This new information put a different complexion on many things which Mayo needed to talk over with Kite. He turned his car towards Wyvering and then remembered that by now Kite should be back in Lavenstock, and with luck, interviewing Danny Lampeter.

Kite was having a successful morning.

Making what was beginning to feel like a habit he ought to kick, he had driven over to Wyvering to interview Macey Smith, and struck pay dirt. After the first token skirmishes, she had admitted to buying some Victorian jewellery during the previous week from a young man answering to the description of Danny Lampeter. Produced them, what was more, in an attempt to show how cooperative she was. Too cooperative, said the nasty suspicious copper in Kite, making an opportunity to have a word with Farrar, whom he could trust to beaver around and find out whatever was to be found that was behind Macey and her son Tigger setting up shop in sleepy Wyvering.

Back to Lavenstock and the run-down part of the town where Sam Biggs's granddaughter had taken up residence. Over a greengrocer's shop, with a flight of stairs leading from a side entrance where the overflow from the shop was piled up, and crates of tomatoes and oranges, onions in nets, sacks of potatoes stood about waiting to be carried in. Kite leaned on the bell and held his nose at the smell of rotting vegetation issuing from two plastic dustbins overflowing with several days' rejects.

It was mid-morning when they got there and he was

prepared for trouble. He had brought Deeley with him, good-natured but solid beef and no messing around when it came to ratbags like Lampeter. Mindful of Deeley's biggest fault, that he was likely to hit out first and think later, Kite said, 'Go easy on him, Pete. We want to take him *virgo intacta*, if you'll excuse the phrase.'

Deeley's round, ingenuous face, red as a farmer's boy's, took on an injured expression. 'As if I would.'

A thick miasma of hamburger and cigarette smoke hit them in the face when at last the door was opened by a big, well-developed girl of about eighteen, adorned with a shaven haircut and a mini skirt so short and tight it had difficulty in covering her bottom. She had a doughy face which she'd been in the middle of making up. The one heavily-shaded eyelid gave her the appearance of having been the loser in a punch-up but Kite thought even Deeley might run if confronted by this Amazon in an alley on a dark night.

He showed his warrant card and told her they wanted to speak to Danny Lampeter. She looked at it without much interest but before she could deny he was there, a voice came from inside the room. 'Who is it, Trace?'

'Police,' Kite said, and the girl shrugged and stood aside to let them in. A stocky, broad-chested, long-haired individual in his early twenties, naked to the waist, looked up from a newspaper propped against a milk bottle on the table.

'What you been up to then, Danny?' Tracey said from behind them.

The rooom was disgusting. A rumpled bed in the corner, a sink under the window piled with unwashed dishes, on the table a meal of sorts which he'd been in the process of eating—breakfast or maybe lunch, whatever cornflakes followed by hamburgers and tinned spaghetti hoops might be designated.

Some remnants of pride prompted Tracey to straighten the duvet on the bed and begin clearing the dishes from the table. 'Never mind that,' Kite told her. 'Sit down while we ask your boyfriend here some questions.'

'He's not my boyfriend—' she began scornfully.

'Shut up, Trace.'

'Danny Lampeter, isn't it?' Kite asked. 'We're here to make inquiries about some goods stolen from the home of the Reverend Mr Willard of Castle Wyvering.'

'Well, you can bloody well go away again. Why should you think I know anything about that?' Lampeter demanded, scraping his chair back and standing up in a threatening manner, muscular brown arms akimbo, the blue tattoos livid, his square jaw thrust forward.

'Watch it, Danny!' Tracey warned.

'Shut up, I said, Trace.' Tracey shrugged, picked up her eyeliner and hand mirror and opted out of the proceedings. Lampeter, however, looking at Deeley, fourteen stones of him leaning on the door, arms folded, sat down again, raking his hands through his unconfined and flowing locks.

'I think you know quite a bit about it. That and one or two more things,' said Kite.

'Dunno what you're on about.'

'Come off it, Lampeter. You're coming with us, whatever, so please yourself whether you spill now and finish your dinner while you talk, or talk later.'

'Oh, ta very much. Somehow I've lost my appetite.'

'Please yourself. Talk here, or at the station.'

'What about?'

Kite told him, succinctly. One, that he was in dead bother for nicking the things from the Willard house. Two, that he'd better have some alibi for the badger shooting. Three, he'd better have an even tighter one for the time of Willard's murder.

To the first, Lampeter made more pretence of not knowing what Kite was talking about. To the second he protested, 'That's a load of old cobblers!' and would have gone on, had he not been silenced by Kite. When the third charge was made, his jaw dropped. 'God Almighty!'

'The Almighty's not going to help you much, Lampeter. And don't tell me you haven't heard about the murder?'

' 'Course I have. I can read, can't I? But what's it to me? I'd nothing to do with it.'

'You high-tailed it from Wyvering as though your backside was afire last Saturday. Just for the fun of it, huh?'

'No law against it, that I've heard. If you must know, I'd had a row with my sis. I'd had it up to here with her, interfering old bitch.'

'That's no way to talk about your sister.' Kite thought of Ruth Lampeter, unlovely, unattractive, lonely, stoutly defending this cretin. 'After all she's done for you. What was the row about?'

'Nothing. Nothing to do with you lot, anyway.'

'Something to do with Willard's murder, was it?'

'No!' Lampeter shouted. Sweat stood on his forehead. 'I swear I don't know a thing about the Rev being murdered, straight up.'

'All right, I may as well tell you that the person you sold the brooch and the other things to last week has identified you, and I'm arresting you on suspicion of theft,' Kite said, and proceeded with the caution. 'Get your hair ribbon on, ducky, and come down to the station.'

Danny suddenly caved in. 'Oh, all right, it's a fair cop. I nicked the brooch and the jet bracelet and things. But I didn't do for the old man.'

'Tape-recorded interview between Daniel William Lampeter and Detective-Sergeant Martin Kite, May 23rd, 1991 at 11.50 hrs. Also present, Detective Chief Inspector Gil Mayo and Detective-Constable Peter Deeley.'

Kite settled himself at the table in the interview room opposite Lampeter. After half an hour, they had a signed confession of guilt about the thefts but nothing more. He was, however, weakening. 'If I tell you something else I know, will you put it down to be taken into consideration?'

'What d'you think we are? The flaming *Exchange and*

Mart? You're in no position to make bargains, Lampeter.'

'Then get knotted.'

There was silence.

'This row you had with your sister. It was about the badgers, wasn't it?' Mayo asked, speaking for the first time.

Lampeter swung his gaze to face the Chief Inspector. 'Might've been.' He shrugged indifferently but his eyes were wary. 'How come you know about that?'

An educated guess, but he wasn't about to tell Lampeter that. 'Never you mind. Now come on, lad, it's in your own interests to tell us what you know. There's been a murder committed and if you don't clear yourself you're in for the chop.'

'It was that Mike Tully,' Lampeter said suddenly, after thinking for some minutes and evidently deciding he'd no option but to come clean. 'Met him and his mate in the Butcher's Arms one night when I'd sunk a few whiskies. He had this Lakeland terrier and he was going on about what a good rabbiter it was . . . We got talking and I just happened to mention I knew where there was some badgers. I didn't know they'd go out and kill the bloody things!'

'What did you imagine they were going to do?' Kite asked. 'Take wildlife photos?'

'I don't see what all the fuss is about, anyway. Two or three badgers. Only a bit of sport, after all.'

Mayo had never seen a badger, except on TV, and he doubted whether either of his colleagues had, either, but this mindless slaughter of dumb creatures for amusement made him want to throw up. Deeley looked as sick as he himself felt. Kite said, 'You're a shit, Lampeter.'

'Here, you lot, I wasn't there, don't start blaming me!'

'Beats me,' Kite said, 'why they stopped at that. Why they didn't stand and watch the dog tear the badgers to pieces. That's the usual form, isn't it?'

'You ever seen what claws they've got, them badgers?' Lampeter demanded. 'You should—Tully says one of 'em

nearly gouged his dog's eye out. Valuable dog like that, he
didn't want it blinded, did he? So they just shot 'em and
left 'em.'

'I don't want to *hear* any more,' Kite said. 'You disgust
me.'

'How did your sister come to know of this?' Mayo asked.

'Because everybody in bloody Wyvering thought it was
me, didn't they? As per usual. And I was getting sick of it.
That sister of mine's not right in the head when it comes
to animals. Reckon she likes 'em a damn sight better than
people,' he added with a perception Mayo wouldn't have
given him credit for. 'You'd think she'd be satisfied with
all them demos, and letters she writes to the papers but no,
she has to be one of the boss women of this society, this
what they call SARA. She'd been looking at me sideways
all week and in the end she asked me straight out, had I
done it. I told her of course I bloody hadn't but when I
told her who had she went off her trolley, just the same.
Seemed to think it was my fault and went on something
rotten about me betraying everything she'd tried to teach
me and all that crap. In the end I couldn't stand it no more
and I pushed off.'

'Selling the things you'd nicked from Willard on the
way?'

'I was a bit short,' Lampeter complained. 'I haven't been
able to get a job since I came out the army.'

'Not strained yourself overmuch trying, I'll bet,' Kite
said.

'SARA,' he repeated later, disposing of a couple of jam
doughnuts with his coffee when Mayo called him in to tell
him what he'd learned from Uttley. 'Obvious, isn't it, when
you know?'

'SARA with a question-mark after it, remember. And in
close conjunction with Sebastian Oliver's visit. Could be
that Willard had learned of Oliver's involvement and was
threatening to tell what he knew?'

'Would he do that? Seeing he thought such a lot of him?'

'If his high moral principles prevented him agreeing to his daughter marrying a divorced man, he'd hardly be likely to stick at shopping Sebastian Oliver, however much he thought of him. It must've been causing him a bit of heart-searching, though.'

'And would it put the wind up Oliver enough to kill Willard for it?'

'It might. Oh yes, it might, if he were involved in that bomb plot.'

'He had an alibi for the time of Willard's death. Which depends of course on Phyllida Thorne. And since she's up to her neck in SARA she'd be only too pleased to give it.'

'It looks,' Mayo said, 'like another ride out to Wyvering. Sebastian Oliver—plus his girlfriend. Not to mention another talk with Danny boy's sister while we're out there.'

Events, however, were to overtake them. It was to be some time before either of them were able to speak to Ruth Lampeter.

CHAPTER 17

Catherine Oliver was in the Rectory kitchen, making pastry. She was well aware of her limitations as a cook and had been pleased if alarmed when Lionel, the previous Christmas, had bought her a food processor—thinking, no doubt, of delicious cakes and even homemade bread. You couldn't go wrong, making pastry in one of those things, everyone said, but Catherine had found she could. Reaching for the off switch now after the required second or two, as the instruction book advised, she decided it couldn't possibly have taken such a short time to bind the mixture together. Perhaps she'd better give it another few minutes, just to be sure. But when she took the dough out and began to roll it, it felt as solid and looked as grey as her pastry always did.

It was no good, she wasn't in the mood for cooking. She couldn't concentrate on anything. What on earth was Sebastian thinking about, taking himself off like that, without a word to anyone since supper last night? And it was now half past three! It wasn't like him. Why?

A few minutes later, she knew, unbelievably, why.

When Kite drew up the car once more in Parson's Place, they found Wainwright there before them, parked outside the Rectory. The constable, looking as though life would have taken a simpler turn had he suddenly been put in charge of the Vice Squad or maybe the whole of the Metropolitan Police Force rather than the lawless parish of Castle Wyvering, took all of three minutes to relate what had happened.

'A goner?' ased Mayo.

'No, sir, not quite, but very bad, according to the doctor. He'd been hit on the temple, see, and must've been laying there all night. They've taken him into the Lavenstock General but they don't give much for his chances.'

'Who found him?'

'Mrs Wentworth that lives up on Main Street, just before she went to pick the kiddies up from school. Apparently the little 'un, young Damian, had been up there yesterday with his dad and lost one of the bits off his remote-controlled car. He was that upset she promised to go and look for it while he was at school. She wouldn't have seen the body if she hadn't been searching around. He'd been thrown into what used to be the moat, where the long grass grows. Rector and Mrs Oliver are both at the hospital.'

And a PC at Sebastian's bedside in case he came round, though according to the medics he wouldn't remember anything immediately previous to the attack if he did.

All the routine steps would have to be repeated, house-to-

house inquiries, taking statements, the whole lengthy rig-
marole. The difference being there was no corpse, this time.
Just a flattened area of long wet grass and weeds where
Sebastian Oliver had lain. Apparently no attempt had been
made to cover him. He had simply been thrown into the
moat from the path and left for dead. The moat was deep,
choked with grass, nettles and giant hogweed, and at that
point shaded by a willow which grew at the side of the path
and overhung the moat, so he'd been effectively hidden
from any casual passer-by.

'Could've lain there for days without being seen, I
reckon,' Dexter, the SOCO Sergeant, informed Mayo,
'except this woman was looking more closely than most.
Lucky he's still in the land of the living.'

But only just. Not giving anything away at the hospital,
they reported his condition as 'unchanged'.

A methodical search of the surrounding area was already
taking place when Mayo arrived. The entrance to the castle
grounds had been put out of limits to anyone except the
police personnel; the few square yards around where the
body had lain and a section of the path had been taped off.
'This seems to be where he was attacked, sir.' Dexter waved
to a point on the path. 'We've found traces of blood and
there's the heel marks showing where he was dragged before
being lifted and thrown down into the moat.'

He had been hit on the head with something hard, heavy
and blunt. Ison, they were informed, had met the ambulance at the hospital, so he would have seen the wound
before it was treated and might, with luck, have some idea
as to what constituted the said instrument of attack.

Later, when Mayo telephoned him from Wainwright's
office, a room built on to the side of his police house, Ison
said he reckoned it must have been something with a
rounded end, a cosh or a sand-filled sock, something like
that. Even one of your police truncheons, he added, risking
a joke. 'Fracture of the left temporal bone, which means

the killer was right-handed. He'll have had a fair amount of blood on his clothes.'

'Apparently Oliver's mother last saw him just after supper last night, Henry, but she heard him go out about eleven.˜Can we assume that's about when he was attacked?'

'If he was, why he didn't get pneumonia on top of everything's a mystery, they tell me that moat's only dry in a manner of speaking. Always damp in the bottom, like a ditch. But yes, I suppose it could've happened about then. Must have a cast-iron constitution as well as a thick skull. It was a blow hefty enough to kill, whether that was intended or not. Not much more I can tell you at the moment, but get in touch if there's anything else you want to know.'

'A truncheon,' Kite echoed, when Mayo repeated the gist of Ison's words, doodling a row of them.

'Wainwright says Mrs Oliver last saw her son just after supper . . . but she's admitted she heard him go out about eleven. Rather reluctantly admitted it by all accounts. Seems she thought he had some clandestine assignment with Phyllida Thorne—which reminds me, we haven't seen her yet. You carry on, I'll go and talk to her myself.' He stood staring down at Kite's doodles. 'While I'm gone, try asking the doc whether a baseball bat would do,' he suggested.

He was back in Wainwright's office within twenty minutes. Phyllida Thorne, he said, had hopped it. Leaving a note saying she'd be back in a couple of days. Taking her little MG and as far as her distracted mother could ascertain, only an overnight bag.

Could she be scared that she was going to be attacked, too? suggested Kite, half way through a mug of Mrs Wainwright's tea and a piled plate of well-filled ham sandwiches made with thick slices from a crusty loaf. If Sebastian had been attacked for what he knew, then it was more than likely she knew it, too.

There was a thought to play with. Phyllida Thorne,

scared! Or even likely, as Kite went on to suggest, to be the one who'd bopped Sebastian on the head? Either possibility seemed to Mayo less probable than the scenario as he saw it.

'It's possible,' he said, taking one of the sandwiches Kite pushed across the desk, reaching for the generous-sized teapot to pour tea the colour of port wine into a second mug. 'But I don't think so. Far more likely little Miss Phyllida's flitted off to warn her fellow activists in London that we may be on to SARA. We need to find her, anyway. You've got her London address and the publisher where she works?'

'No problem. By the way, Ison says a baseball bat could be just the thing, which makes life easier. Can't be many places in Wyvering to look. I've sent some men down to Uplands House to have a shufty at their sports equipment. And just when we thought we were barking up the wrong tree with Illingworth!'

'I want to go through all the case notes again, Martin,' Mayo said, standing in front of the window, looking out on to the village street. 'Everyone we've spoken to, and all the info we have on every single one of them, as far back as we can go.'

Thursday afternoon. The tiny church at Stapley was, if not packed, fairly full with friends and one or two relatives, a representative sprinkling of clergy and a selection of staff and some older boys from Uplands House School. Scarcely a person there who wasn't thinking of Sebastian Oliver, lying at death's door. One or two were also thinking of Cecil Willard, already passed through that same door, and whose funeral service they were here to attend.

'My song is love unknown/My Saviour's love for me/Love to the loveless shown/That they might lovelier be . . .'

The organ was slightly out of tune and wheezed a little, but the St Kenelm's choirboys, brought down for the occasion, sang sweet and true. Laura had arranged to have the funeral over and done with as soon as was compatible with seemliness, without appearing to show undue haste, but she couldn't have borne to have held the service at Wyvering, in the same church where her father had worshipped but had then so horribly died. In any case, he had to be committed to the ground here, the churchyard at Wyvering having long since been filled and recently grassed over.

'*And who am I/That for my sake/My Lord should take frail flesh and die?*'

The choice of hymn must have been Laura's, Mayo decided. He had come to know enough of Willard to believe that he would have turned in his coffin at hearing such an unconventional hymn at his own funeral service. Sitting beside Kite, both of them spruce in white shirts and dark suits, he wondered how the convention that the police should attend the funeral of the murder victim had arisen. Was it expected that the murderer, overwhelmed by conscience at the solemnity of the occasion, would cast himself down before their feet and confess? Give himself away by some other means? It was a disturbing and macabre notion to think that the murderer was here, yet a person who had committed the ultimate outrage, the extermination of another human being, must have passed so far beyond the laws of civilization that he would surely not hesitate to draw the line at attending the last rites of his victim.

For it had to be someone within Willard's own circle who had killed him, and had attempted to kill a second time. Had bodged it and must now be sweating on the top line, praying not for Sebastian's recovery but that he wouldn't ever come round and live to give away the name of his attacker.

He'd made a mistake in trying it on a second time. Mayo thought about the forensic evidence which had just come in regarding Willard's murder: minute traces of the red clay found on the river bank had been picked up near the altar steps, so maybe the assumption that the killer had come in that way was correct. On the other hand, it might be that someone else had gone into the church quite innocently after walking there. The fibres on the altar cushion, however, were a different matter. Some from Willard's tweed jacket, and also a few minute threads of polyester jersey, caught up on the metallic gold cord edging the cushion.

Most of those he'd spoken to in the course of the inquiry were here, except for Sebastian—and Phyllida Thorne, of whom there had been no trace as yet. The Lampeters, too, Danny in custody and Ruth who was being interviewed, possibly at this precise moment, by Fred Uttley. Ruth Lampeter, who was close-mouthed as they come, and an animal rights fanatic into the bargain, a species always so utterly convinced they were right—and in many ways they were —only there was never any room for compromise, nobody else's opinion counted and human life was less precious than that of any animal, even in the interests of *bona fide* medical research; Ruth Lampeter who had stated she wouldn't even keep a pet cat because she thought that deprived it of its natural dignity and freedom. But Uttley was determined he was going to get the bastards who'd blown up the security guard at the Fricker Institute and Mayo decided he'd put his money on Fred, despite the odds.

Jon Reece read the lesson. His voice was strong and clear and the sun streaming through the stained glass haloed his head like that of some stained glass angel . . . No, the analogy was wrong, Gina Holden thought, watching and admiring his striking good looks. More like some pagan god, Apollo surely, god of the sun, poetry and music: golden son of Zeus, who wielded thunderbolts and ruled the heavens.

Jon closed the Bible, paused gravely, stepped down from the lectern and walked back to his seat. Passing the pew where the Head and his wife sat, he smiled at Gina. Dear Gina, how sweet she was. He would miss her when she had gone to Antibes. For a while. Like all the other women friends he'd had, he would soon forget her. As he settled in his seat he felt that he had carried the reading off fairly well. Not a tremor in his voice, despite the emotion he felt. His association with the old man had gone back a long way, and he was upset that it had had to end the terrible way it had. Especially since it had put his own future in jeopardy. But he wasn't at this juncture going to allow thoughts of failure to enter his head. He had planned and schemed for this time. It was unbearable even to entertain thoughts of the prize being snatched from him. He looked at the back of the heads in front, Gina's unfamiliar in her black hat. Richard's pate more balding than ever from here and thought positively: Soon, soon everything will be mine.

The Headmaster was as unaware of Jonathan's gaze on him as he was of the service going on around him. He felt elevated, on another plane, uplifted and at peace because of the decision he had finally come to in the middle of a sleepless night, while Gina slept beside him. He hadn't told her yet, though he was convinced it was the right thing to do for himself, for her, for everyone concerned, the way out of an impasse, no matter what the consequences. He would tell her tonight. As if she read his thoughts she turned her head towards him. Briefly, he touched her hand and then, serenely sure that their relationship was secure enough to weather the shock, that she would support him whatever came about, Richard Holden brought his attention back to the present.

His admiration for Lionel, normally tempered with a slight amused scepticism, was on this occasion unbounded. Sebastian still lay in a coma in the hospital. Catherine would not leave his bedside, but Lionel had insisted that it was his duty, the least he could do, to perform the last rites for Cecil Willard. His rich, musical voice resonated around the tiny church. The last 'Lord have mercy upon us' filled it to the echoes. As he turned to face the congregation for the benediction and raised his hand, the light fell on his face, drawn and pale after the sleepless vigil of the previous night, ascetic as that of some medieval saint. As usual, he took the stage. The congregation shuffled to its knees.

David Illingworth did not kneel but leaned forward in the pew, in the awkward half-sitting, half-crouching posture of the unbeliever, as if not quite denying participation. He despised himself for agreeing to be here at all in the circumstances. He would not have come, had it not been for Laura. He glanced surreptitiously at his wife, kneeling beside him, deep in misery and grief, mopping up yet more tears. His wife! He had not expected, when he had come to Wyvering, battered and bruised by what had happened to him, to fall in love. If the steady, deep content he felt with Laura could be called that. He had 'fallen in love' once before and found it like seaside candyfloss: sticky and clinging, oversweet, unsatisfying and ultimately tasting of nothing.

He thought his life had ended when he left Cambridge. He had breathed the air of academia for so long he had thought he might die without it. Uplands House had been a poor second to that. He had never expected to find a new life waiting for him, heady with possibilities.

He knew now that Uplands House School would benefit with him as Head but it was more than that. He needed the position to bolster his damaged ego and to enable him to give something back for what had happened to Matthew. He needed Laura, too, for a second chance to prove he could be a proper father. And here it was, within his grasp. If, he thought, remembering the interview with Richard the previous evening, he hadn't already muffed his chances by saying too little, or too much. He knew he wasn't good at these things. Immediately, he dismissed such thoughts. What had happened previously in his life had hardened him. With his usual single-mindedness, he intended to let nothing stop him.

CHAPTER 18

It had rained again during the night and the skies were still overcast. Parson's Place had an air of desolation, with a gentle wind soughing through the dripping branches of the mournful yews and making a sad, sighing sound. The ground beneath the cherry trees was littered with a detritus of tattered pink blossom. Not yet having relinquished the key of the church, Mayo let himself in through the main door to wait.

It hadn't changed since Willard's death, except that someone had been in with a broom and a vacuum cleaner after the SOCO team had left it. The same smell of incense, flowers, polish and old stone. No trace of grey fingerprint powder, everything back in its place, dusted and polished. There was a new cushion on the altar, red velvet this time, rather than blue. The clock struck and Mayo checked it as correct by his watch with a sense of *déjà vu*.

A clock, like the elucidation of a murder, would only work if all the pieces were there, put together in the correct order, each piece interdependent upon the next one. And here now in his mind were all the constituent parts of this inquiry: the weapon—the baseball bat—had been found among the Uplands House sports equipment, phone calls had been made, he had spoken to Miriam Thorne. But most importantly, a witness had come forward, in the unlikely person of Tigger Smith. Everything was now laid out clean and shiny, oiled and ready for putting into working order. All that remained was to assemble the parts, set the balance wheel precisely against the hairspring to regulate its beat and wait for it to work.

The search for the goods Danny Lampeter had stolen from the Willards and later sold to Macey had led Kite to make further inquiries about some of the goods she had on sale, not all of which were by any means as innocuous as the ones in the window. In an effort to mitigate his punishment, Tigger had offered some unexpected information.

His statement went like this: 'I was in my mother's shop at five o'clock on the afternoon of the 19th May when I saw a woman going into the church with some flowers. I had never been inside St Kenelm's and always having had a special interest in church architecture, I entered after she'd been in some time and sat down in one of the pews. I did not make my presence known because she was busy arranging the flowers near the altar and I did not wish to disturb her. When she left I was bending down in one of the pews tying my shoelace so she did not see me. I was upset to find that she had locked the door behind her and that I was imprisoned in the church. Then I heard the door being unlocked and an elderly person in a wheelchair came in and went across the front. He did not see me because I had stepped back behind the door when I heard it being unlocked. Almost immediately a man followed him in. I got a look at his face and I saw his back view as he walked towards the front and I am sure I would recognize him if I saw him again. I do not know what happened after that because I left the church immediately.'

Mayo grinned as he read it. No prizes for guessing what Tigger had been up to: slipping in while Mrs Holden had been occupied to suss out the possibilities of the silver and anything else that looked likely.

At that moment, the church door opened and Lionel Oliver came in. Walking slowly, his shoulders bowed, his tall figure elongated in his long cassock, he went straight towards the chancel steps and knelt at the communion rail in front of the altar. Not knowing whether to make his presence known or to tiptoe out and so risk disturbing the man even further, Mayo hesitated too long and the opportunity was lost. Before he could make his mind up, the Rector rose and came back down the aisle, pausing when he reached the pew where Mayo sat, seemingly having been aware that he was there all along

'I've just come from the hospital. There's no change,' he said bleakly. 'His mother is with him.'

He himself was dreadfully changed. The smiling blandness had quite disappeared. He was pale as bleached bone and two deep lines grooved themselves between nose and chin. 'Thank you for coming. I couldn't say what I have to say over the telephone. Perhaps we should go across to the Rectory. We shall be more comfortable there.'

In his study, the Rector switched on an electric fire that wasn't needed and stood in front of it for a while, rubbing his hands as if unable to get warm. Then he sat at his desk and turned his chair round to face Mayo but seemed quite at a loss where to begin. Mayo coughed and set the ball rolling. 'I'm afraid I shall have to ask you a few questions, sir. Perhaps we'd better start by that.'

'What? Oh, go ahead, I don't mind questions, if it'll help you find out who did this to him.'

'Have you heard of an organization named SARA?'

A moment's painful silence. Outside in Parson's Place nothing stirred except Florence, the black Persian, stalking her territory with lofty, monarchical interest. 'Unfortunately, yes, though only recently.' The Rector rubbed his hands across his eyes. 'Yes, I know of it. I learned a few days ago that my wife was, until last weekend, a member. You remember perhaps that she went to a meeting on Saturday?'

Mayo nodded.

'That was a meeting of SARA. She has some inherited money of her own and in addition she has recently written a little book which I am told is expected to bring in more.' He paused and blinked, reflecting perhaps on a phenomenon evidently astonishing to him. 'She had offered to donate to SARA whatever the book might make, plus a considerable amount more—on certain conditions.'

'Which were?'

'I don't know how much you know about this group—
though whatever it is I feel it will not be to their credit. An
ill-conceived gathering of foolish idealists who, I'm sorry to
say, have recently begun to advocate violence to achieve
their aims. Needless to say, Catherine could never have
supported this and she asked for a promise that any money
she put into the funds would not be used for these purposes.
It was made clear on Saturday, I believe, that no such
promises would be forthcoming, and she was therefore
obliged to resign, along with a few more who haven't yet
lost their sanity.'

'And did you know that your son was also connected
with SARA?'

The Rector's eyes closed for a moment. 'Sebastian's con-
cerns are a mystery to me.' He fell again into silence, then
roused himself. 'But that brings me to what I have to say.
Eight years ago, Sebastian was in the sixth form at Halsingbury—you know it?'

One of the better-known public schools, it was located
near the Welsh border and was famous for its successes in
schoolboy rugby internationals and for having numbered a
former prime minister among its pupils. And among its
teachers, a name he had yesterday connected with it. He
nodded, feeling again that sixth sense, a rising of the hairs
on his scalp, telling him that here it was, the end of the
thread which would lead him through the labyrinth and
into the daylight.

'There was—an incident—and he was asked to leave.
You may imagine that as parents we were very much upset,
and of course I demanded to know the reason why. I met
with no success, I was frustrated at every turn, even by my
son. Especially perhaps by my son. Sebastian and I, as you
may have gathered, do not communicate easily.' The line
of pain between the fine brows deepened. 'However . . .
The reason given for his being expelled was that he had
apparently knocked down one of the masters. What
nonsense!'

Mayo could understand the father's difficulty in accepting this. It wasn't easy to imagine that urbane young man rousing himself to anything so uncouth as a bout of fisticuffs. 'You say apparently. Was there some doubt?'

'Sebastian didn't trouble to deny it, but I know my son, Mr Mayo. I am not blind to his faults but he is not, and never has been, given to violence and I am not of the opinion that anyone suddenly acts out of character. I was not even told why he was supposed to have done what he had. The Headmaster, for reasons of his own, refused to try to get to the bottom of it. I was asked to remove my son from the school at the end of the summer term and when I demanded to see the master in question I was told he wasn't available—that he'd already left for an extended holiday in Greece and would not be returning to the school. Sebastian, despite everything I could do to persuade him otherwise, would say nothing. He was apparently quite happy to leave Halsingbury and subsequently, I suppose, he has done no worse for himself than if he had stayed on. There was no alternative but to consider the matter over and done with.'

At that moment, the telephone rang.

Later that afternoon the Rector accompanied Mayo and Kite as they drove to Uplands House School, Mayo showing nothing of the taut excitement he felt, like the rush of adrenalin an actor feels at the start of a play, which told him he was approaching the winding up of the case, with only a few loose ends remaining to be tied up. Kite, impassive at the wheel of the car, gave no indication either as to whether he was feeling the same, though it had been agreed that his role, in this instance, was to be a supporting one, that of silent observer, note-taker, strong-arm support if necessary.

The car drew up on the cobbles outside the old stable block and the three men alighted. A short flight of wooden stairs on the outer wall led to a door at the top, at present standing wide open.

'Come in,' Jonathan Reece invited, charming as usual, carelessly tossing back his hair when he looked up from where he sat and saw Mayo, his hand raised to knock. 'The more the merrier.'

The three men stepped into a room that looked like anything but a converted stable loft. A thick white carpet and modern furniture, a lot of expensive equipment for playing music, stacks of CD discs. In the middle of the room stood Phyllida Thorne.

She was standing directly opposite the chair Reece had just vacated, next to which was a bottle on a small table, and a glass containing a considerable measure of whisky. Confrontation was in the air.

At first sight of Mayo she assumed a defiant look but her eyes widened as she saw that he and Kite were followed by the Rector. 'Sebastian?' There was a new uncertainty in her voice.

'My dear Phyllida, they have just rung to tell me that he came round. Only for a brief moment but we pray and live in hope.'

The kindness of the Rector's tone, the joy on his face, her own relief, made her eyes fill with tears which seemed as unexpected to herself as they did to those watching her. Was it possible the tough case around the dormant flower seeds was beginning to soften? Knuckling this unbidden sign of weakness away, ashamed, she looked like a small, defiant, waif-like urchin. No make-up, her short spiky hair all anyhow, an old pair of grubby jeans and a denim jacket. 'Oh bugger Seb,' she said as more tears rolled, furiously scrubbing at her eyes with an inadequate piece of tissue pulled from her pocket. 'I'm sorry, I'm sorry, I didn't mean . . .'

'My dear child,' said the Rector.

'He thinks he's so clever . . . I suppose he thought he was pulling off another of his smart deals, but oh, he can be such a fool! Why did he have to do such a crazy thing?'

she cried, in an agony of despair and belatedly realized love. But hopefully, Mayo thought, not too belated.

'What are you talking about, Phyllida?' the Rector asked.

'Ask him!' she declared, looking at Reece. 'He knows what I mean.'

'You're upset, Philly,' Reece said. 'You don't know what you're saying. Sit down and have a drink. Let's all have a drink, why not?' With an ironic gesture of his hand, he invited everyone to sit.

Throwing him a glance of the utmost loathing, Phyllida dashed away the last of her tears and picked up her leather shoulder-bag that was lying on a table.

'Don't go, Miss Thorne,' Mayo said. 'I'd like you to be in on this.'

'I've no intention of going. I was only looking for a hand-kerchief.' Having found it, made brisk use of it and tucked it away, almost in command of her emotions once more, she meekly obeyed Mayo's indication that she should seat herself.

Reece spread his hands in resignation. He was wearing black, a roll-neck sweater and jeans. His tall blondness gave him a Teutonic appearance. The black went with his leather chairs and modern furniture, the modern abstracts on the walls. The blondness went with his blue eyes and crinkly smile. But it was a smile that had little humour or welcome in it and though he was affecting nonchalance Mayo thought he suspected what was to come. 'To what,' he asked, throwing himself down in his chair when his offer of drinks was refused, 'do I owe the pleasure?'

'We're here to ask a few more questions about the day Mr Willard was killed,' Mayo said, choosing an upright chair by the dining table.

A raised eyebrow and a glance towards the Rector.

'Mr Oliver has asked if he may be present in view of what we have to say.'

Reece inclined his head, took an unhurried drink, drove his hands into his pockets and leaned back with his legs stuck out. 'Fire away. You won't learn any more than I've already told you.'

'Don't be too sure of that. For one thing, I'd like to talk about your visit to Mr Willard around twelve noon last Saturday, and why you never mentioned it.'

'I wasn't aware that I'd been asked.'

'I'm asking you now, Mr Reece. Please don't pre-varicate.'

Reece shrugged. 'A social visit, off the cuff. A few minutes' chat, that was all it was, on my way to the church for that rehearsal I did tell you about.'

'I don't think it was off the cuff, though, was it? Not when Mr Willard had telephoned you and asked you to call. His reason for asking you was important enough to make you arrange—in the middle of a very busy day—a rehearsal with young Simon Rushton as a cover for going out. You didn't want anyone to know you were visiting Mr Willard because he'd told you he wanted to talk to you about Sebastian Oliver. And I think it was that conver-sation with him that made you decide to kill him.'

Reece had gradually lost his engaging air of schoolboy frankness, but it had been replaced by annoyance rather than fear. He wasn't yet sweating. He gave a short laugh. 'When someone's murdered, there usually has to be a motive, doesn't there? And an opportunity, which I didn't have. Mrs Holden has confirmed where I was when Willard was being killed.'

'Which is no alibi at all. There was nothing to prevent you turning the volume up on your music—anyone calling and hearing it would assume, as Mrs Holden did, that you hadn't heard the doorbell—and then running along the river bank, up the slope that leads to Parson's Place and then into the church. You jog regularly about the village so you'd have a very fair idea what time it would take. You also knew Mr Willard's invariable habit of arriving early for Evensong and that with a reasonable amount of luck you'd have time to do what you'd deliberately decided to

do after your earlier talk with him. The timing was tight
but you knew there'd be no further opportunity to find him
alone, his daughter would be at home and with him the
following day and the all-important governors' meeting was
scheduled for Monday morning.'

'This is ridiculous! Especially since I've already told you
I could have had no possible interest in wanting him dead.'

'Yes, that's what you've said, but it's not so, is it? You'd
a very good reason. It matters very much to you, becoming
the next Head of Uplands House. And Mr Willard supported you in that—until he learned something about your
past so unacceptable that he felt he must withdraw his
support. Something that would give you no chance of being
considered if it was generally known. In fact he wanted to
talk to you about Halsingbury, the school where you both
used to teach.'

'That's going back a few years.'

'I'm not talking about the time you and he taught there
together but later, after he'd left. When Sebastian Oliver
was a pupil there.'

Silence.

'On Sunday morning when we spoke to you, you said
you and Mr Willard had taught together—at Halsingbury
as it turned out. I had been told earlier that was the school
Sebastian had been expelled from, and this enabled us to
establish a connection between yourself and him. I must
tell you that the Rector has told me of the incident which
concerned you both and which resulted in Sebastian being
asked to leave, and in you yourself subsequently resigning.'

From the corner of his eye Mayo saw Philly, perched on
the edge of a sofa, open her mouth to speak, then close it.

Reece's silence lengthened. At last he withdrew his
unwavering blue stare from Mayo's face and fixed it on the
Rector's. 'Have you known who I was all this time—and
said nothing?'

Lionel Oliver replied slowly, 'When you took up the
appointment at the school, there was no reason why I

should have connected John Reece, as I heard it, with Jonathan Talbot-Reece, the master concerned with Sebastian being asked to leave Halsingbury. In fact, I didn't realize who you were until I picked up a manual you had left beside the church organ and saw your name written inside the cover, J. C. R. Talbot-Reece.'

Kite gave a sentient nod over his notes. He'd made a similar mistake himself between John and Jon. For Sara hear Sarah.

'I knew immediately who you were then, of course, and that you'd simply dropped the Talbot. It was a shock.'

But nothing to what Reece's shock must have been on discovering that Lionel Oliver was the incumbent at Castle Wyvering, Mayo thought.

'I'm astonished that you didn't see fit to confront me with it,' Reece said coolly.

The Rector's patrician face showed his anger and distaste. 'Do you think I don't bitterly regret now that I didn't? It was my first impulse. I imagined I might after all now be able to discover what had happened and perhaps clear my son's name. However, on mature reflection I decided to leave well alone, that nothing would be gained but my own satisfaction. Sebastian had put the incident—whatever it was—behind him and if it was anything to your discredit I saw no point in raking it up, simply for the sake of it.'

Reece remained unimpressed by the Rector's charity and consideration, but Lionel Oliver hadn't been looking for thanks. 'As far was possible, I tried to forget it—until I heard there was a strong possibility you might become the new Head at Uplands, since when I've been much exercised in my mind.'

Mayo said, 'I have to tell you, Mr Reece, that I've spoken to Mr Micklejohn, the Head of Halsingbury, and in the light of present circumstances he's been more forthcoming than he was with Mr Oliver. I understand now that the incident concerned examination papers—that you had in fact offered to let Sebastian see them before the exam. He was apparently insulted at the suggestion that he couldn't have passed without cheating if he'd been so minded, an argument developed and there was a scuffle—though I believe it wasn't altogether because of the offer to give him a preview of the papers but rather for the implication of what you expected to follow.'

Reece said thickly, 'I wondered when that was coming!'

'Come off it, Jon!' Philly was unable to keep silent any longer. 'Don't use that as an excuse. Nobody cares nowadays what anybody's sexual preferences are. It was offering to let him see the exam papers that cost you your job at Halsingbury.'

'According to Mr Micklejohn, that was so, but let me finish, please, Miss Thorne,' Mayo said. 'Since it was in Micklejohn's interests not to have a scandal, he agreed, if you would leave the school quietly, Mr Reece, to recommend you to whatever school you moved to, and to say nothing.'

'A highly questionable attitude, if I may say so,' commented the Rector severely.

Reece spun round on him. 'Why should it be questionable? I swear Micklejohn knew nothing whatever about my personal life! I'd never before let it interfere with my job and haven't since. And I don't mess around with young boys, either. Sebastian was different—he was seventeen and I thought . . . Well, I was mistaken, wasn't I? One mistake. But it would've ruined me here. It had obviously suited his corner to leave Halsingbury, so he let people believe what they wanted but it seems he's never forgiven the way it happened, all the same—nor the insult to his precious macho image! When he heard I might be made Head at Uplands he wasn't slow to talk, was he?'

'That wasn't it at all,' Philly said. 'You know what Seb's like. He'd never miss passing on a bit of spicy gossip. He'd already told me.'

'He'd told *you*?' Reece stared at her incredulously for several moments, then said, 'And you really believe he didn't realize where this bit of spicy gossip might lead?'

'Well, he certainly could never have dreamt—nobody in his right mind would—that you'd actually go so far as to kill the old man to stop him using what he'd been told!'

'Just a moment, though,' said the Rector, 'if what you've said is correct, Philly, then when Cecil Willard was killed both you and Sebastian must have known that Reece here, of all people, had a prime motive. Why did you not tell the police?'

Phyllida hesitated, then she said, 'This is where you all came in. I was just about to tell Jon where I'd been these last two days. I expect he can't wait. Well, I've been to London to see Peter Falk.'

Reece did not move but Mayo was aware of his every muscle tensing, every nerve end vibrating. 'Who is Peter Falk?' he asked.

'The man he goes to London to be with every other weekend.'

Reece's colour had mounted and there was a glitter in his eyes, but he said nothing.

'And?' Mayo prompted.

'And Peter confirmed what I'd thought, that . . .' She stopped. 'It's rather complicated.'

'Take your time. There's nothing to rush for, that I can see.'

'Well, as Mr Oliver said, we knew who had a motive for killing Mr Willard but Seb, for some reason, wouldn't go to you—the police. I couldn't understand why, unless he was involved in some way himself, in which case it wasn't up to me to press him. Anyway,' she added with a touch of her old bravado, 'I thought, well, the police are so bloody clever they're bound to find out anyway so what does it matter whether we tell them what we know or not?'

Mayo chose not to comment on this, but waited stolidly for her to go on.

'But then, on Sunday afternoon, I overheard Seb quarrelling with Jon in the garden. I'd gone into the house to answer the telephone and when I came back they were obviously having a big argument. Jon left as soon as I came back and Seb wouldn't tell me what it was about, even though I kind of gathered it concerned me, and that made me so furious,' she admitted, slightly subdued, 'I'm afraid we were scarcely on speaking terms after that.'

'Sunday afternoon,' Mayo repeated. It had been as he thought: Reece's voice had been the one he had heard in the Thornes' garden and later, by the river at Stapley, recalled to whom it belonged. Starting suspicions in his mind which had temporarily been eclipsed by other events, sufacing only after the attack on Sebastian, an act of carelessness which would cost Jon Reece his freedom. Sheer luck had carried Reece through the first crime, where a more carefully premeditated plan might have failed him, the element of luck that was present in all successful crimes, but it had been unrealistic to think it would continue. 'Let's talk about this attack—'

'It was after that I really started to think,' she cut in. 'I remembered that a few weeks back, in London, I was with Seb when he and Jon came face to face with each other for the first time since Halsingbury. It was at a party given by Peter Falk who, incidentally, is a member of—of SARA.' Reece drew in his breath sharply and audibly but she went on, pointedly avoiding looking in his direction and speaking tensely to Mayo, hesitating before uttering the name but nevertheless looking him straight in the eye. No dissembling, prepared to face the music. She wasn't short on courage, whatever else; but then, they none of them were, these blinkered fanatics. What they lacked, among a lot of other things, was a proper sense of proportion.

'Later, we'll go more fully into the matter of SARA,' he said. 'For the moment, let's concentrate on what we were talking about. This Peter Falk, presumably, had passed on the information to Mr Reece here that you were involved in the organization?'

She nodded. 'He tells Jon everything, they've no secrets

from each other—or that's what he said when I saw him in London this morning.' Reece gave a barely suppressed groan. 'Though I don't suppose he'd have admitted it if he'd known why I was asking.'

'And presumably,' Mayo pressed on, 'Sebastian wasn't at first aware that Falk was a member of SARA, or that he'd passed on to Reece that *you* were, otherwise I suppose he might have thought twice about gossiping to Willard.'

'Well, of course he'd have thought twice,' Pyllida said, 'I guess he'd no idea that Jon knew anything about me until after Mr Willard was killed, probably not until last Sunday. When Jon came and threatened him with telling what he knew about me if he didn't keep his mouth shut. He must've been torn between dropping me in it and keeping to himself who the murderer was.'

He said to her, 'All right, but if Sebastian didn't know that Reece was aware of your connections with the organization, why mention SARA at all to Mr Willard?'

She went suddenly scarlet. Whether from annoyance or some other emotion, a deep, painful red spread from her neck upwards. 'I've told you, he didn't go to see Mr Willard primarily about Reece.'

'Well, why then?'

'For advice about me, if you must know! Seb's like a lot more men, he only pays lip-service to women's freedom and he said it worried him, if you please, that I was a member of SARA! That's the only reason he agreed to go to that meeting with me on Saturday, I'm sure, to see how much I was involved. Bloody cheek, as if I'm not perfectly capable of taking care of myself, which is more than he is,' she declared, the hurt in her eyes denying her anger. It had obviously come as a shock that what Sebastian thought and felt about her should mean such a lot to her, and she was mortified that it did. 'So now you know everything.'

Mayo said, assuming his thick-headed copper role, 'Well, no, maybe not everything. You see, maybe we're not as clever as you think we are, Miss Thorne. It puzzles me what Sebastian was doing, arranging, or agreeing, to meet you, Mr Reece, by the castle.'

How the hell, he thought, could anyone be such a fool? Meeting someone you knew to be a murderer on a dark night in a lonely place?

But you could if you were Sebastian Oliver, irrepressibly self-confident, believing you could manipulate the situation to your own advantage because you had the whip hand.

At that moment Mayo felt it was more of an inspired guess than a conscious process of logical deduction which gave him the answer he'd been looking for. Later he was to see that it followed inevitably from what he'd learnt during the conversation. 'He was putting pressure on you, wasn't he?' he said to Reece.

With an angry, sweeping gesture that almost knocked over the bottle on the table next to him, Reece violently denied any such thing. But for the first time, there was a glint of fear in his eyes.

'I think he was. Over Peter Falk—who's no ordinary, run-of-the-mill member of SARA, is he? I think he was the one who masterminded the bombing at the Fricker Institute that killed the security guard.'

'I never told Seb that,' Philly's small voice said into the silence.

But Sebastian was clever. Intuitive enough to put two and two together and make half a dozen. He'd have picked up a hint here, a nuance there, and drawn the inevitable conclusion.

Mayo stood up. 'Mr Reece, I must tell you that there is forensic evidence which will connect you directly with both crimes. For one, there are fibres from a black tracksuit which you sometimes wear for running, but we also have a witness who will testify that he saw you in the church, and—'

'That's impossible!' He was still blustering, but the last revelations had done more than any of the previous accusations to sap his confidence. And now, looking from one to the other, he seemed to sense it was all over, that there was no escape, and his defences suddenly collapsed. 'It's no use trying to explain, none of you will understand.' Sagging almost visibly with the weight of the chip in his shoulder, the schoolboy cowlick looking limp and defeated, he said in a slurred voice loaded with self-pity, 'It's dangerous to be as I am in my profession. There's no room for guys like me. My whole life has been spent denying myself and how I feel and it's so bloody unfair! At least Peter's been free to be himself and work for what he believes in.'

And then with disconcerting suddenness, he jumped up and stood looking from one to the other with a wild look in his eye. 'No! Why the hell should I make excuses? I did what I did. I didn't want to have to kill Willard, I didn't go with that intention, I swear. He wanted me to withdraw my application and I went to the church to plead with him to think again. All I wanted was for him to keep quiet, which shouldn't have been too much to ask. But he wouldn't even listen. And in the end it was so easy. So quick. No more hassle.' He rubbed his hand across his eyes. 'But I'd forgotten Sebastian. It was only afterwards that I remembered what he knew.'

'And decided to kill him, too. That was no spur of the moment decision, you went prepared, with a baseball bat. It was too bad you didn't know that Miss Thorne knew as much as he did, otherwise he wouldn't now be in a hospital bed.'

'He shouldn't have tried it on. I'm the wrong person to put up with that sort of blackmail!' His face had grown red and shiny, the blue eyes hot, a pulse beat in his temple, as if a violence that had been repressed and held down too long could no longer be contained but had to come boiling out, like steam under pressure. Yet the expression on his face was almost exalted. 'What's more, I'm damned if I'll listen to any more of this!'

In a flash, he had made his move. Straight for the door in a few long strides. Out of it, slamming it behind him and over the wooden rails in one leap, never mind the steps. He could easily have broken a leg from that height but he knew what he was doing, how to land, which Kite, following after, didn't—or didn't care to test whether he knew or not. Both he and Mayo were in fair condition but they knew they hadn't a hope in hell. Reece, on top of his form, had a good lead and soon outstripped them both, making for the main school building. The west tower, with its net of scaffolding. The ladders, still in place and Reece swarming up them like a monkey.

Kite had reached the bottom of the first ladder, was about to follow him, just like in the cops and robber series so that the poor dumb cop would be in danger of being pushed off the roof by the bad guy.

But Reece had already reached the top and with scarcely a moment's pause, leaped straight off. Directly beneath him was a pile of builders' sand. Embedded upright in the sand by its spike, ready to be hauled up to the roof, was the new, replacement finial, its leafy crown of acanthus leaves now clearly defined around its central, sharply-tapering boss, pointing in all innocence to the sky.

CHAPTER 19

The month of May had decided to live up to its reputation and bow itself out in a feast of blossom, blue skies and the beginning of a heatwave. Castle Wyvering, peaceful and sleepy in the sun, looked at its best, while Uplands House School on a May morning was incomparable.

'Reece came with the highest recommendation from the Headmaster at Halsingbury,' Richard Holden was saying, 'and I immediately felt he'd fit in here, which he always did. Never thought anything of it when he told me he preferred to be known simply as "Reece" rather than his full name. Less pretentious, he said, and I was inclined to agree.'

Mayo had come to the school to find Miriam Thorne and after speaking with her was leaving when he had encountered the Headmaster on the front lawn, watching as the scaffolding on the west tower was being dismantled, ready to be taken away. Bolts were being uncoupled and planks thrown down to the accompaniment of the sort of language which would certainly have enriched the boys' vocabulary had they been there to hear it. The work was now completed, the damaged tiles replaced and the acanthus-leaved finial upon which Jon Reece's body had been impaled cemented into place on the apex of one of the gables, looking newer than its companions but otherwise innocent of its deadly function.

Holden stood with his hands clasped behind his back, bouncing slightly on his tocs, his gown billowing behind him. There was a subtly different air about him, a relaxation of tension perhaps, a renewed energy.

'But that isn't what you mean, is it?' he went on. 'And the answer is no, I'd no idea he was gay, though God knows that must be the last word to apply. Not at first, that is. Later, I began to suspect.'

'Didn't it bother you at all, sir?'

'I like to think that I'm not prejudiced, and I can assure you there was never any danger at all that any of the boys would be at risk. Had I had the slightest inkling of anything like that he would have had to go. No, I'm as certain as I ever shall be of anything that he was speaking the truth when he said he kept the two sides of his life apart.'

'But when he was likely to be made Headmaster?'

'Well, I didn't know for certain that what I suspected was true and short of asking him outright, which he would have denied, I don't know what I could have done. I certainly wasn't going to conduct any sort of witch hunt.' Holden watched a large lorry doing a reverse turn on the drive, keeping his eye on it to make sure it didn't clip the edges of the lawn with its wheels, then said, 'All right, yes, it bothered me. Look, shall we go into my study? It's too noisy to talk out here and I think there'll be some tea waiting.'

Sitting in the large, comfortable room, with the windows open, tea poured and biscuits handed, Holden leaned back in his chair. 'Sebastian, at least, I gather from Miriam Thorne, is making a good recovery. Showing a tendency to rethink his life and the way it's going too, I understand— but concerned about Philly.'

'Well, she'll have to take the rap, you know, along with the others. With Patman and Quinn and Ruth Lampeter, though even they're small beer compared to Peter Falk. But since she was only involved with setting up the cell here and not with SARA's more militant activities, she should get off comparatively lightly. I thought I'd come along and reassure Mrs Thorne about that while I was here in Wyvering to sort out one or two other matters with PC Wainwright.'

'It won't basically change how she feels about things, you know,' Miriam had said. 'We've tried for years to do that. But maybe she'll cool her opinions down a bit. What happened to Seb has shaken her badly.'

And if Sebastian had the nous to take advantage of that —and Mayo was inclined to think he had his head screwed on the right way, despite appearances to the contrary in the matter of Jonathan Reece—then maybe it would turn out to be a different story. 'She'll be all right,' he said to Holden now. 'And so will young Oliver. Though his memory at the moment is all to pot and he doesn't remember exactly what happened just before he was attacked.'

Jon Reece—or Jonathan Talbot-Reece—hadn't been so lucky. He had died within a few seconds of reaching the hospital. His spectacular leap from the scaffolding on to the stone finial had resulted in multiple injuries, rupturing his spleen and breaking his spine among other things. He had lain a few doors along the corridor from where Sebastian

Oliver was slowly recovering, but had never regained consciousness.

'Thank you for the tea, Mr Holden,' Mayo said, preparing to go. 'I don't suppose we shall meet again but I'd like to wish you well and hope you and your wife will be happy in Antibes.'

The Headmaster took off his spectacles, smiled and said, 'We shan't be going to Antibes, Mr Mayo. I've let myself be persuaded not to retire after all. Not just yet. I've spoken to my doctor and he supports the idea wholeheartedly. It wasn't a severe heart attack I had, just a warning, as they say, and my doctor says there's no reason why I shouldn't live to be ninety—though I shan't inflict myself on Uplands so long!'

'That's a surprise! What does Mrs Holden think of the idea?' Mayo asked, though he could have bet his month's overtime on the answer.

'It was my wife who originally felt I should retire and I went along with her wishes but in actual fact I think now she's rather relieved I've decided otherwise. She knows I shall be happier—and I'm certain *she* will be, staying here.'

'Then Illingworth won't get the Headship?'

'No. No, he won't. But all in all that might be no bad thing. That was partly why I changed my mind when the chairman of the governors sounded me out—before Reece died—on the idea of staying on for an interim period at least, until a more suitable person than either Reece or Illingworth could be found. Like me, one or two of the board members had apparently been having second thoughts, feeling that neither candidate was ideal. Maybe Illingworth can be groomed to take over when I do retire, though frankly, I'm not sure that teaching *per se* is entirely his métier. I can't see him finding it enough of an intellectual challenge in the long run.'

'Never struck me as being the sort to be a schoolmaster, but then, I'm not qualified to say,' Mayo remarked.

'No, though I was very happy to take him, of course,

when he first came here. It's not every day someone with
his background applies for a position at a school like
Uplands. He was quite frank about his reasons for leaving
Cambridge and during his time here he's performed quite
adequately, but that's rather different from being Head of
a school like this. Jonathan would've been the better man
of the two, but . . .' He shook his head.

'It wouldn't have done, though, would it?'

'No, I must admit it wouldn't. Easy, of course, to speak
with hindsight but you know, I liked him, I liked him very
much. I was aware he used his charm quite deliberately to
get what he wanted but I thought it was harmless. I should
have seen the aggression beneath the surface—it was there
in dozens of ways. I always knew he had a bit of a chip on
his shoulder but his kind often do. I'd never have thought
him a potential suicide.'

Yet Doc Ison had said that suicide was a characteristic
of the psychopathic personality. 'Unable to cope with being
thwarted, suicide rather than capitulation. Failure to
develop a sense of moral responsibility, capable of extreme
violence . . . If he was a true psychopath, that is, and didn't
simply have a severe personality disorder, which is more
likely, though it's impossible for me to say, never having
seen him.'

A bell rang somewhere in the distance and as Mayo left,
a troop of small boys streamed out towards the playing
fields with a young master in charge. He saw Laura Willard
—Laura Illingworth—in the distance but he didn't stop.
He'd said everything now that needed to be said. These
people whose personal lives he had so intimately known
were already passing into the limbo of investigations
marked 'Closed'. Already other cases were beginning to
crowd in and push the details of this one to the back of his
mind.

He glanced at his watch. Time before he went home to
pick up some of that special bird seed and fresh fruit for
Bert, who was proving to be a picky eater. As well as being

an obstinate cuss. Mayo was trying to teach him to talk but so far his efforts had been met with nothing but derision. Never mind, he'd grown used to looking for the flash of bright colour in the corner and hearing the screech that passed for welcome when he opened the door.

He found himself smiling as he walked to where his car was parked and drove away under the magnificent line of chestnuts, leaving Wyvering without going back into Parson's Place, driving past the castle ruins and down the hill for the last time, going back the way he'd first come.